The Echo Series

When Angels Cry

Tammy Cheatham

Tammy Cheatham

DEDICATION

To Jean, for raising a man I couldn't help but love

When Angels Cry

CHAPTER 1

Quinto Navarone slammed the ambulance door, leaned around the side of the vehicle, and made eye contact in the side mirror with the driver, "You know where to take them," he said.

Without a word the man nodded and pulled the ambulance away from the white stone portico near the service entrance of Saint Andrew's Children's Home. Once he'd cleared the visitor's parking lot, he glanced back at his cargo. Three young girls, two blonde and one with shiny copper hair, huddled together on the fold out bench in the rear of the ambulance. Grunting, he let his eye's drift back to the road in front of him, and wondered if he could get away with keeping the little redhead for himself. "Nah, won't work. That bastard Quinto would kill me for sure," he muttered.

"You say something, mister?" The pretty little girl with the copper hair asked.

"Yeah, stay in the seat and don't talk. That's what I said," he barked.

While the girls didn't speak to him, Simon heard their muted whispers and sniffles as he maneuvered the ambulance through the streets of Richmond. Thirty long and silent minutes later, he pulled the ambulance to a smooth stop in front of a rundown, abandoned warehouse. Just off Eighteenth Street, in one of the oldest industrial districts in Richmond, forgotten buildings like this one lined both sides the streets for several blocks, and gave the city's drug dealers, hookers and homeless, room to play. But they didn't congregate around this particular building; it wasn't safe, even for them, and they knew it. The square three-story building was dark except for the spot where a single light hung over the door, its beam forming a circling halo on a block of gray cement just outside the entrance. Even though this was one of the few buildings with electricity, the scant light did nothing to improve the building's appearance. Missing bricks pock marked the façade and boarded windows on the lower levels kept nosy looky-loos from spying inside.

Simon shifted the ambulance into reverse and using the side mirrors to guide him, backed up near the door. He didn't see any nosy onlookers but it was better to be safe; after all, those damn homeless people were like cockroaches. For every one that you saw, there were at least a hundred that you didn't. He'd seen them lurking just out of the light, hiding behind trash barrels and burrowed under cardboard boxes, but not on this lot, not if they knew what was good for them. His boss didn't tolerate trespassers here, and the price for getting caught at this warehouse was much too high. Not worth the risk, that was the word on the street.

Leaving the motor running, Simon jumped out and jogged to the back of the ambulance. Twisting a chrome handle, he pulled first one, then both doors, open wide. The girls hadn't moved from the bench seat, but even in the dim light he could see that the two little ones had been crying. Tearstains dampened their cherubic faces and added to the innocence in their eyes.

Simon waved a hand at the clustered girls and ordered, "Come on now girls, hurry over here for me." When they made no move to obey him, Simon reached inside the dark interior of the vehicle and snagged the closest girl, a blonde, by the arm. Her lower lip trembled and eyes widened as he yanked her toward the open ambulance doors. The child had moved only a foot or so when she stopped, and Simon felt the force of someone or something pulling against him. He tugged harder, but not hard enough to bruise the girl. Marks on the merchandise were costly and Simon knew it. He glanced around the blonde to see that the copper-haired girl had taken her friend's hand and was pulling her away from him. The mutinous red haired child had planted her feet and both hands were locked tight around the blonde's wrist. She struggled to pull the little girl further into the ambulance. Simon narrowed his eyes and snarled at the redhead, "Let her go." Then he softened his voice and spoke reassuringly to the blonde, "You want to come with me, don't you honey? You don't want to go back to that place now do you?"

The tiny blonde girl glanced back at her red-haired friend, still struggling to pull her away from the door. She shook her head and tried to move closer to the man; but the older girl wasn't giving. She only stepped closer to her friend, released her grasp on the girl's arm and quickly locked them around the child's waist where she placed one hand atop the other, locked her fingers and held on. The glow from the bare-bulbed light attached to the building shined on the girl's hair and face. Simon could see the determination in her eyes. Before he could move, she yelled, "Let her go mister. This place ain't no better than Saint A's and you'd better take us back right now or you're going to be in big trouble." Speaking to her friend, she pleaded, "Don't go Allie. This isn't a safe place, just look at it! The windows are boarded up or broken and they don't even have the lights on in there! There ain't no parents waiting for us in a place like this."

For a moment, doubt clouded Allie's eyes and she frowned, trying to decide if she should go or stay. Before she could decide, the rust speckled, grey steel door leading into the building opened, and a burly woman with white streaked hair stepped into the light. The woman peered around the man, pushed her glasses up on her nose, and said, "Well now, what seems to be the trouble here?" She frowned at the man and nudged him aside with a bump from her hip before she stepped past him, and opened her arms to the undecided blonde child. "Come here sweet girl. It's time for us to go inside now." The Piper cooed soothingly. Jeri had a way with children, especially little girls. They clung to her and followed her as if she were the Pied Piper.

Allie jerked free from her friend and launched herself at the woman. Tears stained her face and she shuddered in relief, before wrapping both arms tightly around the woman's thick neck, and burying her face against the white uniformed shoulder of the Piper.

One down. Jeri Anderson thought. She gently rubbed the child's back and then extended her free hand to the other blonde child, "Come now, we'll only be here a little while and then a car will come to take us to your new home. You're going to love it there; it's a beautiful farmhouse where you'll each have a room of your own, and best of all, you'll have a real family."

Mesmerized by the Piper's soothing tone, the remaining blonde moved trancelike to the woman's side, and took her hand. That left only the red-haired child in the back of the ambulance. Jeri glared at her, and then turned on the man. "You can bring *that* one, she's trouble for sure; but then Mr. Walker docs like the red hair."

Nine year old Victoria McEvers stepped back, and burrowed further into the darkened ambulance. She quaked, "Take me back to St. A's. I don't want to go to any farmhouse. I already have a family, and my mother won't be able to find me if I leave the city."

Simon planted one big booted foot on the ambulance floor and hoisted his bulk inside, advancing slowly on the girl. His words were cruel and taunting, "You're mama ain't looking for you little girl, she's probably dead on the street by now."

Victoria clinched her fists and warned,

"Don't you say that mister."

Simon snorted, "Why not, Chica? You know it's probably true. Your mama was a junkie and she left you because you were too much trouble."

Unable to control her anger, Victoria flew at the man. She pounded him with tiny fists and kicked at anything she could reach. She raged, "Don't you say that! You don't know my Mama and you don't know me!"

Simon laughed, the sound echoed in the small space of the ambulance. He stooped and wrapped one meaty muscled arm around the girl's middle, hoisting her to his waist. He clamped his free hand over her mouth and moved to the open door. "You're a firestorm alright and I hope you give Quinto hell."

Victoria struggled, her short legs pumped behind him, while her arms wind-milled before him, but she couldn't break free. She clamped down on his fleshy palm as hard as she could. The man flinched but didn't remove his hand from her mouth. Her scream smothered and died behind his hand.

At the corner of the red brick warehouse, Emma Gage-Echo watched the man struggle with a little flame-haired girl before he disappeared inside the building, and then returned a few minutes later, alone. She glanced at her watch and cursed, "Dammit Clay, where are you? You should have been here ten minutes ago." Emma backed out of sight, and watched the muscled man get into the ambulance and drive away. "Shit, too dark to see the plates." She muttered.

Less than a minute later, headlights swept across the empty parking lot, and Emma dodged the piercing glow; thinking that the man had returned. The driver killed the headlights and Emma moved forward. She peered around the corner and watched a different man exit his car and enter the building. This man, tall, thin, and well-dressed, drove a late model Town Car. As soon as she heard the metal warehouse door creak closed, Emma pulled her cell phone out and sent a text to Clay Shuler, the DOJ task force captain. Emma was on loan from the FBI and had been working with the Bureau of Justice Assistance for the last four months. The task force was trying to chase down a child trafficking ring working the inner city. Clay was in charge of the group. *The pick-up is here. Where are you? I can't let him leave with these girls. Hurry or I'm going in alone!* Emma hit send and pocketed her phone.

Emma hunkered in the shadows, keeping her eyes trained on the metal door at the front of the building. She heard the door creak before it opened, and she watched the woman in white step outside. *Looks like a nurse or maybe a nanny.* She thought. The woman still carried one tow-haired child snuggled on her shoulder and pulled the other, with equally white-blonde hair, by the hand at her side. Quietly and efficiently the woman shuffled the children inside the back seat of the car and then slid in herself. The rear car door remained open and Emma supposed that they were waiting for the other child to be brought out; a few seconds later, her thoughts were confirmed when the well-dressed man propelled the red-haired child in front of him, his boots crunched on the pavement, sounding loud in the still night. The child still struggled, but a large bony hand wrapped tightly around her upper arm forced her to move forward. Without turning, the man pushed the warehouse door closed with the bottom of one booted foot. *They're leaving!* Emma thought. *I cannot let him leave with these kids!*

Emma pulled her Glock from the shoulder holster under her jacket, and stepped away from the shadow of the building. The man had his back to her, still struggling to put the last child in the car. The girl's protest muted Emma's steps and she moved forward until she was less than three yards from the target. "Stop!" She commanded, her voice firm but quiet. "Let go of the girl and put your hands up nice and slow."

CHAPTER 2

"You're going to die today bitch. How does that make you feel?" The man said, pointing his gun at her. "You've stuck your nose in my business for the last time." Keeping his gun trained on the nosy bitch, the man stepped closer and smiled down at her. "The last name you're ever going to hear is Quinto. Quinto Navarone."

Emma watched in muted horror, as if her own life were moving in slow motion. She saw her gun slip from her hand and skid across the pavement, watched as her body propelled backward and her feet left the ground. She saw her arms outstretched at her sides like an angel taking flight and somewhere in the back of her mind, she thought, *I'm flying.*

The first shot struck her square in the chest, its fire spread like a hot spark on dry tender before it knocked the angel down to the hard pavement below. *I can't breathe.* She thought, and struggled to suck in a lung full of life-saving air, putrid as it was.

Got to reach my gun. Her mind spun while her eyes frantically searched the ground around her, finally spotting the black and silver Glock 22 near a green garbage dumpster parked at the curb. The angel crawled, tiny gravel on the pavements surface cut through her pants and into her knees. Emma barely registered that the man was still talking, telling her what it would be like to die at the hand of Quinto Navarone.

Hurry Emma, only a few more feet!

The man dragged one blood soaked leg behind him, but didn't slow his advance. He still chattered, telling Emma how he would kill her. Her mind screamed. *Move Emma! Wait, what was that?* Movement near the garbage container flashed in the corner of her eye. *God please not another one.*

A gloved hand reached down and snagged Emma's gun from the ground. The scene suddenly lurched into motion like a high speed movie in her head; shots flashed and echoed into the darkness. One, two, three, four, the rounds stopped, but the metallic click of the trigger dry firing continued. Five, six, seven. Silence.

Emma struggled to stay alert, but knew that she was fading in and out of consciousness. *Who is that? Clay?* She thought. *No...not Clay. A woman...who?*

A statuesque woman with a dancer's lithe body, slipped from the shadows thrown by the garbage container and walked to where Quinto Navarone lay, drowning in his own blood. Careful not to step in the blood pooling on the pavement, the woman spat on Navarone, and then calmly bent and picked up his gun. She tucked the weapon into her jacket pocket before she turned and walked back to Emma. The stranger knelt at Emma's side and placed two leather clad fingers on the side of Emma's neck. She felt for a pulse. "You are alive, that is more than many." She said softly.

Emma tried to sit up, but the effort was too much. She groaned and fell back, "Help m...."

The woman smiled; a sad lifting of the lips at best. Her blue eye's locked on Emma's for a fraction of a second before she reached out and flipped the badge clipped at Emma's waist over, so that she could read it. "Emma Gage-Echo, I have saved you from the devils brother, and now you will owe me. Not today, but soon. I cannot stay with you, but help is coming." She glanced back over one shoulder, and continued, "I hear the sirens already. But first you must have your gun back."

Unable to move, Emma watched in a daze as the woman lifted her right hand making sure to press her index finger around the trigger of the bullet-less Glock before letting it drop at Emma's side. The woman stood and pulled the hood of her jacket tight around her head, and then left as quietly as she'd arrived; she just turned and walked away. A few feet later she slipped behind the green dumpster and disappeared into the darkness.

"No! Wait! Don't leave me here!" Emma fought to stay awake but everything slowly faded to nothing.

Just inside the door of Room 420, the nurse on duty gently shook Emma's arm. "Ma'am, wake up. You're having a dream, that's all."

Someone was holding her arm; a soothing

voice pulled at her, insisting that she return to the present. Emma opened her eyes and found Nurse Webber hovered at her bedside, a worried look creased the nurse's brow, she held an empty syringe in one hand.

"There now. You're awake. Now look around you. You're perfectly safe." Nurse Webber soothed, and pulled the covers up. She tucked them gently around Emma and then continued, "You just close your eyes and go back to sleep, this time you'll dream of better things." The woman's soft humming filled the room and Emma blinked her eyes, fighting to stay awake, the nurse's quiet voice echoed in the small room. "Now you just relax ma'am. It won't be long before your meds kick in and then you'll be able to sleep."

Her voice already beginning to slur, Emma starred at the woman, "I don't want to sleep. I just want to get out of here. I need to go. There are children's lives at stake. I've got a job to do and you people..."

Nurse Webber interrupted her patient before the woman could reach full steam, "Now ma'am, we've been over this before. The doctor will be in to see you tomorrow, and if he thinks you're ready, then he'll sign the release papers. No one but the doctor can do that and you've got to rest now."

Bright fluorescent light filtered into the room when the nurse opened the door, blinding Emma for a moment. Before her eyes had time to adjust, the door closed and she was alone.

Nurse Alice Webber stepped away from the door and smiled at two nurses standing behind the fourth floor station counter. "She'll be down for the night any minute ladies."

The two women behind the counter sighed in unison and smiled back at Alice. The shorter of the two babbled, "Thank goodness you got approval from Dr. Simms to give her that sedative. I don't think I could take another night like the last one. I swear I was tempted to strangle her with the damn call button cord if she pushed that button one more time!"

Nurse Webber rounded the chest high counter and held up the empty syringe before neatly sliding it into a red and white biohazard disposal container attached to the wall. She looked at her friends, planted large hands on her large hips and confided, "It's all in the needle girls. Now that I took care of little Miss Trouble for the night, which one of you is going to pick up our dinner?"

Emma stared into the darkness and felt her body relax; the drugs that the nurse had injected willed her to surrender and let sleep win. *Not yet.* She thought and shook her head. A blinding pain and her own groan reminded her of the concussion they said she had. Emma reached out for the call button controller strapped to the railing of the bed. "You've got to get out of here Emma." She whispered as her fingers brushed, but failed to grasp the controller. "You can reach it, just a little bit further." The movement cost her, fire running the length of her leg stopped her. Letting her hand drop to the cool white cotton of the sheet, Emma closed her eyes as sleep won the battle.

CHAPTER 3

The buzz of his cell phone pulled Tate Echo from a warm and restful sleep. He glanced at the clock radio on the bedside table and silently cursed. *Midnight, damn.* Quietly, he rolled away from the woman at his side, and reached for the phone. Tate slipped from the bed without bothering to dress, and with a quick backward glance at the sleeping woman, he moved to the door then stepped into the darkened hallway.

"Echo here, and this had better be good," he growled.

An unfamiliar voice boomed on the line, "Is this Tate Echo, the Police Chief of Pine Ridge, South Dakota?"

Tate pushed a hand through his too long dark hair, then let it trail to down to his chin and across the stubble growing there, he snapped, "That's right and who is this?" Balancing the phone against one ear, he peeked through a crack in the bedroom door. Tate watched the woman in his bed roll over in her sleep and run one pink manicured hand over his pillow. *Damn.*

"Sorry to call you so late Chief Echo. This is SAC Jackson Pruitt with the Federal Bureau of Investigation. We haven't met, however, I understand that you were once married to Emma Gage-Echo, an agent currently under my command."

At the mention of Emma's name, Tate snapped fully awake. He moved further down the hallway and away from the door before speaking louder, "Is Em okay? Tell me what's wrong." He demanded, a knot of fear already bunching and spreading like a cancer in his gut. Special Agents in Charge did not call strangers at midnight to deliver good news.

Tate listened, the pounding of his heart reached his ears making the man's voice seem hollow and far away. "SSA Gage-Echo has been shot in the line of duty. Currently she's in St. Mary's Hospital in Richmond."

Tate sucked in a deep breath, a living breath, and said, "Thank God, she's alive. How bad is it? Have you contacted her parents?"

The voice on the phone hedged, then continued, "Chief Echo, we've have not attempted to contact Emma's parents. Seems you are the one listed as the primary contact in case of an emergency on her file, and I'm obligated to follow our standard protocol in such situations. I can tell you that Judge and Mrs. Gage are on an extended trip abroad at this time and reaching them will be difficult, should you choose to contact them." His voice dropping to a human but ominous tone, the man continued, "Emma needs family with her now Chief Echo."

Not able to recall his walk to the end of the hall or into the living room, Tate sank down on the sofa. "I'll be there tomorrow." Then recalling that it was already after midnight, he corrected,

"No wait, that's today. I'll be there today."

Tate disconnected the call and leaned back on the sofa. He struggled to push the bile rising in the back of his throat down; silently he struggled with his fear. *Dammit, I begged her to get out of the field, but no, she had to stick her pretty little nose in every high profile case that crossed the threshold.* Shame forced his frustration down only to be replaced with regret, *If I had just stayed, maybe...* He leaned forward and rested his elbows on his knees. Tate let his head sink to his hands as nausea rolled through his gut. Emotion shook him. *His Em. Shot. Fighting for her life in a damned hospital. Alone.*

"I'm on my way Em, just hold on baby." He whispered, his mind spinning with things he had to do before he could leave. Tate stood and then sensed that he wasn't alone. Taralyn Parker stood in the hallway. The blanket that she'd pulled around her shoulders did little to hide the naked curves that had been pressed tightly against him only minutes ago.

"What's wrong Tate? You get a call out?" She asked, her face scrunched with concern.

"Sorry Tara, but it might be best if you go on home." Tate stepped past her in the tiny hallway and turned into the bedroom. He flipped the overhead light on with one hand; its brightness illuminated the room and stopped him cold. Tate took in the scene, a candle on the dresser burned low, its flickering reflection twinkled in the mirror behind it; clothes, his and hers, formed a Hansel and Gretel trail to the bed, and disappeared under a twisted blanket laying in a heap at the foot of the bed. Two pillows rested, side by side at the top of the bed and still bore the evidence of their sleep. *Dammit, how could you have let it go this far Echo?*

Tate followed the trail of clothes across the floor and snatched his pants and shirt from the pile. He pulled them on before moving to the dresser, where he bent low and blew out the candle.

Taralyn slipped quietly into the room and reached for her own clothes. Without a word she walked into the bathroom across the hall to dress. She returned a few minutes later and stood in the doorway staring at Tate before crossing her arms over her chest and finally asking, "You're not going to tell me what this is all about are you, Tate?"

He sucked a breath in and held it for a moment before letting it blow out in a puff of air. He lifted his eyes to meet hers. "I have to go to Virginia. Emma's been shot, and they can't get in touch with her parents. She doesn't have anyone else Tara."

Tara nodded her head and whispered, "I understand Tate. Just tell me one thing, tell me you don't love her, and that you're going as a friend."

"I..." He started and then stopped abruptly. Tate turned his back to her and went to the closet. He pulled a blue duffle bag down from an upper shelf and tossed it on the bed. Unable to meet her gaze, Tate shrugged and then frowned, "I have to go."

Tara sucked her lower lip in between her teeth and stepped close to him. She tiptoed up and gave Tate a quick kiss on the cheek. "Goodbye Tate. I really hope everything works out for you and Emma."

Tara turned away from him and walked to the end of the bed where she dropped to one knee and pushed the blanket aside to search for her shoes. She hooked the shoes with one finger and walked barefoot out of the room and down the hall. Frozen, Tate stood and listened until he heard the front door open and close. Seconds later he heard her car start, and the engine rev as she backed from his driveway.

"Dammit, Echo you should never have slept with her. You know she's had a hard year and what did you do? You took advantage anyway." He cursed while he pulled socks and under- ware from the dresser, and shoved them into the duffle in no particular order.

Seven months earlier Tate, Emma and Martin Crawley, the Sheriff of Shannon County, had worked jointly to solve a serial killer case in Pine Ridge that had lapped over to the county as well. The first victim had been Saralyn Parker, Tara's twin sister. If that wasn't bad enough, Tara just went through a divorce that had her packing up and moving home with her parents.

"Hell, she's ten years younger than you. What the fuck were you thinking Echo?"

He jammed jeans and shirts into the duffle and silently admitted that he hadn't been thinking, not with his brain anyway.

Tate slammed the blue duffle into the back seat of his city issued Range Rover, slid behind the wheel and started the SUV. He cleared the driveway and maneuvered down the dark and empty street with one hand. With his free hand he punched Martin's number on his cell.

His voice coated in sleep, Sheriff Martin Crawley answered, "Crawley here. That you, Tate?"

"Yeah Martin. Look I need a favor. Em's been shot and I'm on my way to Virginia. Can you come by and pick Hercules up in the morning and drop him off with the vet for boarding?"

Hercules had been dropped on Tate's porch by a neighborhood kid seven months ago, and Tate couldn't turn him away. That tiny little bundle of yellow had grown into a slobbering, chewing, monster of a dog that the vet assured Tate was mostly, and he stressed the mostly, French Mastiff.

Martin sounded fully awake now, "Is Miss Emma going to be alright? How bad is it?"

Tate swallowed hard, struggling to force

down the fear that threatened to consume him before he answered, "I don't know. Her SAC wouldn't tell me anything over the phone other than I need to get out there. So you'll get Herc for me?"

Somewhat reassured, Martin appealed, "Aw Tate you know that dog slobbers on everything. Last time he was in my car it took a week to clean up all the drool and he chewed a rear seatbelt almost completely through!"

Tate chuckled and agreed, "Yeah, I know he's a mess, but he's a good dog. Just be sure you put a leash on him and tie it to the child safety seat loops in the back seat. I'm going to call Chad Green and ask him to fill in for me at the office, and then let the mayor know. You good with that, Buddy?"

"You know Chad's been wanting your job for over a year now, maybe he'll get a good taste of it while you're gone and realize it's not all that he thought it was." Martin snorted, then without waiting for an answer he asked, "How long you planning on being gone Tate?"

Tate moved the phone to his other ear and flipped the blinker on for a right turn, "As long as she needs me Martin. I'll be in touch." He disconnected the call and pulled the Range Rover to a stop in the long term parking area of the Pine Ridge Airport. He grabbed his bag from the back seat and jogged into the airport.

Thoughts of Emma consumed him, and everything else slipped away. They'd met in

Virginia when Tate was assigned there following graduation from the FBI academy; she'd thought he was just another green recruit, and had said so. That changed when they were forced to work together on a task force investigating an arms dealer. This particular dealer supplied arms to a drug cartel in South America, and Emma's profiling skills had led them to a break in the case, while his history as a Marine and his extensive weaponry experience made him the perfect choice to infiltrate the organization as a buyer. Together, they'd stopped the sale and arrested the primary supplier in the operation. Together....they'd fallen in love.

Forty minutes later, Tate shook off the past and boarded the plane with the other late night travelers. He took a window seat and breathed deep as the plane ascended. Unable to stop it, his mind moved through the images of their relationship, flickering like old film on a reel...their wedding, their lovemaking, the fighting and the making up. Her smile...her tears. In the end, they'd wanted different things; he wanted a family, a small town and a nine to five job that got him home each night. Em had been on a career path from hell, climbing the ladder, volunteering for the worst of the worst, and taking cases that put her in the line of fire. He couldn't live with the constant knot of worry that had taken up residence in his stomach, and finally threw in the towel. He'd packed up and moved home to Pine Ridge, South Dakota. It was where he'd grown up and where his parents still lived. Some part of him secretly hoped she'd miss him, finally agree he'd been right. But she hadn't. That was almost two years ago, and he had half the dream; a small town and a regular job. But he was missing the most important piece, someone to share it with. No, not just someone. Emma. He was still wallowing in the past when the plane touched down and the overhead cabin lights flickered on.

When Angels Cry

CHAPTER 4

Gregorio Aiden pushed his office door closed and pulled his cell out of his pocket at the same time. Violently, he pushed dial and waited for his call to connect.

A deep timbered male voice answered, and waiving any polite "hellos", said, "Ah, Attorney Aiden, I have been expecting your call. It is too bad what happened to your brother, my condolences to you and your family."

Gregorio leaned back in his chair, pinched the bridge of his nose, and barked, "Quinto was a fool, and the bitch that killed him probably did me a favor." He paused, blowing a frustrated breath, and then continued, "But he was my brother, and I won't allow his death to go unpunished. Handle the problem as quickly and as quietly as possible."

Without saying goodbye, he abruptly ended the call and tossed the phone onto his desk. He unlocked a desk drawer and pulled a manila file folder out. Without any reverence, Gregorio opened the folder and stared at the photos inside. Two blonde haired seven-year olds, and a mischievous looking nine year old redhead stared back at him. He smiled, "Very nice choices for Noah Walker, and a very nice payday for me." He reasoned. "The congressman will be very happy with these three." Gregorio leaned forward and pushed the intercom button that connected him with a young and very shapely secretary just outside his office door. "Jena, get me Congressman Walker on the line please."

"Yes sir. I'll put the call through priority once I have the congressman on the line."

"Thank you." Gregorio spun his black leather chair around and stood to stare out his office window. He watched the street traffic below the high rise building and thought about his brother, and his life, while he waited for the call. *Quinto, you were always a fool and this time you may have put me and our family in the line of fire. I owed you one little favor you said, just one time you begged, and look what it has cost us. You are dead and I am stuck in a partnership with a man I can't trust, so indebted to your partner that I might as well be dead.*

A soft chime sounded and pulled Gregory away from the window and back to his desk. Smothering his own doubt and uncertainty, he picked up the phone. "Noah, I trust that your delivery was all that you expected?" He said.

Noah Walker's southern drawl hissed on the line, "What the hell happened out there Gregory?" Gregorio winced at the Americanized version of his name. Even the nameplate on his door at the prestigious law firm of Jordan, Gilbert, Theisman and Aiden announced him as Gregory Aiden, Attorney at Law, but it still didn't feel as if it fit. He felt like a pretender in this world of wealth and privilege. Walker continued,

"Those girls were terrified, absolutely ter-ri-fied, when Jeri got back to the house with them last night. I had to give the two little one's something to make them sleep, and on top of that, what the hell happened to your man? Jeri said that the last thing she saw was your driver having a shootout with some woman. She had to drive the girls herself or risk everything. I hope you've got a good explanation for this Gregory."

His voice low and consoling, Gregorio empathized, "I understand that there were complications Noah, however, you can be assured that the problem has been taken care of. I have someone on the way to pick up the car and dispose of it as we speak. This was an isolated incident and I trust that we can continue to do business." *Never mind that my fucking brother is dead.* He thought.

Gregorio could almost see Congressman Noah Walker's handsome and calculating face through the phone line. There was no doubt that the man was going to expect a consolation for the mistake that Quinto made.

When Noah replied, his words dripped like winter rain, icy and cold through the phone, "Well now, I do think that we will be able to continue our business relationship. However, I think, and we both know, that there should be a financial adjustment on this delivery." He paused to let his statement penetrate a tactic Gregorio knew that Walker learned as a young politician and found to be well serving even after years of use. "After all, it will be some time before I can actually claim my reward with these three. The carelessness of your man, and the horror that they witnessed, will require that they have a longer than normal," he cleared his throat, "period of adjustment. Currently they are of no value to me, but I can invest the necessary time, assuming that we can reach an agreement."

Bastard. Gregorio fumed inside, but was careful not to let the fire reach his voice, "I understand your frustration with the delay, and can agree to a *minor* adjustment for your loss."

Ten minutes later, the agreement struck, Gregorio hung up the phone, a silent curse on his lips. *Dammit Quinto, your stupidity cost me one third of this shipment. One hundred and fifty thousand dollars gone. All because you wouldn't follow orders. Those girls should never have been at that damned warehouse. I told you it was under observation....I told you.*

CHAPTER 5

Tate followed the signs posted overhead toward the ground transportation area at Richmond International, where he quickly caught the eye of an on duty cabby. He waited while the yellow taxi pulled forward, tossed his duffle in the back seat and slid in. "St. Mary's Hospital on Bremo Road," he instructed the driver.

Once the cab moved away from the curb, Tate let his head sink back against the vinyl seat and closed his eyes. Silently he prayed that Emma was okay. *Just hold on baby. I'm almost there*, he thought. A myriad of possible scenarios and emotions threatened to smother him. *What if she doesn't pull through? Why did I leave her?* Tate pressed his fingertips against his closed eyes and pushed back the tears that threatened to spill. *You know why you left, but was that really the best thing? You should have just stayed and waited for her to come around, and then you would have been there when she needed you. This wouldn't have happened...if you'd just sucked it up and stayed.*

Fifteen minutes later, the taxi pulled to an easy stop in front of the entrance at St. Mary's. The hospital, a six story, brown brick, T-shaped building, was both old and new. The updates and add-ons made in recent years were clearly distinguishable against the original design of the building. Tate tossed a twenty over the seat to the driver, stepped out, and walked away without waiting for change.

Daylight struggled with darkness and seemed to be winning the battle. Soft tones of pink and yellow lightened the morning sky and formed a halo over the sun's globe as it fought to rise and rule the day, but Tate didn't notice the sun's battle, he only heaved his duffle up on one shoulder and walked through the frosted glass doors marking the entrance of the hospital. He stopped at the information desk and smiled at a thin fortyish woman with bottled-red curls and asked which room Emma was in. Following the woman's directions, Tate stepped into the elevator and pushed four.

Silently and quickly the conveyance moved upward toward the fourth floor. Gratefully he was alone for a moment and tried to brace himself for what he might see. Was Em even conscious? Did she know where she was? Who she was? Would she know him? All these questions swirled through Tate's mind and knotted his gut.

The elevator doors slid open soundlessly, and Tate turned right down a dimly lit hallway, and followed the signs showing room numbers until he reached room 420. Emma's room. Unsure what he would find inside, Tate took a deep breath and reached for the door handle. A shrill and nasal-voiced nurse behind a high counter stopped him.

"Sir! Sir you can go in there. Visiting

hours won't begin until nine." Nurse Webber said in her most authoritarian voice. She moved from her seat behind the counter to where Tate stood, just outside Emma's door.

Tate's back stiffened and he straightened to his full six feet plus. Stone faced he turned steel grey eyes on the bossy nurse and scowled, "Lady, if you think that I'm going to wait for two and a half hours before seeing my wife, then you'd better go call security, because it's going to take more than a frown and some finger wagging to keep me out of there."

Tate wasn't sure which word in his threat had made the difference to this woman, but something had. Her frown turned into a full blown smile making her look younger and sympathetic, and most of all willing to bend a few rules. "Well now. We didn't know that Agent Echo was married." Nurse Webber whispered.

Relaxing his posture, Tate shifted and softened his voice, "I got here as quickly as I could. How's Em doing?"

Glancing at her friends behind the counter Nurse Webber winked and clicking her tongue, she reached out to pat Tate's forearm. "Don't you worry a bit Mr. Echo, she's going to be just fine now that you're here. I wouldn't be surprised if she's not released after the doctor sees her today. You go on in, but if she's sleeping, please don't wake her. The poor thing keeps having nightmares, and on doctor's orders we've had to sedate her."

Noting the nurse's name, Tate replied, "You have my word on that Nurse Webber. I won't wake her. I just need to be in there when she does wake up."

Tate stepped into the barely lit room, paused to let his eyes adjust, and then released a breath that he hadn't known he was holding. The knot in his stomach softened, letting go of at least some small portion of the fear that he'd carried inside since he'd gotten the call from SAC Pruitt. *Em's going to be okay. Thank God for that!*

Tate dropped his duffle soundlessly near the door and moved to Emma's bedside. He stared down at her and frowned. Even in sleep, Emma's forehead was creased with worry, and one white knuckled hand gripped a bar on the bed rail as if she were afraid of falling. *Still beautiful...still mine.* He thought, before reminding himself for the millionth time that they were divorced.

Tate reached out and pushed a strand of silky mahogany hair behind Emma's ear then bent and dropped a feather-light kiss on the worry lines creasing her forehead. He smiled when the lines relaxed and a small breath escaped her lips. "That's it Em, no worries. I'm here now." He whispered. He moved a blue and chrome plastic chair closer to the bed and sat, allowing his body and mind to relax for the first time since he'd gotten the call from Emma's boss. He gently pulled Emma's hand into his own and turned it palm up. Without thought or hesitation, Tate pressed feather light kisses to Emma's soft skin and whispered, "I have never been so scared in my life Em. I don't know what I'd have done..." his voice cracked and trailed off. The silent tears that he'd refused to allow for the last seven hours, threatened to come again, and this time he let them.

Reassured that Emma was safe and alive, Tate let his head rest on the edge of the bed, next to Emma's hand. He drifted into a restful sleep and woke sometime later when Emma turned in her sleep. Seconds passed before she turned again, this time she cried out, begging for help from some unseen person. The pain and desperation in her voice shook him. Emma was normally a controlled professional that wouldn't give in to fear or pain, and Tate knew that whatever she'd been through had been a lot worse than just being shot. *And you weren't there Echo. You should have called, and then you would have at least known the mess that she was in, the risk. You let her down...again. And this time you almost lost her for good.*

Tate comforted her the only way he knew how. He lowered the bed rail and carefully lay on the edge of the bed, gingerly he gathered Emma against him as closely as he could without causing her pain. Almost immediately she stilled, one hand coming to rest on his chest. "That's it Em. Sleep baby, I've got you now."

Since receiving the midnight call from SAC Pruitt, Tate had run on adrenaline and coffee. The frantic fear of not reaching Emma in time and the trip to Virginia was a blur. Now that he'd seen her, exhaustion pulled at him and Tate drifted to sleep. His Em was safe and right where she belonged, in his arms. Just holding her close and knowing that she was safe was enough. Nothing else mattered, not the past or even the future. For this minute in time, Em was safe, and he was here to make sure that she stayed safe.

Nurse Webber pushed the door to Emma's room open, just wide enough to see inside. She smiled when she saw the couple spooning on the bed, both of them sound asleep. She turned to face her friends and crooked her index finger, motioning them over. Alice Webber moved back just far enough that they could peek into the room. The trio in white let the door gently close and walked quietly back behind the sterile counter, the only sound heard was their white soled shoes squeaking on the tile floor.

"You know that's against the rules Alice." The shorter nurse admonished.

"You're right Cynthia, but I say we look the other way as long as *that* woman is sleeping."

The trio locked eyes and nodded at each other, together they'd formed a silent pact and all turned back to their files and monitors, forgetting what they'd seen in room 420.

CHAPTER 6

Congressman Noah Walker pushed the white wood double doors to his three story farmhouse open and stepped inside. He stopped in the foyer to hang his coat and savored the smell of something baking. *Probably cookies.* He thought. Somewhere in another room he heard a television playing and children laughing. *His girls!* He walked quietly down a short marble-covered hallway and stopped in the doorway of the large two-story family room located on the east side of the house. Noah smiled, crossed his arms over his chest, and leaned on the door jamb. Silently he admired his girls.

Clustered around a wall-mounted television, two young girls sat cross-legged on the floor, they bumped shoulders and chattered about some program they were watching. The cathedral sized windows lining one wall let the morning light pour onto the floor where the girls sat, bathing them in its warm glow. Behind them on the sofa a girl of about fourteen sat, head down reading a book, soft brown hair shrouded her face.

Noah cleared his throat and watched the girls turn in surprise. That surprise turned to delight and they squealed and jumped to their feet to greet him.

"Daddy's home!" A girl of ten yelped and launched herself at Noah.

Catching the child to him, Noah pressed her small body tight against his own and covered her mouth with his. He sucked her bottom lip into his mouth, lightly pinching it between his teeth. He let one large hand drift down to cup her bottom and felt the heat in him rise. He drew back and smiled at the girl.

"Now that was a king's greeting indeed Nora. Thank you."

The Virginia congressman set Nora down, and turned to the other girl who waited to greet him. Folding his five foot nine inch frame down, he dropped a chaste kiss on the forehead of an eleven year old blonde-haired and blue eyed beauty. "That's not fair!" She cried. "I want a kiss better than you gave Nora. I *am* older you know."

Noah laughingly joked, "I didn't know that Chloe! You're older than Nora? How could I have forgotten such a thing? Come here and show me how to kiss you correctly." He dropped to his knees and watched Chloe slide closer to him. He allowed the girl full control of the kiss, she was the teacher today.

Noah remained motionless as Chloe wrapped her arms tight around his neck and pulled him toward her. Inches away she opened her mouth and he could practically feel her anticipating the kiss she was about to deliver.

"I am a better kisser than Nora," she whispered against his lips.

Without acknowledging her comment, Noah moaned when the girl slid her tongue seductively into his open mouth and flicked it against his own tongue. Silently, he begged her to battle with him. He needed her to take control and give him what he most desired. The girl rubbed her budding body against the now hard portion of his anatomy, teasing him, taunting him.

Seemingly satisfied that she'd done a better job than her rival, Chloe pulled back without letting go, and stared at Noah. "How was that Daddy?" She asked.

Noah pulled the girl close and buried his face against her check. He dipped his head and nipped at a barely budding breast hidden under her thin cotton shirt. He replied in a thick whisper, "That was perfect Chloe, just perfect. Thank you."

Across the room, fourteen year old Bethany stood, cleared her throat and frowned at the younger girls. "You girls run into the kitchen and let Ms. Anderson know that Daddy's home. If you're lucky those cookies she's been working on are out of the oven and you can have some."

The girls nodded and raced out of the room, their voices echoed back as they argued over who would get the most cookies.

Bethany locked eyes with Noah and flipped her dark hair back over one shoulder. Slowly she walked toward him. Tight low rise jeans hugged her dancer's legs and paired with a yellow off the shoulder crop top, the outfit offered Noah a peek-a-boo view of her taught abdomen as she advanced. The girl slid up to him and casually placed one hand on his shoulder, and allowed the other to run a trail down his chest before dropping to cup his dick through the light-weight wool dress pants. Coyly she smiled up at him then squeezed. She cooed, "Welcome home Daddy."

Noah groaned and pulled her roughly against him before lifting her small frame and forcing their bodies to meet at the most crucial juncture. Viciously his mouth covered hers in a brutal and exciting kiss. A kiss designed to punish the girl for teasing. She loved it and responded with a harsh kiss of her own.

Bethany, the oldest of the girls at the Walker farm, was unquestionably queen bee. The younger girls mimicked her and sought her out for advice, and while she loved the adoration of the other girls she craved the power that came from pleasing Noah. She'd do anything to earn his pleasure.

Noah was first to break the kiss. He looked down at Bethany and sternly ordered, "Go to your room Bethany."

With a smile Bethany pulled his hand up to her face, slipped one of his large fingers into her mouth and sucked deeply before letting his hand drop and leaving the room. Noah watched as she climbed the stairs, the swaying hips of the woman-child held him in place until she disappeared from sight.

CHAPTER 7

Sun filtered in through the closed blinds and begged Emma to wake up. Still under the effects of the medicine that Nurse Webber had administered the night before, she opened one eye and frowned. *I'm still in the hospital.* She thought. Then she felt it, rather, she felt *him.* Coming fully awake she froze. *There's someone in the bed with me?* Emma let her eyes move downward and stared at the definitely male hand resting possessively just under her breasts. *I know that hand!* She thought. "Tate?" She whispered, her voice hoarse from sleep.

Tiny kisses on the back of her neck confirmed it and grinning for what felt like the first time in weeks, Emma burrowed deeper against Tate's warm body. *I'm safe, really safe.* She thought. Contentedly Emma closed her eyes and drifted into a restful sleep, her first in days. This time her dreams were filled with the past; their past, and while the dreams were different they were almost as disturbing.

Sometime later, the rattling of dishes outside Emma's room woke Tate, and careful not to disturb Emma, he slipped from the bed. Tate stared down at Emma and for the first time noticed the dark circles under her eyes, the paleness of her skin, and the large bandage on her hip and lower back. Tate gently pulled the covers up and tucked them lightly around Emma's sleeping form; at last he was certain that in time, she would be alright. He walked on stocking feet to the door and picked up his duffle bag. Careful not to wake Emma, he walked into the tiny bathroom set in the corner of the room and quietly closed the door before flicking the light on.

He stared at his reflection in the mirror and said, "You're a mess Echo. You can't let Em see you like this." He rummaged in his bag and pulled first his toothbrush, and then a disposable razor out, and set them on the edge of the small sink.

He's gone. She thought. *Maybe he wasn't here at all. Maybe it was just a dream.* Rolling to her back, Emma winced at the pain in her hip but didn't turn over. She let one arm rest over her eyes and tried to separate her dreams from reality.

"You awake Em?" Tate's deep timbered voice sounded in the small room.

Now that sounded real. She thought.

Emma slowly pulled her arm down and opened her eyes. She stared at Tate leaning against the metal frame of the bathroom door. She sucked in a deep breath and felt tears pooling in her eyes. *He's here and he's just as gorgeous as he ever was.* She took in his dark hair and freshly shaved face. Grinning she exclaimed, "Tate! I thought I'd dreamed you!"

Tate gave her his best smile; a dimple dotted one clean shaven cheek as he walked toward her. "Snuggled up in that little bed with you I had a few dreams myself, Sugar." He bent and dropped a kiss on her lips, and then he stepped back to really look at her.

Satisfied that his earlier assumption that she would heal was correct, Tate demanded. "Tell me what happened, Em."

Before Emma could explain how she'd landed in St. Mary's Hospital, the door opened and a thirty something doctor walked into the room. With a straight white toothed grin he asked, "Agent Echo, how are you feeling this afternoon? I see you have a visitor today. That's always a good thing."

Tate stepped forward and extended his hand to the doctor. He introduced himself, "Tate Echo. And you are?"

The doctor grasped Tate's outstretched hand and replied, "Dr. Brett Simms. Very nice to meet you, Mr. Echo. We're very happy that Agent Echo has family with her now." He turned to Emma and continued, "And if everything checks out with your CT scan today, I don't see any reason that you can't be released, now that your husband is here to help you at home."

Emma tried to sit up and failed. She winced at the pain in her leg and then leaned back on the raised bed. She didn't miss the 'husband' comment but if that meant she could leave the hospital today, she wasn't going to argue the point, "So you'll be releasing me back to duty? I have..."

Dr. Simms laughed and glanced first at Tate, and then turned back to Emma. "No release for duty yet, Agent Echo. You'll need some home health care visits to assist with dressing that wound and..."

Cutting the man off Emma said, "No. I can do it myself."

Dr. Simms smiled indulgently and continued, "Now Agent Echo, you can't even see the bulk of that wound, and it's going to need cleaning and dressing every day for about two weeks."

Raising a hand, Tate interrupted, "I'll be able to dress the wound, Dr. Simms."

The doctor turned to Tate and chided, "Now Mr. Echo, we really should have a qualified professional stop by to care for Emma's wound; we can't risk any infection or other problems that might land her back in here. There are several qualified home health care agencies in Richmond, and I'm confident that we can find someone suitable for her."

Tate's smile didn't quite reach his eyes, and his tone did nothing to hide his coldness when he responded, "I am a certified critical care paramedic and I *will* be responsible for Em's care. Now if you could just get that CT set up and send Nurse Webber in here with some directions on my wife's care, we'd like to leave now."

Surprised at the unforgiving firmness in

Tate's voice, Dr. Simms lifted an eyebrow and then raised his hands in defeat. He locked eyes with Emma, frowned and said, "I'll have someone from Radiology down to pick you up in about ten minutes for the CT." Turning back to Tate he continued, "Nurse Webber's shift ended a couple hours ago, but I'll send in the RN on duty to provide you with your initial supplies and directions. You are to bring her in immediately if she gets a fever, or if the wound shows any signs of redness or infection, understood?"

Tate nodded and replied, "Understood, and just so that we're clear, I want to assure you that I would do nothing to compromise Em's care. We'll follow your direction explicitly."

An hour and a half later, and finally cleared to leave the hospital, Emma stood alone in the tiny bathroom praying that she could get her clothes on without help. One step at a time Emma. Just one step at a time. She silently demanded.

She pulled the strings that tied in front of the hospital gown, and let the garment slide off her shoulders and onto the floor. Emma leaned against a small chrome sink jutting from the wall and stared at herself in the mirror. Gingerly she touched the angry blue-black bruise just above her left breast. "Damn good thing you had that vest on." She whispered. Without attempting to put her bra on, she pushed her arms through the sleeves of a button down shirt, the movement cost her, and Emma sucked her bottom lip between her teeth struggling not to cry out. She breathed deeply, in and out, willing the pain away. "You're half way there." She muttered.

Tate's voice seeped into the small bathroom. "Two minutes Em, and then I'm coming in there whether you like it or not."

"Back off, Echo. I can do this." She demanded, and sat on the closed toilet. Emma pushed first one foot then the other into her jeans and pulled them onto her legs before standing up. She sucked in a deep breath, clamped her teeth together and fought to ignore the throbbing pain in her leg when she pulled the jeans up and over the bandaged wound. Beads of sweat popped out on her colorless face, while her fingers fumbled with the snap on her jeans. Giving up on the snap Emma turned the faucet on and used a shaky hand to splash cool water on her face.

The bathroom door opened and Tate poked his head in the small space, "Time's up Em." He looked at Emma's ashen face, still wet from the splashing she'd done and he spewed, "Why the hell do you have to be so stubborn? You look about ready to pass out." Tate slid an arm around Emma's waist and guided her back to the bed. He stood back and watched her sink onto the mattress and close her eyes. *She's in pain...bad pain.* He thought. Tate stepped closer, pushed her damp hair back from her face and whispered, "Just give it a little time Em, you don't have to be strong all the time. I'm here to help you, if you'll just let me."

When Emma didn't respond Tate dropped into the hard blue chair and watched her struggle to control the pain. Her eyes were closed; one white-knuckled hand gripped the bed rail while the other hand flexed open and closed in time with her breathing. He knew the look, and he knew that this was not the time to raise hell about her stubbornness, or anything else. He silently shook his head and leaned back in the chair to wait for Emma to deal with the pain in her own way.

One, two, three... Emma silently counted. *You can do this. Just concentrate and breathe. In and out, in and out. That's it.* She encouraged herself. With a final deep breath she pushed past the pain and managed to sit up on the side of the bed. A few minutes later the door opened and a man pushing a wheelchair padded into the room, his white shoes squeaking on the tile floor.

Emma insisted, "I won't be needing that...*thing.* I am perfectly capable of walking down to the lobby and getting into a cab!"

The aide gave her a big, white toothed grin and bent to lock the wheels of the chair in place before he replied, "Hospital policy ma'am. All patients are escorted to the lobby, and all are required to ride. It's not so bad. If you'll just have a seat, I'll get you out of here as quickly as possible. We could even pull a few wheelies if you're up to it." He joked.

Tate bit back a smile and watched Emma ease down into the chair, her jaw clinched in aggravated acceptance. He moved to open the door and walked a few paces behind as Emma was wheeled away.

The elevator doors opened and the trio moved back to allow passengers to exit. A tall blonde, broad shouldered man in his early forties was last to step out of the conveyance. He carried a foil wrapped bouquet of fresh blooms, "Emma, I was just on my way to see you!" He stopped in front of her and bent to kiss her cheek, laying the flowers in her lap as he did. "You've been released, that's wonderful."

Emma smiled at the man and then remembered Tate standing at her side, "Clay Shuler, I'd like you to meet Tate Echo. Tate, this is Clay, he's the captain of the task force that I've been assigned to. Tate's in town to help out while I recover."

The two men shook hands, but there were no warm smiles. Clay shot Tate a look and then turned to Emma, "Emma," he chided, "if you needed help, all you had to do was ask. I'd have been more than willing to help you out, and you know you're always welcome at my house."

Emma looked embarrassed, "I appreciate the offer, but I think I'll be more comfortable at my own house."

The aide behind Emma cleared his throat, Emma glanced back at him and said to Shuler, "I'm sorry to rush, but we have a taxi waiting downstairs. It was really sweet of you to come by and check on me and thanks for the flowers."

Clay smiled and stepped back so that they could enter the elevator. "I'll catch the next one. And Emma, do take care and call me if you need anything at all."

Tate nodded his goodbye and followed Emma into the elevator.

Once the doors closed Emma muttered, "That was a little awkward. I never would have pegged Clay for the hospital visiting or flowers type. Maybe he just feels guilty because he was late getting to the warehouse that night."

"Maybe so." Tate said tightly. Silently he thought that maybe the man had thought a hospital visit would get him a 'come over to the house' visit, and that would lead to a bedroom visit. He'd seen the type before, the predatory look around the eyes, the posturing that screamed "back off" to any other male in the county. *Fuck Shuler*. He thought.

CHAPTER 8

Simon Alvarez sat on a stone bench near a fountain just outside St. Mary's Hospital, waiting. He was good at waiting. He'd already learned from a rather talkative aide that the woman who killed Quinto would be released today, and when she was, he intended to follow her and kill her. *And then you will leave the country with a fat wallet, compliments of Mr. Aiden.* The matte black, Kel-Tec nine millimeter in his boot was loaded with a fresh clip, and his Harley, just twenty feet away, waited with him.

Simon looked up when the double glass doors under the portico slid open, he watched a male aide push a scowling young woman out of the hospital. A large man dressed in jeans and carrying a blue duffle bag followed a few steps behind them. The man with the duffle moved around to help the woman out of the wheelchair when a yellow cab stopped, its rubber wheels squeaking on the brick driveway.

This is it, Simon thought, already moving toward the waiting motorcycle. He pulled the chin strap of his helmet tight and flipped the dark shield down to cover his face before slinging one leg over the powerful machine.

When the cab moved out of the hospital parking lot and onto the highway, Simon pulled his bike out three cars behind it. He followed at a discrete distance, but never lost sight of his prey.

Tate settled in the back seat of the cab next to Emma and watched her closely. He didn't like the ashen color of her face, or the pain that he saw in her eyes. "You doing okay, Em?" He asked quietly.

With a barely perceptible nod to indicate that she was fine, Emma turned her head and stared out the window, wondering how this was going to work. Seven months ago, she'd gone to Pine Ridge, South Dakota to help Tate with a serial killer case, and it had taken all the will power she possessed not to fall in bed with him every time he looked at her. *Now here we are again. And he's being so damned nice.* It was one thing to push him away when he was being his usual arrogant and bossy self, but saying no when he turns on the charm and makes a point to be so caring, well that was going to be more than hard, it would be torture.

Tate scooted closer to Emma, leaned over and whispered in her ear. Low enough that the cab driver couldn't hear, he said, "I think we've picked up a shadow, black Harley, matching helmet, left lane."

Emma glanced around the driver and scanned the road behind them in the side mirror of the cab. "I see him." Speaking to the driver she instructed, "Take a left here please."

With a nod, the driver flicked his blinker on and moved over one lane before completing the turn.

Without turning around, Emma watched the motorcycle behind them discretely. She saw the biker drop back a few lengths, and then complete the turn behind them.

"You recognize him or maybe the Harley?" Tate asked.

Emma didn't take her eyes off the mirror but she shook her head in response to Tate's question. To the driver, she said, "Please pull over at the coffee shop on the next corner."

Tate nodded his head and confirmed that he understood the plan. He scooted back across the seat and let one hand rest on the door handle, ready to get out as soon as the taxi stopped. He'd pretend to go in for coffee and try to get the license plate on the Harley as the shadow drove by.

Simon slowed the Harley and watched the man get out of the car and then look back inside to say something through the open window to the woman. *Maintain speed and drive right by.* Then another thought slipped in. He could circle the block and take the shot now. She's alone, well except for the cab driver, but then smart cabbies never see a thing – at least the ones who care to keep breathing don't. *Not a good idea Simon. You've got to be sure she's dead.* He scolded his desire to rush and be done with this mess. He had to be patient and be sure this little loose end would never come back and bite him in the ass. Simon stared straight ahead and maneuvered the motorcycle past the cab and took a right at the next corner, intending to double back.

Tate leaned casually against the side of the taxi and watched the Harley move past them and then turn right at the next corner. As soon as the big black machine cleared the corner, he jumped back inside the cab, slammed the door and bellowed, "Move! Take a left at the next corner and a right at the one after that."

The taxi shot out into the street, a horned blared behind them. "You people in trouble?" The cabby asked, nervously glancing back at Tate and Emma in the rearview mirror.

Emma managed a weak smile for the man, and said, "Nothing to worry about. That motorcycle that passed us back at the coffee shop seems to be following us, and we'd rather he didn't."

The cab driver frowned at her, "I don't want no trouble in my cab, so maybe I can drop you..."

Tate interrupted the man, and snapped, "You will drive." He pointed at Emma and continued, "This woman is with the FBI and she was recently shot on duty. You will drop us when and where we tell you to, and not one inch before then."

The driver nodded nervously and maneuvered the cab around a corner before he risked a glance back at Emma, "This man, the one on the motorcycle, he wants to shoot you?"

He asked.

Emma leaned forward and read the drivers name from his certification card. "We're not sure exactly what he wants Mr. Sperraza, and we would prefer that he not get the chance if shooting me is his plan."

Mr. Sperraza flashed a yellow toothed grin at Emma in the mirror and bragged, "Ah, no worries then. I know the city better than anyone, and I will make sure that he does not follow us. You will be safe with me."

Tate continued to watch the mirror and toss an occasional glance out the back window, watching for their shadow. "I think we lost him."

After a series of twists and turns rivaling a corn maze, Mr. Sperraza turned the cab left on a quiet street lined with centuries old Sugar Maples, Sycamores and Post Oak trees. He pulled the cab to a stop in front of a mid-sized white bungalow with gray trim, and without turning the motor off he stepped out and opened the rear door for Emma. "Here you are Miss, safe and sound, just as I promised."

Emma smiled up at the man and gingerly stepped out of the cab. "Thank you, Mr. Sperraza, we couldn't have made it without you."

At the rear of the cab, Tate rolled his eyes. "Go inside Em. I'll grab our bags and be right in." He pulled some cash from his wallet and handed the money to Mr. Sperraza. Quietly Tate spoke to the man, "Look, I appreciate what you did for us. I'd like you to take the same route back, I know it will take longer but I don't want anyone to be able to back-track and find us here. Can you do that for us?"

Mr. Sperraza nodded his understanding and took the money that Tate held. He smiled up at Tate and said, "You can count on me sir."

Two blocks down the tree lined street, Simon Alvarez toed the Harley backwards, tucking it out of site in an alley littered with refuse and empty crates from a street side restaurant. *They thought they were so slick, but all they are is dead.* He grinned at the thought.

CHAPTER 9

Gregorio Aiden took the white stone steps two at a time and entered his house through the kitchen door. A round woman well into her fifties stood at the kitchen sink. She looked up in surprise when he entered, but smiled. Gregorio raised a questioning eyebrow at the woman and pressed one finger to his lips. She smiled broadly at his unasked question, and pointed through an open door and mouthed, "The dining room".

Gregorio silently walked to the doorway of the bright yellow room and slipped behind a small dark-haired child sitting on her knees in an ornate dining room chair. He slipped his hands over her eyes and leaned in close. "Guess." He whispered.

Itasca Aiden laughed, she loved this game. She already knew who it was, but guessing a few times was always more fun. She reached up and gently traced her fingers over the large hands that covered her eyes. Thoughtfully, she said, "It's not Mrs. Calder; her hands are soft and smell like lemons." She ran her small hands over his fingers and paused to feel the large onyx ring that he wore, she continued, "It's not Nana Navarone because she has more rings on her fingers. So…it must be Daddy!" She exclaimed before jumping from the chair and wrapping her arms around the Gregorio's legs.

Gregorio lifted the child into his arms and kissed her forehead. He pulled back and looked at her. "Tassie Aiden, I think you grow an inch every day when I'm away at work!"

Tassie hugged him tight, laughed, and then suggested, "You could stay home and watch me grow Daddy." Without waiting for his response, the child continued, "Want to know what I did today?"

Gregorio shifted his daughter to one hip, nodded, and listened to her chatter about her day while he walked to the family room. He knew that his mother would be waiting in the family room; she always waited there for him to come home. Holding Tassie closer and smelling the baby shampoo scent of her hair made him think of the three little girls that he'd sent to live with Noah Walker.

He'd always consoled himself with the thought that the children he placed were not on the streets, they had nice homes and good food. Wasn't that enough? He pulled Tassie closer, and let himself think for just one second, of the horrors that they faced inside their beautiful homes and with their full bellies. He'd convinced himself it was a good trade off; their innocence for a better life. But was he any better than that pedophile Walker? After all, he'd sent them there. Gregorio sighed, knowing that he didn't have a choice, not now. He shuddered and vowed that nothing like that would ever happen to his daughter, not his beautiful Itasca.

Theresa Navarone set aside her book and stood when Gregory entered the room. She looked up at him, frowned and said, "Put that child down Gregorio. She is four years old and much too big to be carried. You spoil her more each day and that is not good for a child."

Gregorio dropped a kiss on his mother's cheek and retorted, "Itasca is indeed four years old, but she is not too old or too big to occasionally be carried by her *father*. As for the spoiling? She is my only child and I am inclined to spoil her for many years yet."

The older woman took her seat, picked her book up and muttered, "That she is your child is certainly questionable."

"Tassie, will you go and ask Mrs. Calder to bring us a glass of lemonade? I would like to speak with Nana Navarone for a moment." Gregorio sat Itasca down and watched her run to do his bidding.

At the doorway, Tassie looked back at her daddy and blew him a kiss. She didn't make eye contact with her grandmother.

Certain that Tassie was out of earshot, Gregorio knelt at his mother's side and took her hands in his. Turning them, he looked at the wrinkled skin and dark spots that marked her more with each passing year. With a deep sigh he started, "Mother, in your heart you know that Itasca is my child. She is not to blame for the circumstances that kept her from us for two years, and I want you to stop referring to her as *that child.* We are family and I ask very little from you, but this I demand. I will not allow you to hurt Tassie."

Theresa pulled her hand free and wiped at some unshed tear before softly reprimanding him, "Quinto has been dead for four days and my heart is broken, but all you can think of is your *Tassie.* Why haven't you found your brother's killer? Isn't that what is most important now?"

Gregorio's jaw clenched with frustration, his mother had always found a way to divert any conversation about Itasca, and she hadn't failed this time either. He stood and looked down at his mother, "I have promised you that I will find Quinto's killer, and I will keep my word to you. Now I want your word, your promise, that you will treat Itasca with the love and attention that she deserves as my child. She *is* your only grandchild and that should be important to you now more than ever."

Without giving him the promise he'd asked for, Theresa watched Mrs. Calder enter the room. The servant carried a silver tray topped with a picture of lemonade and a plate of cookies; *that child* closely followed her. *Thank God they came back before she had to make a ridiculous promise to Gregorio.* "Ah, your refreshments have arrived Gregorio. I think I will retire to my room and rest a bit." Theresa rose from her chair, carefully placed her book on a side table and left the family room without looking at Itasca.

CHAPTER 10

Tate watched the yellow cab pull away from the curb and wondered if they'd actually ditched the shadow. He thought he'd caught a glimpse of the big black Harley when they'd exited the freeway but he hadn't seen him again. He didn't want to alarm Emma, but to the unseen enemy, he challenged, *Bring it on you bastard. I'll be waiting for you.*

Tate picked up the bag that contained the dressings and medicines for Emma's wound, slung his duffle over one shoulder and walked to the house. Emma had finally moved out of the apartment that they'd shared and bought a house; a vintage bungalow just outside Richmond, in what most considered to be the historical district. *Maybe she's changed too*, he thought. When they'd been together it had always been his dream to ditch the apartment, buy a house, get a dog and have a couple kids. *Maybe she's ready now.* He pushed the door open and stepped into a small parquet floored entryway. The first thing he noticed about Emma's house was the alarm panel on the wall, made note of the brand and model, *Best available, that's good.* He heard Emma's voice coming from the adjoining room, she was talking to someone on the phone. Tate followed the sound of her voice.

"What do you mean 'suspended'?" Emma thundered into the phone. She paused, listened, and then continued, "You know as well as I do that he *did* have a gun. How the hell do you explain the fact that I was *shot?*" Tate watched her nod her head as if the person at the other end of the line could see her, before she said, "I told you there was a woman there. She emptied my gun on him, and then put it back in my hand. She even told me that I *owed* her a favor." She paused, listening to whoever was on the phone, and then continued, "Of course there was GSR on my hands. I never said I didn't shoot him, I did. Once, in the leg, but I didn't kill him and I didn't empty my Glock on him."

Tate leaned against the door frame and watched Emma's face turn a bright red. *She's hot.* He thought.

Emma listened but said little more before she disconnected the call and turned on him. "Can you believe that shit? Suspended! I have never shot anyone without just cause and they damn well know it."

Tate dropped the bag containing the medical supplies on the table and pulled Emma by the arm, leading her to the sofa in the next room. "Sit down Em. I'm going to grab a glass of water and your pain meds and then we can talk about this. You know that Pruitt, assuming that's who you were talking to, is just following procedure. The facts will come out. Just sit here and relax a minute, and I'll be right back."

Tate returned a few minutes later with a glass of water and an opaque brown bottle of pain medicine. He handed the water off to Emma, dropped down on the sofa with her, and opened the prescription bottle, shaking one capsule out for her.

Emma leaned back on the cushions and Tate moved to give her room. He pulled her feet into his lap and unconsciously massaged her toes. The simple action opened a floodgate of memories. Evenings spent together on the sofa, telling each other about their days, sharing their dreams or just feeling the closeness of each other with no words passing between them. Expelling a long breath, Tate said, "Tell me what happened that night, Em."

Emma closed her eyes and reveled in his touch. "Mmmm...I've missed those foot massages, Tate." She allowed herself to enjoy the feeling a moment more then pulled her feet back from his grasp. She opened her eye's but didn't sit up. "It's a long story and it's not over yet. I've been assigned to the Bureau of Justice Assistance for the last four months, working as part of a specialized task force to break down a trafficking operation. Rumor on the street is that some guy calling himself 'Captain' heads it up. We got that from an informant early in the operation but so far, we haven't gotten a glimpse of Captain and a few weeks later the informant OD'd down on Eighteenth Street, not too far from where I was shot in fact."

"Drugs?" Tate asked.

Shaking her head Emma continued, "Kids, mostly young girls but some boys too. It makes me sick to think about it, some of the ones we found were as young as six." She rose up on her elbows and stared at Tate, "These demented bastards are selling kids to some perverted sexual deviants. I can't even imagine what these kids are going through."

Tate leaned back and propped his feet on the coffee table, he resisted the urge to touch her and put his hands behind his head. He encouraged her to go on, "So what were you doing alone at that warehouse the night you were shot? Where was the rest of the team?"

Emma leaned back, sighed and said, "I got a tip from a street informant that there were kids being held in the warehouse, so I called Clay, and he was supposed to meet me there, well, him and the rest of the team. I waited for over an hour and he was a no show, so I slipped to the back of the building hoping I could get inside, or at the least hear something that would warrant calling in the Richmond PD."

"And did you?" Tate asked.

Emma nodded and closed her eyes, remembering that night. "I stood at the corner of the warehouse and watched an ambulance drive in and drop three little girls; two blondes and a red-head. There was a middle-aged woman already inside the warehouse and she came out when the ambulance backed up to the door. I couldn't hear what they were saying, but she only talked a minute or so, then she led the two blonde kids into the building. She must have said something to reassure them because they went without any problems." Emma chuckled, "But the red-head kid put up a fight. From what I could see she totally lived up to the 'red haired' fiery reputation. The driver finally had to pull her out of the ambulance and carry her kicking and yelling into the building."

Already knowing that she hadn't, Tate forced his anger down and asked anyway, "So then you called Richmond PD?"

"No. I sent a text to Clay; I thought we had some time before the pick-up came. I didn't think they'd move the kids right away." Regret filled her eyes and Emma's voice thickened, "If I had called for back-up, chances are those girls would...."

Tate interrupted her, his voice icy, "Don't go there, Em. It won't change anything." Silently he acknowledged that it might have changed everything. Emma probably wouldn't have been shot, the girls probably wouldn't have been taken. Anger threatened to overtake him but he pushed the thoughts away, knowing that it was too late to change what had happened now and thankful that Emma was alive. "You should have called for the damn back-up and Shuler's not much of a leader if he didn't even bother to show up."

Emma sat frozen, she knew that Tate was right, but she hated hearing the words aloud, seeing the anger flash in his eyes and knowing the effort that it took for him to remain as calm as he was right now.

At her nod, Tate continued, "So what about the ambulance, you get a tag or anything on that?"

Emma shook her head, "Not a damn thing. It was too dark to see the plates and there wasn't any logo or identifying info on it. White for sure, but nothing more. The guy driving was dark skinned, probably Hispanic. I caught a quick glance when he went into the building."

"What about the woman? You get a look at her?" Tate questioned.

"White woman, white uniform. Like a nurse or maybe a nanny. Probably in her late forties or early fifties."

"So what happened next?" Tate interrogated. Unconsciously his hands drifted back to her feet.

"A few minutes, maybe five, passed, and a dark sedan, a Town Car, I think, pulled up. One man inside, dark complexion, late twenties or early thirties, well dressed. He got out and went into the warehouse for no more than two minutes, then the woman came out with the two blondes, and they got into the car. Then the man came out pushing the little red haired girl in front of him, she was still resisting, but the kid didn't have a chance." Emma swallowed hard, her voice barely audible. "I had to stop them. I couldn't just stand there and watch them leave with those kids."

Tate's hands stilled on Emma's feet, he probed, "All this time passed and still nothing from Shuler. Incredible. So that's when you made your move?"

"Yeah, I stepped out and identified myself, then I ordered him to let go of the girl. He shoved the kid toward the car and turned on me. I moved back for cover, but he'd already fired, so did I, but I think my shot only grazed his leg; he didn't go down. His first shot hit me in the chest, thank God for the vest. My gun flew out of my hand when I hit the ground and the bastard kept coming. I remember seeing the woman get out of the backseat and drive away with the girls. Then he was right in front of me, screaming at me, telling how it was going to feel to die. He kept saying that the last name I would ever hear would be Quinto Navarone."

Agitated, Tate stood up and paced the small space in front of the couch. He paced and tried to tap down the emotions that threatened to spill from his soul. Fear, anger….relief…boiled together and formed a volatile cocktail inside him. *She could be dead now, you could have lost her. She knew to wait for back-up…FBI rule number one, no grandstanding. She's right here in front of you and you still have a chance to make things right.* He stopped in front of her and struggled to keep his voice even. "So, we know how you got the chest wound, how about the one on your thigh? The bastard shot you again when you were unarmed and missed so badly that he only hit your leg?"

Emma sat up and continued, "No, or at least I don't think so. The chest shot knocked me down. I was crawling or scooting toward the curb, my gun was near a garbage dumpster there. Before I could reach my gun, a really tall woman stepped out from behind the dumpster, picked up my gun and unloaded it on him. I think that the thigh shot happened when he fell and reflexed on the trigger going down."

"So tell me about the woman." Tate prompted.

"She didn't say much, but I'm pretty sure it was personal for her. She unloaded my Glock on him, and then kept dry firing the gun after he was down. She walked over to him, pocketed his gun and spit on him before putting my own gun back in my hand."

Tate whistled through his teeth, dropped into a chair across from her and said, "Clearly it was personal for her. Maybe she was his wife or lover, or one of the kids was hers. Doubtful that she was just a Good Samaritan who just stepped in to save you. Did she say anything to him? I mean we both know that woman usually kill for emotional reasons, that's why there are fewer female serials, so, what was her emotional reason?

Emma nodded her agreement, "She didn't say a word to him. She kept dry firing my gun after he was down like she wanted to keep killing him, or make damn sure that he was dead."

Tate frowned, "You said she told you that you owed her a favor, what'd she ask for?"

"Nothing. She flipped my badge over, looked at it and then told me that I was alive and that was more than some others. She said that I owed her, not then, but someday soon. I was fading in and out but I remember her telling me that help was on the way. Then she just walked away. Disappeared behind the dumpster."

Tate turned the event over in his mind trying to make sense of it, "So we can assume that whoever she is, at some point she's going to want something from you. She's got your name and she's got a gun. Scary combination, Em. She could have killed you just to make sure there were no witnesses. I have a hard time understanding why she wouldn't, I mean no killer walks away and lets the one person who can identify them live."

Emma nodded, "I thought about that too. I mean, clearly she hated Navarone but I don't think she's a killer...yeah, she killed him, but for some reason I think she had to do it. Again, back to the 'something personal'."

"You listed in the phone book?" Tate's voice was calm when he asked the question, but inside his stomach roiled, his heart pounded in his ears and his mind spun. *Thank God for whoever this woman was. Without her, Emma would be dead...and where would that leave you, Echo? How would you make it through even one day knowing that you should have been here to protect her?* He had no answers.

Emma rolled her eyes at him, "You know I

wouldn't do that. Even if I wasn't in the Bureau, I wouldn't want every crank caller or telemarketer on the planet calling me."

Tate saw the exhaustion on Emma's face and knew that her pain meds would kick in soon. He ordered, "Lay back down, Em. You rest a while, and then we'll work on getting a description of the woman for Pruitt. Blankets in the hall closet?"

Emma nodded, stretched out on the couch and closed her eyes. A few seconds later Tate returned with a light blanket and tucked it around her.

Tate stared down at Emma and thought that how some things never seem to change. They'd been divorced for a while now, and still she had the power to make him feel more than anyone else. "I still love you Em," he whispered.

CHAPTER 11

Noah Walker descended the stairs and pushed a hand through his damp hair. Today's tryst with Bethany confirmed what he'd already known. It was time for Bethany to go. *She's too old, too crude....just too...too everything.* He pondered a moment. *Now how to make her disappear?* He'd been in this situation before, a girl on the brink of womanhood was just more than he wanted to deal with, in fact, any grown woman was more than he wanted to deal with. *Is it the loss of innocence, the mature body? What is it that's such a turn off?* Noah admitted to himself that he knew the answer to that question. It was everything and more. He couldn't look at an adult woman's body and find the same thrill that his girls gave him, it wasn't that he hadn't tried when he'd been younger...he just couldn't.

Jeri Anderson smiled at Noah when he entered the kitchen. She leaned against a speckled- granite topped counter and watched over his girls. Noah winked at her. He depended on Jeri, but more than that, he trusted her.

Jeri had been his lifeline from the time they were kids. She was always there to pick him up and make things right. He'd been five when they'd met, and Jeri was his sister Sara's best friend. Sara had been six years older than him and their mother had forced her to take Noah everywhere that she went, and Jeri was right there with them...until the accident.

The memory seeped in, and Noah let it come. He could see the three of them riding down the blacktop road on their bikes as if it were yesterday. It was summer and they'd ridden their bikes to the lake every day. Sara's legs were long and tanned as she pumped the bike, making it go faster. Her hair flew loose and blonde behind her in the wind. She always had to be first. Noah's hands grasp the counter in front of him and his eyes closed. He saw the truck, heard Jeri scream and watched helplessly as his sister's body flew through the air and landed in the weed filled ditch. He'd run all the way home, his heart pounding in his chest, to get his mother, but when he'd gotten there she wasn't in the house. At least that's what he'd thought until he heard the laughter coming from her bedroom.

The memories flew through his head now and Noah was powerless to stop them. He pushed the door open and stopped. His mother glanced around the body of the man poised atop her, and spied him in the doorway. He could still remember her words, *Come in here Noah. Sit down here on the bed next to me. This is a beautiful thing.* Noah ran that day, but he couldn't outrun the memory, not then and not now. His mother's short legs wrapped around some man's hairy back, his chest pressing her breasts flat while he pumped and grunted above her. His stomach roiled at the thought, flabby untoned, flesh on flesh...it was vulgar and even at five, he knew that he would never touch a woman that way...never. Jeri had tried to explain it to him but it was just too much for a five year old.

Noah shook his head and turned around to lean against the counter next to Jeri, who even now, was a nice looking woman, and even though she had been his first love, his confidant, his protector, he couldn't think of her as anything but a trusted friend. He shook off that vile day and forced those memories back where they belonged, his mother was a whore and there was nothing more to consider. That is what happened to women once they were grown and what he didn't want to witness happen to his girls. He would enjoy them while they were fresh and innocent and then someone else could ruin them. He watched Chloe pulled a cookie sheet from the oven, and place it on the cabinet where Nora and two other girls stood waiting with a spatula and a tray.

"Those smell wonderful girls!" He said. "I hope you saved some for me."

Chloe giggled and placed one hand provocatively on her hip, "Daddy, you know that we can't have cookies until after dinner."

Noah stepped closer to Chloe and dropped a kiss atop her head. From the corner of his eye he saw the two new girls shy away. Both of them moved to Jeri's side, the shorter of the two popped a thumb in her mouth. *Endearing.* Noah thought. He stepped closer to Jeri and locked eyes with the taller of the two blondes, "I wouldn't want to spoil our dinner, so I will wait.

First we have dinner, then cookies and then what would you girls like to do?"

Nora and Chloe spoke at once, "Fashion show!"

"Ah, fashion show it is. How about you two go upstairs and work on your costumes while I talk to Ms. Anderson."

The two girls ran from the room chattering to each other about the evening entertainment and the costumes that they would wear.

The congressmen dropped to one knee to be at eye level of the younger girls so they wouldn't fear him. He reached a hand out. Gently he cupped the cheek of the smaller blonde. "What's your name sweetheart?" She had the most incredible blue eyes....just like Sara....

The child smiled shyly, pulled her thumb from her mouth and answered, "I'm Allie." She glanced at the girl next to her and whispered, "This is Ivy."

"Allie and Ivy, you *are* a beautiful pair. Now tell me, would you like to play fashion show tonight or would you like to help me judge the best costume?"

Ivy stammered, "I want to dress up."

Allie grinned and echoed Ivy's answer, "Me too. Nora showed us how."

Noah kissed each girl chastely on the

head, and said, "Very good. Why don't you join Nora and Chloe and work on your outfits until dinner. I can't wait to see what beautiful surprises you have for me!"

The girls stepped away from Jeri, joined hands and whispered to each other as they walked away. At the doorway, Allie stopped and looked back at Noah, "See you later...Daddy." She said shyly.

Noah winked and agreed, "Yes, and I'll see you later too." Noah sighed with relief. The girls would fit in nicely. Already they wanted to please him. Once the girls had left the room Noah turned to Jeri, "What about the other one? Where is she?"

Jeri frowned and said, "That one is a terror. She doesn't even try to fit in. She constantly talks about her mother and getting back to St. A's. I tell you, she's going to be trouble Noah. We should have left her at the warehouse or gotten rid of her."

Noah snagged a cookie from the nearby platter and shook his head, "You know I love a challenge Jeri, and on top of that we haven't had a red-haired angel at Walkers in a very long time. Which room is she in? I think I'll have a little talk with her before dinner."

"She's in the pink room." Jeri informed.

He turned to leave, then stopped and waited until Jeri's eyes met his, "Later tonight we need to talk about Bethany. It's time." At her nod, Noah left the room.

Noah climbed the stairs and wondered what the best way to handle this stubborn child would be. It wasn't as if he hadn't had this issue before, but then each child was different. He needed her to trust him, depend on him, and most of all, he needed her to be willing to do anything...*anything* for him...anything *with* him. He smiled. Noah was smart enough to know that you didn't get that kind of adoration by planting fear and so far he'd never had to be the authoritarian with any of his girls. If it ever became necessary, then that was Jeri's job. In fact he'd often thought that keeping his girls happy and willing was a lot like his political career, tell them what they want to hear and if it doesn't work out, never admit any responsibility for failure.

The farmhouse had nine bedrooms and none of them, except his and Jeri's, would lock from the inside. Reaching the door of the pink room, he rapped a brisk knock and without waiting for an answer, turned the knob and entered the room. The blinds were open and standing in front of a set of lace covered double windows, stood the most adorable fire-haired girl that Noah had seen in a very long time. *She will just have to adjust to her new home because I won't let her leave.* He thought.

He cleared his throat and waited for the child to face him. When she didn't acknowledge him, he walked to where she stood and silently admired the view from the window.

"The garden is beautiful this time of year don't you think?" he asked softly.

Nothing.

"Would you like to take a walk outside with me?"

The girl turned and locked the most intense set of green eyes on him. Noah smiled at her and reached out, lightly touching her hair. "Come with me, please. My name is Noah, but all the girls here call me Daddy, it would make me really happy if you did as well. What's your name?" Noah asked, reaching for her hand.

The girl jerked her hand free. "If I tell you, will you take me back to St. A's? I need to get back before my mother comes." Her voice quivered.

Ah, a little deal maker. He thought. "Walk with me and we'll discuss it." He took her hand again. "Now what's your name?"

"Victoria." The girl spoke softly. "Victoria Elizabeth McEvers."

Noah led the girl down the stairs, and kept his tone comfort filled as he said, "Victoria, what a lovely name. I think I'll call you Tori. Would that be alright with you Tori?"

Jerking her hand free again, Victoria crossed her arms over her chest and seethed, "My name is Victoria Elizabeth McEvers. I have a mother, and I want to go back to St. Anthony's."

Noah dropped down and sat on the stairs. He pulled her down next to him. "Let me explain something to you Tori. This is going to be hard, and I'm sorry that I have to tell you but...well, your mother is dead. She died the day before you were brought here."

Victoria jumped up and screamed, "No!" She pointed a finger at him. "You are lying! My mother is alive and she's coming back to St. A's to get me. I don't believe you."

Without standing, Noah brushed a strand of hair from Victoria's face and consoled her, "I know that this is hard for you, but think about it. Would the nice Sister at St. A's have really let you come and live with me if she knew that your mother was coming back for you?"

He could tell that he had her attention now, "There was an accident and your mother was hit by a taxi when she crossed the street, it happened right in front of St. Anthony's. I'm surprised you didn't hear the sirens yourself. She was coming to see you, but didn't make it."

Victoria melted helplessly into a puddle of tears and heartbreak right in front of him.

He gently continued, "Your mother loved you dearly, Tori. She wanted you and was coming to get you. But now that just isn't possible and you know you mother would have wanted the best for you, right?"

The child was motionless as if stunned. Noah gave her a moment to process what he said and then pressed the point. "This home is a wonderful place for you to grow up where you will be well cared for and loved. Your mother would be relieved to know you are here with me."

He watched Tori closely knowing his words were hitting their mark. *Step one, a broken spirit. She'll have to depend on me now. I'm all she has.* He thought. Noah slid an arm under Victoria's legs and effortlessly lifted the girl. He didn't say anything else as he walked through the kitchen and out the back door. When he'd reached the garden, Noah sat down on a sun drenched white stone bench.

He held her tiny body tightly against his and whispered soothing words while she cried. "Everything is okay, Tori. You've got me now and I'll take really good care of you. It's what your mother would have wanted. She loved you, and would have wanted you to have the kind of life that I can give you. It's my job to take care of you now that she's gone, and I promise you that I will."

Noah rocked her gently and waited until Victoria's sobs slowed to a hushed hiccupping before he spoke, "Tori, I want you to know a secret, an important secret." He cleared his throat and continued, "You are my daughter, I don't mean like the other girls, the adopted girls. I mean you are my flesh and blood. Your mother was my lover and I am your father."

When the child didn't speak, Noah

continued, "Do you understand what I'm telling you Tori? You are my child and this is your home, you will live here, with me, forever."

Without looking at him, Victoria nodded her head and buried her face tightly against his shoulder. Something about this didn't seem right to her; didn't feel right. *He lies, my mother told me all about my father and she never lied to me.* She thought. *And if he lies about being my father, he's probably lying about my mother too.* She couldn't believe her mother was dead because deep down she knew she wasn't. It just wasn't true. She didn't know how or why she felt as she did, but she knew this man was a liar. The way they were put in to the car at night, and driven here where no one would see them still bothered her. Nothing about this man or this place seemed right and if her mother had died she would have known somehow. Victoria's heart soared! Now convinced that nothing about the story he was telling her was real, she still had to find a way out of this place. Maybe if he thought she believed him and was upset she might get a chance.

Victoria lifted her tear stained face and looked at Noah with piercing green eyes, "You're my father? My real father? Honest?"

Noah smiled at her and nodded, "I am. I need you to keep this a secret just between us Tori. If the other girls knew, then their feelings would be hurt and they might even be jealous of you. You want your sisters to love you right?"

She nodded and whispered, "It will be our secret and I won't tell the others, not even Allie, and she's my best friend."

Noah pulled her into a tight hug and breathed in her young girl scent. He thought, *it won't be long before you're mine heart and soul.*

Setting her on the bench beside him was almost painful, he wanted her close, really close, but he knew that this was not the time. "The other girls are preparing for a fashion show after dinner. I know that you've had a rough day today, so you can sit with me and help with the judging if you'd rather not participate. How does that sound?"

"I'll sit with you, Father, but I don't feel like dressing up right now." Victoria refused to call him daddy like the other girls and she knew about the fashion show, she'd heard Nora telling Allie and Ivy about how all the girls would dress up and do the model walk for Daddy. She'd even seen some of the clothes in the closet in her room. She would *never* wear see-through panties and nightgowns in front of *anyone! What I need is a telephone, and I can't find a phone if I don't ever come out of that room.*

When Angels Cry

87

CHAPTER 12

Satisfied that he knew where to find the woman, Simon slid his helmet on and flipped the dark shield down to cover his face. He started the bike with the push of a button and muttered, "Let them get comfortable and then I'll come for a visit. A short and painful visit." He laughed and jammed the Harley into gear. The big black machine moved smoothly into the light traffic on Bellevue Street, and Simon drove away.

Standing at the end of the alley, concealed by a rack of red milk crates, Wynter Burgland watched Simon Alvarez watching the man and woman. "Another of Gregorio's men." She whispered. When the motorcycle and man left the alley, Wynter ran forward, and watched to see where he went. She breathed a sigh of relief when he turned away from the woman's house. She ducked her head and rounded the corner of a street side coffee shop where she took a seat near a large square window overlooking the street.

"Black coffee." She said when the waitress stopped at her table. Wynter stared out the window and wondered how long it would take before the man on the motorcycle returned to deal with Gregorio's little problem.

"Thank you." She smiled when the waitress returned and set a steaming cup in front of her. Sipping the hot drink she pulled a note pad and pen from her purse and dropped it on table next to her coffee cup. *What should I say?* She wondered. She stared at the paper and struggled to find the right words. Finally she picked up the pen.

Her hand shook and her mind spun, the words came and went in a jumble of fear and anger. She knew what would happen to her if Gregorio found out that she had helped the woman that he thought had killed his brother. It was simple, she would disappear, just as so many problems had disappeared before her, and since she had no family, no network of friends, no lover...there would be no one to look for her. But then, she reasoned, he would kill her anyway once he found out that she had been the one to kill Quinto. She struggled to balance her fear with her sense of what was right.

"You can't just do nothing. You have to tell the woman that she is in danger." Resolved to the task, she wrote.

Wynter finished her coffee and left the shop with the note tucked safely in her jacket pocket. She walked down the street on the opposite side of the woman's house in no particular hurry.

"Emma Gage-Echo, you are in serious trouble." She muttered, knowing that Gregorio would stop at nothing to kill the woman who murdered his brother *and* even worse, interfered in his business. *Too bad he doesn't know that it was me who killed Quinto.* She thought. *Maybe I should tell him, and then kill him when he comes for me, that would solve two problems. The woman would be safe and Gregorio will be gone. I still have Quinto's gun.* She patted her purse and was reassured to feel the bulk of the gun inside. Wynter shook her head and scolded, *You know that won't work. Itasca is my flesh and blood, but she could never love a mother that killed her father.* Disgusted with her own thoughts, Wynter plopped down on a metal bus stop bench at the street corner and waited. She unconsciously fingered the note in her pocket.

A man appeared in the window of the house and she watched him closely. Who was he and how would she get past him to talk to Emma Gage-Echo without being seen by Gregorio's man? Tate felt at home in front of the black and chrome range in Emma's kitchen, he flipped a grilled cheese sandwich with one hand, and held his cell phone in the other.

"I'm not sure when I'll be back Martin. Em's in some pretty heavy shit here. We picked up a tail as soon as we left the hospital today, and I expect we're going to have an unwelcome visitor or two at some point. Even if she weren't hurt, I couldn't leave her to deal with what I know is coming at some point, and as long as she's in danger, I'm going to hang around."

"You take good care of Miss Emma and don't worry about things here." Martin demanded. "It's only been a couple days, but so far Chad hasn't let the job go to his head and things are running pretty smooth."

Pushing the skillet off the red-hot, flat surface burner, Tate scooped the sandwich up and dropped it onto a waiting plate. "That's good. I was a little worried about leaving him in charge, but I was more worried about Em. Hell, I'd have left the chair empty if I'd had to." Cautiously Tate asked, "How'd it go with Herc? You get him over to the vet okay?"

Martin snorted a reply, "You know damn well that I got that dog to the vet like I said I would, and you also know that it took me two hours to clean all the slobber out of my car. I don't know why you keep that slobbering bag of bones. He's just a big mess waiting to happen."

Tate bit back a laugh and said, "I appreciate it buddy and I owe you one. I've got to go now but call me if anything big comes up."

"Will do, and you tell Miss Emma that me and Barb are praying for a quick recovery, and tell her that I'm still saving her a spot on the County force. Any time she wants to leave that job, she's got one waiting here."

Tate disconnected the call and pocketed his phone. He deposited the sandwiches on the dining room table and went to see if Emma was awake. He stepped into the living room and spotted her sitting up on the couch, "You're up, good. I made us some of my famous grilled cheese sandwiches. You ready to eat?"

Emma nodded and stood up. She swayed, immediately overcome with dizziness she grasped the cushioned arm of the sofa for support while she waited for the spinning to stop. Tate was instantly at her side, he wrapped a supporting arm around her waist and Emma leaned into him. "No more pain meds Tate. I can't think straight, and right now I need to be able to do that."

Tate took Emma's arm, and led her through the living room and into the dining room. He helped her settle in a chair and empathized, "Once you get some food down, you'll feel better. As for thinking, you're suspended, remember? Right now, the only thing you need to think about is getting well. I mean it Em."

A groan escaped when Emma sat in the stiff dining room chair, and she moved to adjust the cushion so that it supported her wound. She narrowed her eyes at Tate and said, "Like I could forget that I'm suspended Echo. That doesn't mean that I can just forget about the case, I've got to figure out some things, so that I'm ready when the time comes. I need to find out who that woman is, and what her role in this mess is. More importantly, I need to know where she is. She may be the only one who can clear this up."

The doorbell chimed and Tate's reply died on his lips. His body tensed. "You expecting company?" He whispered. Without waiting for an answer, he pulled his service weapon from its shoulder holster, and with a stern glance at Emma, he ordered, "Don't move." In an instant he was down the hall.

Tate cautiously stepped to one side of the front door and peeked out one of the small round windows stacked on either side of the door. He wasn't surprised when he didn't see anyone; he'd been expecting unknown and unseen company since they'd left the hospital. Something crunched on the floor near his foot and he glanced down and saw a folded piece of yellow paper on the entryway floor. He scooped the paper up and tucked it in the back pocket of his jeans, before cautiously opening the door. Tate opened the door and glanced in both directions and then stepped out onto the porch, leading with his gun. He moved silently to the north end of the raised wooden porch and pivoted to look down the north side of the house, nothing. Following the same path back to the door he repeated the process on the south side of the house.

No one. Adrenalin pumped through his body as he listened and watched while the seconds ticked by. He took in every detail but nothing along the street seemed out of place. Letting out a breath, he whispered, "Time to check the rear." Tate entered the house and closed and locked the door behind him, before moving through the living room and back to the kitchen where he repeated the process out the back door.

Emma felt useless sitting at the table while Tate secured the house. *I should be the one protecting my own damn house. This isn't his battle, it's mine.* She thought. Her patience was thin, but Emma waited for Tate to finish his recon and return to the dining room before she asked, "Who was it?"

"Not sure. I didn't see anyone but someone was here, they left you a note." He reached in his pocket and pulled the lined yellow paper out, and handed it to Emma.

Emma snatched the paper and unfolded it. She scanned the note and then held it out to Tate. "It's her, I sure of it. The woman. The one who shot Quinto Navarone. She was here."

Tate took the note from Emma's outstretched hand and asked, "So I'm guessing it's time to pay back the favor?"

Shaking her head, Emma answered, "More of a warning."

Flipping the paper open, Tate read the brief note to himself. *The motorcycle man knows where you are and he is dangerous, but he is not the one you should be most afraid of.* He let the paper drop to the table. "Pretty cryptic warning.

Emma took a bite of her sandwich, looked thoughtful for a moment, then nodded her agreement, "You'd think that if she knows so much about what's going on, that she could just spit it out and save us all some time. I already assumed that the guy on the Harley was just handling the dirty work for someone in a power position. In the last four months we've stopped two deliveries but only managed to catch one runner, and he turned up dead in his cell before we got anything useful from him."

Tate picked up his sandwich but hesitated and said, "So if her note is correct, now we have two unknowns that know exactly where you are. I get that the Harley guy may have been a better shadow than we knew and followed us from the hospital without being seen, but how did the woman know where you live? Hell, at this rate, anyone and everyone could be camped across the street." When Emma didn't comment, Tate continued, "What happened to the runner you caught? The other guys in lockup figure out that he was a diaper sniper?"

"Not that we're aware of and he hadn't been released in with the general population yet when he died. Appears he had a heart attack, at least that was the ruling. I never really believed it. I think someone made sure he had a heart attack, but there wasn't anything on the tox screen to support it. He lawyered up the minute we cuffed him, and we never got to conduct a full interview. Clay and the guy's attorney went in the interrogation room with him; came out a few minutes later saying he wouldn't talk, and then less than an hour later he was dead."

Tate's senses tingled, "Why would Shuler be in the cell with an arrestee and his attorney. That's not protocol. Most attorneys would have balked and called attorney and client privilege. No cops allowed."

Emma nodded, "The guy asked to see Clay. We thought he was going to try and cut some kind of deal. You know, give us a name for a little consideration at trial time. Probably would have worked too, if he'd lived. We've been chasing our tales on this ring for months and that kind of break could have had some very powerful negotiation possibilities for the perp."

"He asked to see Shuler by name?" Tate questioned, an uneasy feeling settling over him as he waited for Emma's response.

Emma shook her head. "Don't go there Tate. Clay was the arresting officer, the head of the task force, and the guy knew it. I've worked with Clay for months now and I trust him, but more than that, I trust my own instincts and my training as a profiler."

Tate nodded and flicked the note that lay on the table with one finger, "Well, this note is definitely in a female's handwriting, but that doesn't guarantee that it's from your shooter woman." Emma opened her mouth to speak but stopped when Tate held up one hand. He continued, "I agree that the note's most likely from her, but we don't have any concrete evidence to support that, not yet. What I do know is that if we can trust the woman, assuming it's her, then your house is not the safest place for us to be. If she knows where we are and the Harley guy knows where we are, then sooner or later, one or both of them are going to show up here."

Emma tensed, mentally preparing for the battle that was sure to come. "You're right. Sooner or later, someone will probably show up here, I'm counting on it. I know it's not what you think is best, but I'm not leaving Tate. This is my home and if they want to bring the war here, then I'll have the advantage. *No one*, and I mean no *one*, is driving me from my own home." Before Tate could protest, she continued, "What we need to do is to locate the woman. Clearly she knows things; things that could help us break this case. Even if she doesn't, I still need her statement to clear my name and get back on the active duty list."

Tate pushed his dark hair back from his forehead, pinched the bridge of his nose with two fingers, and sighed, "Just think about it Em. Laying low in a nice hotel for a few days would give you time to recover. You're not up to fighting the war right now. Retreat, give yourself time to heal, and then take control of the situation. You know, live to fight another day." He locked eye's with her, recognized the look harsh look that she gave him, the stubborn set of her jaw and the unmovable resolve to do it her own way.

Emma's face softened, but her voice was firm. "I can't Tate. I can't just go hide and watch from the sidelines while someone else does my job. You, of all people, know what I'm saying is right. You have to understand how this makes me feel." She reached across the table and closed her hand over his much larger one, and squeezed. "I can't let these people win. They've already tried to kill me, got me out of commission, and off the case. I'm pissed Tate. It's personal now."

"Put yourself in my place Em. If this were anyone else, you would be the first person to demand that they go to a safe house with a twenty-four hour protection detail stationed on them. That's standard protocol. I know it and you know it. Why should it be different just because you're an agent? Why Em?"

"You know why. I'm not 'anyone' else. I'm a trained agent with the FBI." Quietly, she continued, "I'm me and I don't hide when there's trouble. You know that."

Tate blew a breath and threaded his fingers with hers. "I knew I wouldn't be able to talk you into leaving, and I guess I can't blame you. Echo's don't run, but they do prepare. If we're going to stay here, then we need to secure the parameter and the house. Lay in some supplies and stock up on ammunition. And yes, we do need to find the woman."

Finished with her sandwich and relieved that Tate wasn't going to put up more of a fight about leaving the house, Emma stood, dropped a kiss on his head then took her empty plate to the sink.

"Damn, I wish I'd brought Herc with me." Tate muttered.

Emma laughed. "I heard that, and how is my sweet little Hercules?" Emma recalled how the puppy had been dropped on Tate's porch and how taking him out for a potty break had almost gotten her killed. She was in Pine Ridge, working on a serial case with Tate and the

Caching Killer, so dubbed by the press, had snatched her right out of Tate's backyard. She hoped talk of the dog would lighten the mood.

Tate turned in his chair so that he could see her through the open door. The mental list of things to do, precautions to take, as well as safeguards to put into place, grew faster than he wanted but he smiled at her, and then he lied, "I should have taken that dog to the pound the night that kid dropped him on my porch, and you know he's a long way from little or sweet. If he can't eat it or chew on it then he slobbers on it. I've had to replace just about every piece of furniture in the house and according to the vet he's still just a pup, meaning that there's still time for him to chew, eat or slobber on the things he missed the first time around."

Emma smiled, relieved that the tension between them had lessened. "You know you love that dog Tate Echo."

Grinning back at her Tate admitted, "Yeah I love the damn dog,"... *but I love you more.*

Tate stacked his plate next to hers in the dishwasher and then nodded his head toward the hallway and her bedroom, "It's about time to change those bandages Emma. You get undressed and I'll grab the supplies. After I secure the house, I'll meet you in the bedroom."

CHAPTER 13

"What do you mean you didn't finish the job? I don't have time for these delays and complications!" Gregorio thundered into the phone.

Simon shuddered and stammered, "It was too dangerous, too many people around in the day time. I know where she lives now, and I will go back and finish the job when I am certain that I can do so without anyone seeing anything. There is a man with her, a big man. I'm certain that he is a cop or ex-military, maybe both."

Gregorio interrupted him and raged, "I don't give a damn who's with her. Kill them both if you have to, just make sure she's dead and do it soon."

Even through the invisible phone lines, Simon's voice was liquid ice, "I assure you that I will kill her, but I am not being paid to kill the man too."

Gregorio clutched the phone tighter while his other hand rhythmically flexed open and closed, he scowled, *More money, it's always about the damn money. The asshole hasn't even stopped to think that I could just have him killed too.*

His voice low and quiet, Gregorio ordered, "You will be compensated appropriately for the job. I will even agree to a bonus if you can tell me in twenty four hours that it is completed.

Now get it done."

Slamming the phone down, Gregorio pushed back in his chair and swallowed the remaining two fingers of whisky in his glass. The liquid burn couldn't match the fire of his anger. *Idiot. He is no better than Quinto, I should get rid of him now, before he does something stupid.* Gregorio stood and refilled his glass from the bar in his office.

Two drinks later he silently admitted that for now, he needed Simon. "I will let him live for a while, then when I no longer need him I will make sure that he is taken care of." He slurred and reached to turn off the light on his desk, planning to call it a night. The ringing of his office phone stopped him. "This better be good news." He muttered and snatched the phone up. He growled, "Gregorio Aiden."

Noah Walker's voice boomed into the room. "Gregory, how's my favorite attorney?"

Realizing who it was, Gregorio wished he'd let the machine pick up. His voice sounded tired even to him when he answered, "I'm fine Noah. What can I do for you?"

The congressman laughed and then answered, "Today I am calling to do you a favor Gregory. I have a little something that I'd like to *give* you, a gift of sorts. Can you have someone come out and pick her up?"

Gregorio leaned back in his chair. His voice was laced with suspicion when he asked,

"A gift you say? Would this be a little bronze haired gift?" He'd heard about the problems Simon had with the little redhead and he was fully prepared to take her if Noah had decided that he couldn't use the child. There was always a market for porcelain skinned redheads, especially young ones and sometimes older ones too.

Clearing his throat, Noah chided, "Definitely not. My gift is a little larger, a little older and has outlived her usefulness here."

Damn. It's got to be Bethany, that's too bad. But she is still marketable and will certainly help to offset the consolation that I had to make on that last blotched order. "Give me two days to make the arrangements and then I'll send a car. I have a contact in Texas who can take this one and she'll be far enough away that she won't cause any problems here. I'll call you when the transport is in place." Even though he was pretty sure he knew the answer, Gregorio asked, "I'm guessing that she was one of mine? What's her name?"

"It's Bethany, and no need to call me. Just make sure your contact in Texas knows that she is never to return to Virginia. Jeri will make sure she's ready to go, so call her when the car is sent."

Gregory disconnected the call and pulled a file folder from a locked drawer in his desk. He flipped the folder open and stared at a photograph of a beautiful brown eyed six-year old. "Bethany. Almost fifteen now, absolutely gorgeous, and already too old for Noah Walker. That's a shame but you'll do just fine in Houston...once you get used to the streets."

Bethany's leaving? Hope flared somewhere deep inside her. *He does let people leave!* Nine year old Victoria squatted on the floor outside Noah's office and strained to hear the rest of the one-sided conversation. *Never to return to Virginia? He said we were adopted and now he's giving her away? Maybe Bethany's from Texas and now she's going home?* Victoria pushed back the questions, and prayed. *Please don't let him find me. I've got to use that phone or I'm never going to get out of here.*

After her talk with Noah in the garden, Ms. Anderson had stopped locking her in at night and tonight she planned to find a way out. She realized that the call was ending and slipped into the coat closet in the hallway, she quietly pulled the door closed. Victoria clutched a small flashlight that she'd taken from a drawer in the kitchen and waited until she saw no light filtering in around the closet door. She made herself count to ten real slow. *Just wait. You don't want to get caught,* she thought.

After what felt like an eternity, Victoria stood and slowly turned the knob, opening the door just a crack. Satisfied that the house was now dark, she slipped out of the closet and quickly walked to the office door. She stopped and stared at a small square keypad on the wall next to the door, a red light silently flashed its warning. She tried the handle anyway. "Locked. There's got to be another phone in a house this big." She muttered.

Victoria slid on sock feet across the white marble floor, and made her way to the kitchen. She'd seen an alarm panel on the pantry wall yesterday when she'd asked for chips and been told to get them herself. *Maybe I can turn it off.* She thought. The flashlight flickered across the floor as she hurried to the pantry. She tiptoed and stared at the white box mounted on the pantry wall. *Too high to reach.* Victoria pulled a step stool from where it was tucked under the bottom shelf in the pantry and placed it on the floor in front of the panel. She climbed up and stared at the red lights twinkling on one side of the box. The pale green screen glowed and flashed the one word that Victoria didn't want to see. *Armed.* She stepped off the stool and slid it back to its place just as the kitchen lights came on.

"Who's in there?" Ms. Anderson asked.

Victoria jammed the flashlight into her pocket and called out, "It's me, Victoria. I...I was hungry." She rounded the corner of the pantry and saw Ms. Anderson dressed in a fuzzy blue robe and standing next to the sink.

Jeri crossed her arms over her chest and said, "I see. It's well past bedtime and I don't normally allow anyone to be up after hours, but if you're hungry I guess we can make an exception this once."

Victoria sighed in relief and forced herself to smile at the woman, "Can I have cookies?"

Jeri nodded and said, "Sure, grab the milk from the fridge and I'll get us a cup."

CHAPTER 14

Determined not to rush Emma, Tate busied himself loading the dishwasher and now added detergent before he closed it and pushed start. "You about ready Em?" he called out.

The reply was muffled but firm, "I don't need your help, I've got this."

Damn the woman is stubborn. He snatched the bag containing gloves, ointment and bandages from the counter top and stomped down the hall to Emma's bedroom. He pushed the door open and froze. In front of a mirror attached to the closet door, Emma stood, naked from the waist down. Her shirt, hiked up and bunched under one arm, provided Tate with the most amazing view. The curve of her back, her long and shapely legs and her softly rounded ass were gloriously bare and undamaged. The air left his lungs in a whoosh and Tate wondered if he'd died and gone to heaven. Unable to do the gentlemanly thing and turn his head, he raised his smoky eyes upward and managed to meet Emma's blue ones in the mirror.

Emma twisted trying to see her wound in the mirror and finally let the shirt drop, effectively covering herself. "Ok, so I can't do it."

Tate grinned and held up the bag of supplies. "You forgot these too. Get on the bed and let me help you Em. I've already seen the good side of things, so let me see the rest. I did promise Dr. Simms that I'd take care of you."

She didn't say anything, just growled and moved carefully to the bed. "You even *look* like you're enjoying yourself and I'm going to shoot you Tate."

Tate sucked his bottom lip between his teeth and tried not to laugh. He knelt at the side of the bed and gently lifted Emma's shirt, pushing it up just far enough that he could see the entire wound. She'd already pulled the bandage off. Angry red and blue marks peppered the back of her right thigh and the outer side of one cheek of her butt.

"Except for the one place that they stitched, it looks like road rash Em. If I didn't know you were shot I'd guess that you slid from a bike on one side of your butt." He pulled on a pair of sterile gloves and squirted antibiotic ointment from a silver tube on one hand before gently massaging it onto the wound. Using small circular motions he slowly rubbed the entire area and mentally cursed, *Damn these gloves, I can't feel a thing.* That wasn't entirely true; he could feel the growing bulge in his jeans. *Just think about something else. Anything else.* He coached himself. *Not only is she off limits Echo, she's hurt and you're an asshole for even thinking of touching her that way.* Finished with the medication he pulled a cotton bandage free from its package and gingerly spread it over the deepest of the small puncture wounds before pressing the sticky edges gently against Emma's skin.

Emma sucked in a deep breath and held it. Tate's touch was light, rhythmic and so familiar. She wasn't sure what hurt more, the wound or knowing that the hands that carefully touched her were his. Emma closed her eyes and silently prayed. *God, please help him hurry up and get through before I turn over and...well, you know.*

Tate stood and turned so that Emma wouldn't see the bulge in his pants and shoot him. "All done." He said, walking to the door while he stripped the gloves from his hands. "I'm going to wash up and give you time to get dressed."

Emma released her breath in one long sigh and rolled to one side, covering her eyes with an arm. "Get over it Emma. You know it won't work no matter how bad you want him" she whispered.

"You say something?" Tate asked from across hall.

"Uh, no. Just muttering to myself about...oh never mind." She shot back. Emma stood up and snatched a pair of sweats from the dresser. She gingerly pulled them on and straightened her shirt before leaving the bedroom. Just as she reached the doorway to the living room, she heard her cell phone ringing from somewhere in the kitchen and detoured toward the sound. She stopped, surprised when she heard Tate answer the call.

"Hello." A pause. "Yeah, this is her phone. She's not available right now, who's calling?" Tate glanced up when Emma entered the room. "Hold on, she just walked in." He covered the phone with his free hand and whispered, "Clay Shuler."

Emma grabbed the phone and frowned at Tate. "Hello Clay."

"You got a call screener now Emma?" A deep male voice asked.

Not bothering to answer the question, Emma asked, "Tell me that the Internal Affairs investigation is over and I'm back on the case."

"Can't do that just yet. You know how it is when IA gets a bone. "

Tate pretended not to listen while he wiped down the counter and bagged the trash. He tossed a glance at Emma and could tell that she wasn't happy with whatever the task force captain was telling her on the phone.

Emma made no effort to hide her frustration. "It's been four days and I need to get back on the case. Those assholes over at IA know damned well that I didn't shoot an unarmed man. You and I both know that those kids could be anywhere by now."

Clay cut in, "Hold up Emma. I know you want to get back to work and we want you back, the team needs you, but you're not the only one working this case. The rest of us, the team, we're still out there, still working to catch these bastards." Emma heard him suck in a breath. "I'm trying to keep you in the loop so that when the IA investigation is over you'll be up to speed." He paused, "That's really why I'm calling. We've got three more reported missing and I'm pretty sure that are the same three you saw at the warehouse the night you were shot."

Emma sucked in a quick breath waiting for him to continue. When he didn't she prompted, "Go on."

"We picked up an alert from the Richmond PD yesterday for three girls missing from St. Anthony's Children's Home, you know, the one over on Eighth Street. Just so happens that these three fit the description that you gave to the IA rep. when you gave your statement."

Tate moved around Emma and pulled a dining room chair out, pointing for her to sit. She sat, and then asked, "Two blondes and a red-head? Somewhere around seven to ten years old?"

Clay confirmed the description, "Bingo. The director at St. A's says that they were missing the morning after you saw them at the warehouse. He reported the girls to Richmond PD as runaways but didn't seem overly concerned. We reviewed the initial report from the interviewing officer and two of the girls had been there for several years and they'd never had any problems with them. The kids were identified as Allie Barrow and Ivy Tambrey, both seven years old and blonde; the red-head is Victoria McEvers and she's nine."

Pushing her hair back, Emma raged, "Dammit Clay I should have saved these girls! Now we may never know where they were taken."

Clay cleared his throat and softened his tone, "This is not your fault. Hell I should have gotten there sooner and given you the back-up you called for, then *we* could have saved the girls and you probably wouldn't have been shot either, but that's not what happened and we can't spend our time rehashing what's over and done."

"That's just it Clay. It's not over and done. Kids are going to keep disappearing and being forced to endure God knows what unless we stop it." Emma felt, rather than saw, Tate move behind her. His hands moved to her shoulders, massaging the tight muscles there before they drifted to her equally tense neck. She forced herself to concentrate on what Clay was saying instead of how good Tate's hands felt.

Clay's voice dropped. "I know how you feel and I want to catch the bastards too, but right now all I can do is keep you filled in and keep the pressure on the bad guys. I also wanted you to know that the local media will be running pictures of the girls, TV and newspaper. I didn't want you to see them on the news and freak out. Hopefully we'll get a hit and someone will have seen them. Kids don't just disappear and if we get really lucky maybe the national news will pick it up. I know we don't usually want the media in our business, but if it helps save these girls then I'm all for it. I'll call you if I hear anything more and Emma, get some rest. We need you at 100% and back on the team."

"Thanks, Clay, and I appreciate you keeping me up to date on the case. You'll let me know if you hear anything on the IA investigation?"

"You know I will, but I expect that Pruitt will know before I do. Oh, and Emma?"

"Yes?"

"Well…if you need anything, give me a call okay? In fact, you could send Echo home and let me help you out for a few days. I…I want to help and it would be so easy to keep you in the know about the case if you were here. You know, here with me." He stammered.

Emma held her breath for a moment, and then replied, "We're good for now but I appreciate the offer. Talk to you later." She clicked the phone off and deposited it on the table. *What the hell was up with Shuler? He'd never hit on her before and now he seemed to be pouring it on by the bucketful.* She let herself relax into Tate's massaging hands. After a few minutes, a satisfied moan escaped her lips.

"Bad news?" He asked.

"Still nothing from IA on my investigation

but they did pull a lead on the three girls that I saw that night. Appears they were runaways from St. Anthony's Children's Home."

Dropping down into the chair beside her, Tate asked, "So they ran away the same night that you saw them? That seems pretty strange."

"Kids run away from facilities like St. A's all the time. What's strange about it?" Emma asked.

"I just mean that it seems pretty unlikely that they would run away and then get picked up by traffickers all in the same night. Most runaways end up on the street for a while before some street pimp puts them to work. How old did you say these kids were?"

Emma jumped up, almost knocking the chair over behind her and replied, "Little. Too little for street work. Two seven year olds and a nine year old. Shit, what if they didn't run away? What if someone took them straight out of the home? The numbers I saw show most actual runaways are teens or preteens, these kids in no way fit the national average. I want to go over to St. A's and ask a few questions, you in?"

Tate nodded his agreement, "I'm in, but it's too late today. You do know that if word gets back to your SAC that you're poking around on this case that you're going to catch hell."

"Yeah I know, but right now it's more important to find these girls."

"Agreed, finding the girls is top of the list." He looked thoughtful. "The whole thing stinks. I mean why would kids this little just take off on their own?"

Emma drummed her fingers on the table top, "Top of my head I'd say that if they left voluntarily then they were running to something, or they were running away from something. We need to find out which it was, and that's only if they left on their own."

Tate stood up and pushed his chair in, "First thing in the morning we'll check it out, now I think you should hit the hay. It's been a long day and you are still recovering. I need your alarm code and once I've checked the house, I'm off to bed too."

Emma tiptoed up and planted a quick kiss on Tate's jaw. "We make a great team Tate. You always seem to come up with something that helps me fill in the holes." She turned and walked toward the hall, her voice trailed back, "Codes an easy one to remember, oh seven, eleven, oh seven. See you in the morning."

Tate smiled, *She still loves me. Why else would she use our anniversary as her alarm code?* Just as quickly, his anger surfaced, "Yeah she loves you. She loves you so much that she's going to sit right here and let herself be a target for some asshole that wants to kill her." Love was never the question between them, it was just never enough. *Nope, not on my watch.* Tate made a quick run through the house and checked all the windows, secured the doors and left both the front and back porch lights on before setting the alarm.

He dropped down on the bed in Emma's guest room, and toed his boots off, pulled his toothbrush out of the duffle and walked in his stocking feet to the bathroom. He'd just turned the water off when he caught the rumbling sound of a motorcycle in the distance. The sound was distinct. *Definitely a Harley.* Tate thought. He reached out and flicked the light switch, throwing the bathroom into darkness before he slipped out and made his way through the pitch black house to the front door. A dark house hid their movements from anyone watching – the darker the better.

Tate peeked out the same window he'd used earlier and while he could no longer hear the rumble of the motorcycle, he felt the fine hairs on the back of his neck rise and knew that the guy was out there somewhere in the shadows of the quiet street. "Come on you bastard. I'm waiting for you." He whispered.

CHAPTER 15

Simon Alvarez killed the engine on his Harley and let it coast down the darkened street in front of the woman's house. He knew the black bike would be impossible to see on a moonless night, and coasting assured that the powerful machine didn't wake anyone in the sleepy neighborhood. The Harley might not seem like the best choice for someone in his profession, but it was a matter of perspective, and he knew that in a chase, nothing on four wheels could touch him. He could maneuver in and out of places that even the smallest car couldn't go. The shadows thrown by the large trees lining the street would help to further conceal him. Three houses beyond *her* house, he pushed the big Hog over to the curb, and dropped the kickstand. He slid his helmet into the oversized black leather saddle bag on one side of his motorcycle, and crossed the street.

Simon walked in the shadows of the trees lining the neighborhood until he was directly across the street from the woman's house. He stopped there and stood behind a huge sycamore tree, entirely concealed from anyone on the street, or across the street. A few yards away, a streetlight on the corner dropped a soft round circle of light below it, but the glow didn't reach far enough to give his position away.

He reminded himself, "This is the woman that killed Quinto Navarone. She is not weak." He watched the house for several minutes and saw no signs of anyone moving about or even awake, the house was dark and still. He slipped out from his hiding spot, and jogged across the street careful not to let his boot heels touch the pavement. The rubber soled riding boots he wore made very little sound. He took a similar post in the woman's yard and continued to watch the house for signs of movement. *Maybe I should just burn the house down with her and that man, assuming he's still there, in it.* He considered it and decided that a fire wouldn't be much fun. He wanted to face the bitch and remind her of Quinto before he took her down and he didn't need a whole fire department showing up as witnesses.

Tate stood immobile at the small window, and he didn't flinch as a dark figure run across the street and into Emma's yard. When the runner ducked behind a large tree, Tate took a chance and stepped away from the window. He made his way soundlessly back to the bedroom, stepped into his boots and shoved his service weapon into the waistband at the small of his back, no time for the holster. He'd just turned to leave the room and Emma stuck her head inside the door. She gripped her personal gun, a Glock 19, in one hand and let it hang loosely at her side.

"What are you doing?" She asked in a whisper.

Tate stepped close and kept his voice low, "We've got company outside. So far he's hunched behind a tree just watching, but I don't intend to give him the chance to do more. I'm going to slip out the back and try to circle around behind him."

"I should be the one to go; it's me he's after," Emma whispered angrily.

Tate glared at her in the darkness and asked, "Can you run?"

Emma stared at him blankly.

"Well can you?" Without waiting for an answer he brushed past her and checked the window to see if the man was still in place. A sliver of movement from the corner of the house confirmed that he'd moved.

"He's moved closer to the house. Disable the alarm, Em." Tate ordered in a whisper.

Emma nodded and hurried to the alarm panel; punched in the code and when the red light on the keypad turned green, she silently gave Tate a thumbs up.

In the kitchen, Tate stood to one side of the back door, his body flush with the wall. He reached back and grasped the gun from his waistband, pulled it around and flipped the safety off. He slowly turned the door knob and eased the door open. The porch light could give away his position but he knew that turning it off would definitely draw the perpetrator's attention, so he left it on. Tate silently slipped out the cracked door then immediately dove to the left, away from the porch and out of the light. Behind him Tate heard the soft click and knew that Emma had locked the door behind him. *Good girl.* He thought.

Tate stood totally still and breathed deeply, forcing his heart to slow its jackhammer pace. He calculated the time since he'd looked out the window last and figured not more than forty five seconds had passed. *Plenty of time for the asshole to have made it around the house, if that was his goal.* Knowing that either porch light would give the intruder away, Tate took a calculated guess and decided that a bedroom window would be the most likely point of entry. *Away from the lights and out of view of the street traffic.* Tate kept his back flush against the cool siding of the house, and side stepped his way to the corner. He stopped and counted to three, and quickly took the turn, his gun leading the way. The man he'd watched run across the street now stood at Emma's bedroom window, and was so intent on getting it open that he hadn't seen or heard Tate round the corner of the house.

A large oak on the corner of the yard swayed in the evening breeze, letting the glow of a streetlight flicker across the side yard. Disbelievingly Tate watched a second UnSub hug the shadows at the front corner of the house and slide toward the man at the window. *Dammit! He's got help. Is she hiding from her partner or has she seen me?* Even in the dim light Tate knew that this second perpetrator was a woman. *Time to shake the party up.* He thought.

Tate stepped out from his position at the corner of the house keeping his gun leveled on the man at the window and said, "Drop your weapon and step away from the window." Glancing at the woman he ordered, "You, step over here next to your friend. I want you both where I can see you."

The man turned but didn't step into the light or raise his face Tate.

"He has a gun!" The woman screamed.

Tate thought for a moment she was talking to him. *Was she?*

Without a word the man took a step toward Tate and pulled a gun free at the same time.

Without hesitation, Tate dropped to one knee and fired. His shot hit its mark and pushed the man's body backward with its force. The intruder seemed to melt. He slid down to the dew covered grass under the window and came to rest with his back against the side of the house. Tate ran forward and kicked the man's gun away before turning to deal with the woman. "Dammit! She's gone," he cursed.

He took a second to feel for a pulse at the man's throat, there was none. Certain that the man wasn't going anywhere, Tate took off. *What the hell just happened here?* He thought. *Whose side is the woman on?* "Got to find her and get this figured out." He huffed. He turned the corner of the house and ran headlong into Emma. The force of their bodies colliding knocked her down, flat on her butt.

"What the hell are you doing outside?" Tate demanded, and then saw her wince in pain. He quickly kneeled. "Are you okay Em? Are you hurt?"

"I'm okay. I just lost my breath for a second. I heard the shot, are you okay?" Emma looked up at him with worried eyes.

Tate frowned at her, "Dammit Emma, you're hurt and I don't need to be worried about you and a loose shooter." She glared at him and refused his help getting up. The last thing he needed was her pissed off. He used the only logic he knew she would agree with. "Em, you know you aren't 100% and worrying about you is distracting." He paused a minute. "There are two of them Em."

Her gaze snapped back to his and worry creased her brow. Her eyes quickly scanned the area just as Tate's did.

"I shot the guy that I saw sneaking across the yard, but there was a woman too." Tate extended a hand, and pulled Emma to her feet. "She couldn't have gone far. You didn't see anyone when you came outside?"

Already turning to go inside Emma called over her shoulder, "No, no one. I'm going to call in Richmond PD, but then I'm coming back to check out the guy you shot."

Tate knew that it would be a waste of breath to argue with her. "Fine. Bring a flashlight when you come back Em."

Overhearing Emma's plans to call the police, the woman crouched lower in the shrubbery. *I've got to get out of here! I cannot be here when the police show up and hiding in the shrubbery is not hiding at all.* She heard footsteps approach and froze.

Tate walked the perimeter of the house and found no signs of the woman. The man hadn't moved. "Dammit. Where the hell could she have gone? I know I'd have seen her if she hit the street." He looked up when Emma came around the corner of the house, the glow of two flashlights leading her way. Tate reached for one of the lights and said, "Stay here while I search the other side of the yard. I can't believe she got away clean and we didn't see or hear anything. She's got to be hiding."

Sirens wailed in the distance. *It's now or never, and you can't get Tassie back if you're locked up in jail.* The woman peeked out of the hedge and saw the man swinging his light back and forth across the yard some thirty yards away. Counting to three she pulled herself up and ran without looking back.

Wynter sprinted across Emma's front yard and she didn't slow down or look before she ran into the street and made it to the yard on the other side. *Faster! You've got to go faster!* Reaching the back of the property, she didn't hesitate at the fence that separating the yard from the alley behind the house. She grasped the top of the fence with both hands and vaulted over, dropping to the other side and landing in a squat.

Tate saw a flash out of the corner of his eye. "Stop!" He yelled and then took off at a run. He cursed. "She runs like a damn gazelle and these boots are not helping." Tate was in the middle of the two lane street that separated Emma's yard from the one on the other side, when he saw the woman take the fence. The hood of her jacket fell back and the scant light revealed a mass of long blonde hair flowing in the dark night. She matched the description Emma had given him of the woman who saved her. If that was true, why was she running?

The next few seconds were a blur. Headlights rounded the street corner and a car screeched to a stop only a few feet from him. Tate froze when he saw the light bar blinking a fast red and blue atop the car. A spotlight attached to the driver's side mirror temporarily blinded him and Tate instinctively raised his hands. A voice boomed, "Don't move. Drop the gun and keep your hands where I can see them."

The door of the police cruiser opened and a twenty-something officer in blue jumped out and immediately hunkered down behind the open car door, his gun pointed straight at Tate.

Tate saw his chance of catching the woman and finally getting some answers fade into the distance as the woman was quickly engulfed in the dark of the alley.

Turning to face the patrol car, his arms raised, Tate yelled, "I'm a police officer. I'm going to bend over now and lay my gun on the ground."

CHAPTER 16

"Bethany you can't take all these clothes with you. It's just a weekend trip." Jeri Anderson lied. "One bag and that's it. Now put the rest of these things back where they belong and finish getting ready. The car will be here for you soon."

"But I don't know where we'll be going or what to take! I want to look nice." Bethany pouted, and dropped an armful of clothes onto her already cluttered bed.

"I'll be back in a few minutes and I expect to see this mess cleaned up and your bag packed. It's a special privilege to be given a weekend trip and you can't keep the driver waiting." Jeri glanced at the other five girls in the room and ordered, "You girls leave Bethany alone to pack and come downstairs. She's certainly old enough to select her own clothes for a weekend trip and it's time for school work, I believe we have science and history today." Jeri left the room without closing the door, she fully expected the younger girls to follow her downstairs. She'd been home schooling Noah's girls for years, and took a great deal of pride in teaching them. She'd always told Noah that even if the girls never left Walker Farm that they still needed the structure and discipline that came from having regular work and assignments.

Chloe and Nora stood and motioned to Allie, Ivy and Victoria, "Come on. Like Ms. Anderson said, Bethany doesn't need you little girls helping her pack." Chloe said. Chattering the girls slid from the room. Victoria followed behind them until they reached the top of the stairs, then she turned and ran back to Bethany's room.

"What do you want?" Bethany demanded.

"Did you come here from Texas?" Victoria asked.

"Not that it's any of your business but I've never been to Texas in my life. I've always lived right here, this is my home. Why do you care?"

Not sure if she could trust the older girl, Victoria hedged and then decided to take a chance and tell Bethany what she'd heard. "Look I overheard a call last night and you're going to Texas and you can't ever come back."

Bethany dropped the shirt she'd been folding and spun around grabbing Victoria by the arm, she spewed. "What did you say?"

"Last night I sneaked down to the kitchen, and *Daddy*," the word choked her, "well, he said to someone on the phone that you weren't to ever come back from Texas."

Bethany let her hand drop from the younger girl's arm and sank down on the bed. When she looked up, Victoria could see that her eyes were filled with tears. "You're sure about this? You didn't make it up?" Bethany questioned.

Victoria bobbed her head and swore, "I'm positive and I don't make things up. He said you could never come back to Virginia."

"Shit, this cannot be happening. I won't go." Bethany flopped back on the bed.

"What do you mean, what's happening?" Victoria asked and stepped closer to the older girl.

"There were others...you know, other girls. They were older than me. One day they were here and then they were gone. I barely remember the last one." Pulling a deep breath in Bethany continued, "Look, you've got to get out of here before it's too late, before you're too old. He doesn't like the old ones." She choked back a sob. "The old ones...like me."

Victoria frowned and plopped down next to Bethany on the bed, she said, "I want to go back to St. A's. My mother *is* going to come back for me." Dropping her voice to a whisper she continued, "She promised and my mom always keeps her word to me."

"I can't help you now. I can't help anyone, not even myself. Go downstairs before Ms. Anderson comes to get you. Keep her busy, I need some time alone, okay?" Bethany pulled a tissue from a box on the bedside table and blew her nose, her hands shook. "Go. Okay? Just go."

At the door Victoria turned back to look at Bethany. She didn't seem so old and mean now, she just looked sad. Sad and scared.

"Victoria?" Bethany's voice quivered.

"Yes."

"Before long, he's going to want you to spend the night with him. Don't do it. I don't have time to explain it all to you but trust me; you don't want to be there. Hide or better yet, get sick, just don't go in that room with him, and Victoria, the next time you're allowed outside, tell Ms. Anderson you want to feed the ducks and go check out the gazebo at the pond, okay? I used to go there every day...when I was younger. Now go. Go downstairs...before she comes back."

Victoria nodded and pulled the door closed behind her. At the top of the stairs she stopped and listened. *Bethany's crying?*

Jeri Anderson looked up when Victoria entered the dining room and said, "So you decided to join us after all?" She wondered where the child had been, but smiled at her anyway. "Have a seat next to Chloe, we're doing Science and Nature now and then we'll move to History. You know Tori, it's important that you keep current with you studies and being late is not the way to do that."

With a slight nod, Victoria slid into a chair. She didn't bother correcting the woman about her name. Instead she flipped the book in front of open and asked, "Can I feed the ducks today?"

"Probably not today, you're already behind the other girls with your work and feeding the ducks is a reward that you have to earn." Seeing the disappointment on the girls face, Jeri softened her tone and continued, "If you work really hard to catch up today then I bet you can have an outing tomorr...."

A crash from somewhere outside interrupted Jeri. "Now what was that? You girls stay here and continue your work while I check."

The girls looked at each other but didn't move. As soon as the door closed behind Jeri, Victoria pushed her chair back and ran to the window over the kitchen sink and looked out into the garden.

Tears clouded Victoria's eyes and she thought she would throw up. She ran to the door and struggled to get it open. Her hands fumbled with the door before she gave up and sank to the cool tile floor. Sadness and fear overwhelmed her and tears ran freely down her face.

"Oh no! No! Bethany..." her scream pulled the other girls from their seats. They pushed and vied for a spot at the window trying to see what Victoria was screaming about.

The door that wouldn't open for Victoria flew open and Ms. Anderson ordered, "Step away from the window, all of you." When the girls didn't rush to obey her, Jeri screamed, "Now! Go to your rooms now!"

Allie and Ivy moved to stand beside Chloe, their eyes were wide with fear and when Chloe took their hands and began leading them away, Nora followed a few feet behind. That's when Jeri noticed Victoria on the floor. The child sat with her knees drawn up and rocked, sobbing and saying Bethany's name.

Shit. She saw. Jeri squatted in front of Victoria, and brushed the child's hair back. Softly she asked, "Victoria, I need you to go up to your room now. Can you do that for me?" She grasped the girl by the arms and lifted her to her feet. "I'll be up to check on you in a few minutes, just go to your room for now." Jeri waited until Victoria left the room before she went back outside to deal with the problem in the garden.

At the window in her room, Victoria peeked through a gap in the lacy rose-colored curtains and watched Ms. Anderson and the man who takes care of the garden spread a faded quilt next to Bethany's crumpled body. *They didn't even call 911. Everybody knows you call 911 when there's an accident.*

Victoria turned to see who was there when her room door opened. Chloe stood just inside the doorway. "This is your fault, you know that, right? You were the last one to talk to her and you must have said or done something to upset Bethany. I hate you!"

Shocked, Victoria moved to the bed and sat down on its edge. Tears filled her eyes and ran down her cheeks. *I can't tell her. She wouldn't believe me and she might tell.*

Chloe stormed across the room and grabbed Victoria's arm. "Did you hear me? I hate you!" She hissed.

"Let go of my arm. Now." Victoria demanded.

"Or what? You'll push me out of a window too?" Chloe sneered. "You've been nothing but trouble since you got here. You are not my sister, and I'll find a way to make you pay, just you wait and see."

Victoria knew that it was wrong but she wasn't going to let Chloe push her around. She let her hand cover Chloe's and pulled one finger up and back. Without letting go of the finger she stood and used her grip on Chloe's finger to push the girl away. "I didn't push Bethany; I was in the kitchen with you and everyone else. You are right about one thing though, I am not your sister and I won't ever be."

"Girls! What's going on up there?" Ms. Anderson's voice rang up the stairs.

With a look that promised that this wasn't over, Chloe stepped away from Victoria and moved to the open door. "Nothing's going on. I was just checking on Tori because I heard her crying. She's okay now."

Jeri reached the open door, took a look at both girls and said, "Thank you Chloe, it's very nice of you to check on your sister." She wrapped an arm around Chloe's shoulders and led her away from Victoria's room. "Now please go check on the younger girls, they may need a big sister right now too."

Chloe nodded and walked across the

hallway to the other bedrooms. Jeri turned to Victoria. "Are you okay, Tori?"

Without speaking, Victoria nodded and sat down on her bed. She was relieved for once that Chloe was such a good liar. She didn't need this woman questioning her any more than necessary.

"Why don't you lay down for a while before dinner and I'll call you when it's time to eat." Jeri suggested as she pulled the door closed.

Victoria lay back on the bed as her head swam. This was a very dangerous place and Bethany's accident proved it. Bethany had been trying to tell her something but what was it? Victoria had no desire to go anywhere with Daddy and Bethany's warning gave her a least a little strength knowing that whatever happened in that room was bad and she had to stay away. But why did Bethany want her to go to the gazebo? There had to be a way out of this house and maybe Bethany was trying to tell her something. She had to find out and soon.

CHAPTER 17

"Gregory Aiden calling, sir." The smooth and sexy voice of Shawna Thompson, Noah's assistant, slid through the intercom.

Noah turned in his chair and replied, "Put him through Shawna and you can go ahead and leave for the day. Pull my door closed on your way out please." Noah trusted Shawna with any of his political business, there wasn't much about his congressional dealings that she didn't know of, and understand. She'd been his personal assistant for over five years and he often got the feeling that she'd like to be more than just his assistant. Ultimately, and even though she was a curvaceous and beautiful twenty nine year old, she was just too old.

Gregory didn't waste time with polite conversation. "What the hell is going on out there Noah?" Without waiting for a reply he continued, "When my driver showed up to pick up your *little problem,* he said that Jeri and your gardener were digging a grave! A fucking grave!"

"Slow down Gregory. It was an accident, a tragic accident, nothing more. Seems our Bethany may have found out about our plans to send her to Texas, and she jumped from the second story window." He paused. "It is a tragedy and I really haven't come to terms with it all yet."

"Don't pull that sympathetic political bullshit on me Noah. I know that..."

Cutting the attorney off, Noah snapped, "She was dead on impact, Gregory. There really wasn't anything else we could do given the circumstances, and you of all people should understand why. Clearly, we couldn't call the authorities in."

Gregory fumed, "I cannot believe that you would be so callous about this Noah. You can't just bury someone in the middle of your yard like that! What about the other girls? They had to have heard or seen something. What are you telling them? Shit!"

"This really isn't any of your concern Gregory. I have complete trust in Jeri and she will handle the girls, as for the gardener, he won't be a problem.

"You may not consider it an issue Noah, but if any of this ever leaks, my partner..." Gregory's words faded.

"Unless you or your driver let it leak, then I have no worries. You know as well as anyone that sometimes ugly things happen to beautiful people, even children. As for your partner, the elusive Captain, tell him or don't; that's no concern of mine. Bethany has been...was...mine for the last eight-years, and now she's gone. That is not your business, nor is it your partner's. Now instead of focusing on what cannot be changed, why not focus on finding a replacement for dear sweet Bethany? I have a room empty and waiting, and Gregory, this time I think I'd like a son."

Gregorio winced at the use of his partner's name. The Captain wasn't his real name of course, but using it loosely could be just as dangerous, and deadly, as using the real thing. "Fine." He growled. Gregorio hung up and shook his head. Had he really just agreed to find a little boy for that sick bastard? Noah's appetites were getting stranger, more deviant, and he seemed to think less and less of the consequences should someone overhear or find out. This was getting out of hand, but Gregorio had no idea how to stop it now. The only option left was to find exactly the right opportunity and then the next time that phone rang, Noah would hear nothing but the beating of his own sick, perverted heart.

CHAPTER 18

"All right mister, stand up nice and slow and then turn around. Put your hands on top of your head and walk backward toward the sound of my voice." The police officer stood from behind his car door and pulled a pair of cuffs from his belt. "Stop right there." He ordered. "Now drop your left hand and put it behind your back."

Inside Tate fumed, but he did as the officer ordered. *He's just doing his job. Playing it safe. You'd do the same thing and you know it.* He told himself. Tate waited until he heard then felt the cuffs click into place before he spoke. "My name is Tate Echo, I'm the police chief of Pine Ridge, South Dakota and my wife, Emma, called 911 to report an intruder and a shooting. The intruder is on the north side of the house and he's dead."

Two Richmond patrol cars slowed and stopped at the curb in front of Emma's house, their red and blue lights shooting across the dimly lit yard and into the trees. The patrolman nodded at his back up and said, "Check the north side of the house." He pointed at Tate and continued, "My runner says we've got a one eighty seven."

Tate turned his head and spoke over his shoulder, his tone laced with aggravation, "The perp was breaking into the house and when I confronted him he showed his weapon. I shot him in self-defense. Ask my wife."

A few feet away from Tate and the officer, she spoke, "That's ex-wife, officer. I'm Emma Gage-Echo" She paused then added, "FBI Special Agent Gage-Echo, and this man," She nodded at Tate, "is Tate Echo and he has correctly identified himself as the police chief of Pine Ridge." She extended her hand to the patrolman and leaned in so that she could read the name on his badge. "Thank you for responding so quickly Officer Whitman." At first she'd been relieved when she saw Tate in the street, but as the officer held him at gunpoint and then cuffed him, it was hard not to find it a little funny. Tate must be livid because the cops had allowed the woman to escape, although he was doing his best not to show it.

Tate turned and faced Emma and Officer Whitman, he scowled, "Look, if you two are through with your chat I'd appreciate it if you'd get these cuffs off me."

Emma forced herself to hide her smile.

Officer Whitman glowered at Tate, and said, "I'll un-cuff you if and when I'm ready sir. You can start with telling my why you were running away from the crime scene."

"I was chasing a woman who was in the yard. I don't know if she was helping the guy I shot or just passing by, but she hid, then she ran."

Officer Whitman pulled a cuff key from the key keeper attached to the right of his belt buckle and unlocked the cuffs on Tate's wrists.

"So you're saying this runner, a woman, was either involved or a primary witness to the shooting?"

Seeing that Tate was only seconds away from a full on explosion, Emma stepped in. "That's correct officer. She was only feet away when Tate shot the UnSub." A porch light across the street flicked on and Emma's neighbor stepped out on the porch in his pajamas and slippers.

She said, "I see that we're drawing an audience, could we please step inside to finish the questioning Officer Whitman? I'm sure I could come up with a fresh cup of coffee for you.

The officer gave her a brisk nod and followed Tate and Emma toward the house. They'd just reached the porch when one of the two street cops who'd arrived last rounded the house and said, "Guys dead alright. I'm calling in the crime team and coroner and Eli's going to stay with the body."

Three hours later, Tate and Emma watched as the patrol cars, crime team van and City of Richmond morgue vehicles drove away.

Tate pushed the door closed and turned to Emma with a sign of relief, "Let me take a look at your wound Em. You were limping and I saw that face you made when you sat down at the table."

"It's fine. I landed on my ass when I fell

earlier is all."

"You mean when I ran you over coming around the house. Now drop those sweats and let me have a look."

Rolling her eyes, Emma turned down the hallway, her voice echoing back. "I'm going to let you have a look, but only because I'm too tired to argue with you, so don't think that you've won any major battles here Tate."

Tate followed her into the bedroom and pulled on a pair of sterile gloves. His eyes roamed over the back of her sweatpants where blood oozed from her wounds and soaked the material. He stood by the bed as she moved the pants out of the way. "A couple of the stitches have come loose, Em. I think you should go in and get them re-stitched."

Emma rolled over and patted the side of the bed, she waited for Tate to sit down and said, "Not happening Echo. They were going to pull the stitches out in a few days anyway, so now they have less to do when the time comes. Just tape it closed and let it be, it's been a very long night and I'm not going to the ER and sit for hours over a couple of stitches."

Knowing that she was right about the wait in ER and seeing the fatigue on her face, he nodded and did as she asked.

When Tate finished with the taping and a fresh bandage, Emma shimmed the sweat pants up her body, but didn't get up. Tate lay back on the bed next to her and opened his arm; inviting her to snuggle. Surprised, he watched Emma roll toward him, fitting her body in the curve of his arm, her head rested on his shoulder.

"Thank you for being here tonight Tate. I..." Her words died away when Tate pulled her closer and rested his chin on her head. Closing her eyes, Emma breathed in the scent that was unchanging, all male and all Tate. Silently she wondered to herself just how many times she'd lain just like this, snuggled up to the man she loved, safe in his heart and his arms. She slid one arm across his chest and sighed. There was no need to finish her sentence. He knew.

Afraid to speak and break the spell, Tate pushed a lock of dark mahogany hair back from Emma's face then dropped a chaste kiss on the forehead. He pulled her closer and closed his own eyes, Tate thought to himself. *Moments like this may be all we'll ever have.* The thought no sooner took root before it was pushed aside with another. *I hope not.*

Hours later, Emma woke to the smell of fresh coffee. She struggled to wake fully and finally forced one eye open. Tate stood in the doorway to her bedroom with two steaming cups in his hands. The last thing she remembered was being together on the bed; she was wrapped in Tate's arms feeling loved and loving. "How long have I been asleep?" She asked.

Tate extended her one cup of the dark brew and replied, "Only a couple hours. You ready to take a walk?"

"Let me brush my hair and grab my shoes. I want to see if that motorcycle is parked around here somewhere before one of the neighbors calls it in or has it towed. Then I want a shower before we visit St. Anthony's."

"I already had my breakfast and shower. You're breakfast is waiting in the oven. Should be good until we get back from our walk."

With a wince, Emma stood and walked to the bathroom still sipping her coffee. Tate had always been the early one. When they'd been married he'd always been up hours before her so he could take a run in the park near their apartment before the rest of the world woke up. "You ever sleep?" She mumbled as she passed him.

He laughed and turned down the hallway, his boots clicking on the smooth wood surface, "I'll be in the kitchen when you're ready."

Fifteen minutes later, Tate and Emma left the house just as the morning sky turned pink with the new sun. They didn't have to go far, just three houses down they found the big Harley parked against the curb. Emma pulled a tissue from her pocket and tried the latch on the saddlebag. It wasn't locked and she pulled it open.

Tate reached in and pulled a plastic document holder out of the saddlebag and handed it to Emma. "Let's see who this baby is registered to." He said.

Emma pulled the registration paperwork from the holder and flipped it open, "Registered to one Simon Alvarez, 2111 Post Oak Lane, Richmond. That's not too far from here." She said.

Tate took the paperwork from her and placed it back in the bike, "Em, you know we can't go snooping around at his house. Cops are probably there right now."

"So we wait to snoop at his house for a couple of days, there are other ways that I can find out who Mr. Alvarez is without running into the Richmond PD. After all, the man tried to kill me. I think I deserve to dig into his business a little. I need to know why he was after me and if he was working on his own or for someone else."

Tate shook his head and said, "I'm betting he's a hired hand. I seriously doubt that the head of a child trafficking ring is going around personally killing people who get in his way."

"Agreed. I'll do some database creeping on Mr. Alvarez as soon as we get back from St. A's. Who knows, maybe we'll catch a break and find out who he's working for. Too bad you didn't catch our lady friend. I'd really like to know what her interest in all this is. Was she with him or was she trying to get him too? She ran for her life when the cops showed up so she may be underground and hard to locate. For whatever reason, she saved me not once but twice."

Tate laced his fingers with hers as they walked, "I can't get a grip on that either, not yet anyway. It's like she's appointed herself as your guardian angel. She saves you from Navarone, warns you about the guy I shot last night, and then hangs around in your yard and warns me that he's pulling a gun seconds before I shoot him. Hell, maybe she's the acting angel for us both."

Emma nodded her agreement. "I just wish we could talk to her and find out why she's helping us and why she seems to know so much about the bad guys."

Tammy Cheatham

CHAPTER 19

Victoria flopped down on the bed and
covered her eyes with one arm. *Mama would say
'Run Vic! Run!'* "This place is evil Mama. Please
help me get out of here. I don't know what to do
Mama." She whispered.

Unsure how long she'd lay there, Victoria
scrambled up when a soft knock sounded on the
door. Victoria watched the Piper enter her room
and take a seat next to her on the bed.

Jeri smiled, "I thought you'd want to know
that Bethany is going to be just fine. The driver
who was supposed to take her to the airport
took her to the hospital instead. It wasn't as bad
as it looked Tori. Just a few bumps and
bruises."

Swallowing a lump in her throat, Victoria
looked at the woman and hoped her voice didn't
give her thoughts away. "She's really going to be
okay? I thought...I mean...I..."

Jeri patted Victoria's leg, "She is going to
be fine. Just like I said, she's bruised and needs
a few stitches, but that will heal. Bethany was
very lucky and when she's well enough she'll still
get her trip. There's nothing for you or the other
girls to be worried about."

Afraid to speak, Victoria nodded.

"I'm going down to make us some lunch,
you'll let the other girls know about Bethany and
then all of you will come and have something to

146

eat, ok?"

"Okay." Victoria squeaked. When Ms. Anderson left the room, Victoria went to the window. Her mind spun with details from the day, things she'd been told and things she knew. *Total lies. She thinks just because I'm a kid that I don't know crap when I hear it. Well I do.* She stomped her foot against the soft carpet in silent frustration. *I saw all that blood, and I saw them wrap Bethany in that old blanket and put her on the gardener's cart. He drove away to the woods, not the driveway. I am not the stupid little girl she thinks I am.*

Victoria willed herself to be calm, she had to play the part, make it sound real; her life depended on that. She took a deep breath, and went to Chloe's room first. She spread the lie that Ms. Anderson had told. She watched the other girls squeal in delight at the news and wondered. *What's wrong with these kids? How can they just believe anything that woman says? Don't they have brains?*

Downstairs, Victoria slid into a chair at the big table in the kitchen and looked at the food on her plate. She felt sick, she *needed* to throw up. Fighting the nausea, she looked at the Piper and said, "I don't feel good." She pushed the plate away from her to the center of the table and she leaned back in her chair. "I'm going to be sick."

Jeri pulled a paper towel from the roll and ran it under cold water and squeezed the excess out, efficiently she shook the towel open and went to Victoria's side. Wiping the child's face, she cooed, "You've just had a stressful day Tori. You'll feel better if you eat."

Fat tears welled in her eyes and Victoria looked up at the woman. She gulped for air, "I can't breathe! I need some air, please help me!"

Jeri rushed to the control panel in the pantry and disabled the alarm, and then pulled Victoria by the hand out to a bench in the garden.

"You're hyperventilating. Sit here and bend over with your head down," Jeri ordered. That's it; just keep your head down for now. You're going to be fine, you'll see." Victoria did as she was told and forced herself not to pull away when Jeri rubbed her back. "I'm going to step inside and get you a glass of juice and I'll be right back. Are you okay to sit here by yourself for just a minute?"

Without speaking, Victoria let her head bob. As soon as she heard the door open Victoria raised her head slightly, her eyes snapping to the place where Bethany had lay just a couple of hours ago. The sun hitting the white stone walkway only emphasized the pinkish glow on the pale rock; she knew the stain was Bethany's blood. Fear threatened to consume her, her body shook violently and she rocked trying to control it. Victoria clenched her jaw and silently swore, *I will survive this, I will get away and I will find my mother. I won't let them keep me, I won't*

believe their lies. I am going to leave this place!
Victoria could almost hear her mother telling her
that they could survive anything for a little
while; they just had to focus on each other and
wait it out. *That's what I'm doing mama, I'm
waiting it out.*

The sound of the door opening gave
warning that Ms. Anderson was returning and
Victoria let her head drop further between her
legs.

"You can sit up now Tori." Ms. Anderson
handed her a small glass of apple juice. "Just
sip on it and I know you'll feel better soon. I
think that you should lie down for a while after
you finish your juice. A good rest always helps
when you feel badly."

Warning bells sounded in her head and
Victoria stared at the glass in her hand. "I'm not
thirsty." She tried to hand the juice back but
Jeri closed her hand around the glass and gently
pushed it back toward her.

"Just a few sips and then you can come
inside and rest."

Taking a tiny sip of the juice Victoria
shuddered, remembering the fogginess of her
first days here, the days before they'd let her out
of her room. *There was always juice, apple juice,
on my breakfast tray.*

"Can I have crackers to go with my juice?"
Her tiny voice pleaded.

Glancing back at the house and then at the juice, Jeri relented, "Sure, That might help to settle your stomach. I'll get them for you, but I want you to finish that juice, okay?"

Victoria nodded and took another very tiny sip and then let it run from her mouth back into the glass before she lowered it.

As soon as Ms. Anderson opened the door, Victoria dumped all but a sip of the apple juice on the grass under the bench. She counted to three and then followed the path back to the house.

Jeri turned in surprise when the door opened. Glancing at the almost empty glass in Victoria's hand she smiled. "You feeling better now?" she asked.

"A little. I think I'd like to go to my room now, okay?" Victoria answered and slid the juice glass onto the counter.

"Of course it's okay, it's just what you need right now." She handed Victoria a plate with crackers on it and continued, "Take these with you in case you fill sick again and I'll be up in a little bit to check on you."

Victoria took the plate of crackers from Jeri and walked out of the room. At the bottom of the stairs she smiled.

CHAPTER 20

Emma's personal car, a steel gray Toyota Camry, was small and Tate had to move the seat back to accommodate his long legs. Emma provided the directions and he drove to St. Anthony's Children's Home. He parked in front of the facility and turned to Emma, "You ready for this?"

Emma nodded and replied, "So how do you want to play it?"

Tate leaned around and pulled his cap from the backseat, flipped it on his head and frowned, "I think we better stick with the official titles. Let them think that you've been assigned to the case to search for the missing girls. Hopefully we won't have to explain who I am since I don't have the official creds to pull off being FBI anymore."

Emma pushed the car door open and agreed, "Works for me. Just flash your badge while I'm talking and I doubt they'll push to see it up close. I suspect they're going to be pretty tight with details about these girls, but I don't think we could pull it off if we go in as a married couple looking to adopt and then try to ask questions about the missing girls."

They met at the front of the car and Tate said, "What I'd really like is to get ahold of their records for the last couple years and see just how many kids have come up missing from here. I can't believe that it was just coincidence that these three ran away and you see them with a trafficker the same night. That's just too coincidental to be anything other than planned."

Emma stared up at Tate. "Okay, how about I go in to talk to the director alone, in my official capacity of course, and you stay in the reception area and put some of that Echo charm on whoever's manning the desk."

Tate gave her a dimpled grin and dropped a quick kiss on her upturned lips, "I hope it's not a sinfully ugly nun dressed in full habit, those girls are tough to crack. Or worse yet, a man."

Emma laughed, "Let's go see what we're up against and just for the record, I hope she is very homely. It's always harder to charm a beautiful woman, so the plainer she is, the better for us."

The building, a brown stone monstrosity built in a half triangle stood ominously, two wings splayed off to either side forming a V. "Looks like something out of Middle Age Architecture class doesn't it?" Tate asked.

Shadowy darkness covered one side of the building, while sunshine bathed the other with bright morning rays, it was like evil and goodness had faced off and waited to see who would win. Lodged between the two wings, the main entrance stretched upward where it peaked with a bell tower topped with an iron cross. The bell tower stood between the wings, an impartial judge, as if waiting to see who would win. An oval portico supported by two faded brown brick columns covered the ground level entrance and Tate pulled one of the heavy wooden doors open for Emma to enter before him.

"Creepy." Emma whispered. She couldn't imagine how intimidating this building was to the children who called it home.

Inside, the foyer continued in the oval shape that began at the door, making the entrance seem lonely and hollow. Polished granite flooring stretched the length of the hallway and glistened in the light from a lone window at one end. Emma paused to read a name plate attached to the first door inside the building. She looked at Tate, and said, "This is it."

Emma straightened her jacket, and then clipped her badge on. She pushed the door open, stepped inside, and stopped in front of the only desk in the room. The woman at the desk looked up. Emma flipped the leather holder containing her credentials and picture ID open and held it out. "Hello, I'm FBI Agent Emma Gage-Echo and I'd like to speak with the Director of Children's Services please."

The woman behind the desk glanced at Emma's badge and stood up to inspect Emma's picture ID. Satisfied that Emma was indeed who she said, the woman closed the holder and handed it back to Emma. "Do you have an appointment with Dr. Garrett?" she asked.

Tate recognized that this was the opportunity to doing a little of the charming that Emma suggested and stepped closer to the desk. He picked up the black plastic name plate from the desk and pulled out his best Hollywood smile, knew that his dimples were shining and said, "Mrs. Sharon Porter, lovely name. It is Mrs. isn't it?"

When the woman blushed and shook her head to indicate that she wasn't married, he continued, "Well then, *Miss* Porter, I'm sure that you can help us. We don't have an appointment, but it is very important that Agent Echo speak with the director, I'll just stay out here and keep you company. That is, if you don't mind." Placing the placard back on her desk, Tate leaned closer to the woman. "Could you help us out by checking to see if Dr. Garrett is available?"

Emma rolled her eyes when a slow blush crept up the woman's face and tinged her cheeks a rosy red. Miss Porter who had to be at least 35, maybe 40, looked wide-eyed at Tate, and then she giggled. "Let me check the schedule and see if there's possibly a break or cancellation, maybe we *could* squeeze you in."

Tate winked at Miss Porter, and continued, "That would be wonderful Sharon. It is okay if I call you Sharon, isn't it?"

Emma stepped back and gave Tate the room he needed. He immediately took a seat on the edge of Miss Porter's desk, and leaned casually near her while she checked the schedule on her computer.

Tate is so obvious it's ridiculous! Emma thought. *Oh well, he's blocking me from her view and that means I have a chance to look around.* Tall puke green, metal file drawers, the horizontal kind, lined the wall behind Miss Porter's desk, six in all. An event calendar hung slightly crooked on the wall next to the door. Dates were marked very neatly with black ink and extremely precise handwriting. *Probably Miss Porter's handwriting.* Emma guessed, as she quickly scanned the current month and didn't see anything of importance to her case, not that she thought there would be. *I need to see what's in those cabinets.*

"Oh, Agent Echo." Emma turned at the sound, Miss Porter's sing-song voice interrupting her thoughts.

"Yes?" Emma answered.

"We are very lucky indeed. Dr. Garrett will be able to see you today. He has someone in his office now but his lunch appointment called a little bit ago and cancelled, so if you could wait half an hour we could squeeze you in."

"That will be fine, and thank you." Emma replied, and then moved to take a seat across from the reception desk. She gave Tate a look and flashed her eyes from him to the file cabinets, hoping he would take the hint. He did.

Tate stepped back and cleared his throat.

He smiled at Sharon Porter and let his voice drop, "I don't suppose you could give me a quick tour of the Center while we wait? I studied architecture briefly in college and I would love to see the rest of the building."

Sharon glanced at her watch and beamed up at Tate. She replied, "Well it is almost my lunch time. I don't suppose it would hurt to take a few extra minutes. Let me just forward the office phone down to the registration center, they can pick up any incoming calls for Dr. Garrett while I'm out." Almost as an afterthought she turned to Emma and asked, "Will you be joining us, Agent Echo?"

Emma smiled at the woman's obvious attempt to be coy and answered in her sweetest voice. "No, I'd better wait for Dr. Garrett; I'd hate to miss my opportunity to talk with him. You two go ahead and maybe I'll get to see the building some other time."

Tate pulled the door open, crooked his arm and extended it to Sharon. "Lead the way then, lovely Miss Porter."

There was that school-girl giggle again. Miss Porter slipped her hand through Tate's arm and led him out the door.

As soon as the door closed behind the touring couple, Emma stood and peeked out the frosted glass pane on the windowed door. She watched Tate and Miss Porter stroll down the hallway and turn the corner. Without them in the room she could hear low-toned voices coming from the next room, presumably Dr. Garrett and his appointment who, judging from the timber of both voices, was also a man. Confident that she had some time, Emma turned the swivel lock on the brass knob. *No interruptions please. I've got to see what's in those cabinets.* She kept one ear open for any change in the voices or other signal that the meeting in Dr. Garrett's office was ending, and moved to the file cabinets behind Miss Porter's desk. Each lateral drawer sported a tag indicating the alphabetic range in its confines. Emma let her fingers run across the drawers and stopped when she reached "M". *The red-haired girl's last name is McEvers.* She thought. Emma tugged at the drawer and was disappointed, but not surprised, to find it locked. She moved to the next drawer and the next quickly and found them locked as well. *Crap.*

She turned to the reception desk and muttered, "Now where would Miss Over-Organized keep her keys?" She moved to the reception desk and tugged the thin drawer in the center of the desk, it easily slid open. Emma was surprised, and quickly scanned the space for keys. *Nothing, dammit. She probably wears them on a chain around her neck!*

Voices from the next room grew louder and closer. Emma quietly pushed the drawer closed and rushed across the room to take a seat. She had just sat back and crossed her legs when the door opened.

A squat man, almost as wide as he was tall, and definitely more fat than muscle, stepped from the inner office. He wore a tight blue suit and black shoes with a full coat of street dust on them. His tie, a red and white striped, was loosened at the collar and swung like a pendulum from his thick neck. He was closely followed by another man; Emma quickly decided that this man was the Dr. Garrett that she'd come to see. *He fits the director image*, she thought. Tall and well-built for a man clearly over fifty, a touch of distinguished gray at the temples of his short-cropped hair, and unlike his guest, the presumed Doctor wore a dark suit that fit him well, a matching tie with subdued hues of gray and black and a pair of Rockport dress shoes that you could see your face in. Emma stood when the two men stepped into the outer office, but she didn't approach them.

The well-dressed man glanced at Emma, one eyebrow lifted in silent question but he didn't acknowledge her in any other way, he just turned to his guest and shook the other man's hand. "Thank you for coming in today Mr. Baskin, we are always happy to work with the staff over at the Child Protective Services division, and if I find any additional information that could help you, then I will certainly give you a call."

The man called Mr. Baskin turned toward the door and Emma thought, *Damn, I forgot to unlock the door.*

When the man reached the door he turned

back to Dr. Garrett and said, "You do that Garrett and remember, we've got availability to house some of these kids in real homes. I got people out there that want kids..." He glanced at Emma and scowled, then cleared his throat and continued, "Just call me when you have more than you can handle here and we'll get them placed." He turned the door knob and pulled the door, it didn't open. He frowned and tried again, "You locking people out now Garrett?"

Speaking up Emma smiled and quickly said, "Oh I think Miss Porter may have locked the door when she left for lunch."

The man gave a "Hrmp", unlocked the door and left.

Emma moved forward and extended her hand to Garrett. "Hello, I'm FBI agent Emma Gage-Echo and I have just a few questions for you." She paused and produced her badge for him to see. "Miss Porter indicated that you might be able to spare me a few minutes since your scheduled lunch appointment cancelled."

"Of course, Agent Echo. I assume that you're here regarding the run-away girls and even though I've already spoken with the police, I'd be happy to answer your questions. Please join me in my office." He pulled the door open and waited for her to enter. Closing the door behind them, Dr. Garrett gestured to a chair, and once Emma was seated, he crossed behind the desk and took his chair. With a tight-lipped smile he asked, "Now, exactly how can I help you today Agent Echo?"

CHAPTER 21

"Yes I do understand that we have an agreement but..." Pinching the bridge of his nose, Gregorio frowned but didn't interrupt the voice on the other end of the line.

"I expect delivery as promised Gregory and I don't care what you have to do to make it happen. I have clients just as you do and without this shipment everything is at risk and you'd damn well better believe that if I am at risk, *you* are at risk. You've been totally isolated from the ugly end of our partnership, sitting there in your million dollar house with your pretty little family; on the other hand I've had to feed both ends of the monster and cover your ass too."

Gregorio decided that the best appeal was one of adoration, "I know that you have sacrificed to keep our venture going and that you have taken more than your share of risks, but..."

The voice cut him off, cruelly, the man on the phone spat, "No buts. You have one week to make this happen or I will crush you. You defy me on this Gregory and it's not just your home or your job that you're risking, it's everything...think about that...everything. The next time that you call me, make sure it's to set up the delivery and not to cry about complications on your end."

The phone clicked and went to dial tone.

Gregorio cursed and placed the phone in its cradle, and then reached for his drink.

Gregorio downed his drink and poured another. How the hell had he let himself get so deep in this mess? It started off innocuously enough; he'd forged some adoption papers for a friend of Quinto's, no big deal really. He'd just made partner at the firm and looking back he supposed that he was 'feeling the power', and after all, he was certainly in a position to push a little paperwork though the court system. At the time, he was certain that he was helping both a homeless child and a childless couple. Yeah, they'd gone about it the wrong way, but the end result was a win for everyone....and the pay was amazing...*Don't forget that Gregorio.*

The ice in his drink tinkled against the crystal glass, and Gregorio's mind fast forwarded two months from his first deal with the devil.

Quinto had strolled into his office looking like the street thug that he was, and dropped a packet of papers on his desk. "Take care of it Gregorio. The Captain finds you to be an asset to our team, and this will be both your test and your biggest payday."

The papers slid out of the accordion packet and Gregorio recalled his shock at seeing Noah Walker's name listed as the adoptive parent. He glanced up at Quinto and pushed the paperwork back across the desk, silently refusing. He didn't know where these girls had come from, but he knew they weren't babies, knew that Walker had no wife, and knew that this was all kinds of wrong.

Quinto had laughed at him, "Oh no, brother." He said firmly and pushed the papers back in front of Gregorio. "There is no option to refuse. Your life and mine depend on how well you handle this job." His brother grinned at him, "Don't you want to know about the money, brother? It's three times what you earned with that silly little baby adoption....three times, Gregorio. Think about that."

In the end, he'd done what was demanded of him, that time and more times than he wanted to remember. He'd pocketed the money, built a fortune, and tried to justify his actions even though he suspected what was happening to those children.

Then Tassie came along, his beautiful baby girl. He'd do anything to keep her safe, to make her life the best that it could be...anything. Somewhere he'd lost himself and he knew it, just as he knew that there was no going back. He just had to play along until the time was right.

What the hell am I going to do? He's not going to let this go. I can't risk Tassie. Damn you Quinto, I need that baby you promised me.

The phone rang again and interrupted Gregorio's frantic thoughts, "Gregory Aiden." He answered.

Nothing.

"I can hear you breathing, Wynter, why don't you talk to me? Don't you want to know how Tassie is doing?"

A gasp spewed through the phone line and Gregory smiled. "I think it's time we worked this problem out. Wouldn't you like to see your daughter? I'm sure we can reach a solution that will work for us both if you'd just talk to me."

Hesitantly at first, then stronger, the female voice on the phone agonized, "There is no solution unless you are ready to give me my daughter."

"Ah, you know that I would never give *my daughter* to you or anyone else. Tassie belongs with family and..."

"I am her mother! There is no closer family than that." Wynter hissed.

The chair squeaked when Gregory leaned back in it and crossed his legs, "Yes, you are her mother, and while that is a fact, it is also of little consequence to me. I don't wish to have the same argument with you...again." Pausing for a breath, Gregory continued, "I supposed you have heard about Quinto's unfortunate death?"

Wynter gulped and tried to keep her voice steady. *He can't know. Not yet.* "Yes, I heard that he was dead, but that is not my concern. I need to see Tassie."

"It's been months since you've seen your daughter, what makes you so sure that she will remember you? It would be easier if you just let her forget that you are her mother, I will marry someday and then she will have the mother she deserves, and for now she has me and her grandmother."

Knowing that his words had the desired effect, deeply hurting the woman on the phone, Gregory smiled. "Cat got your tongue?"

Wynter spoke with firm resolve, "I will never let her forget that I am her mother." Then she pleaded, "How can you be so cruel Gregorio?"

He laughed, not a happy sound, "I didn't force you to leave my home or to leave our daughter behind when you left. That was your choice."

Her voice begged him to understand, "You know why..." Her voice fell before she continued, "Please just let me see her....please."

Gregory smiled at her obvious defeat, and cooed, "I can make that happen for you Wynter, but I will need something in return. A favor of sorts. In fact that's exactly what I need. A very small favor."

"No." Wynter's reply was firm. "I won't help you. I cannot help you that way."

"Hear me out before you decide. If you don't help me, then you will never see Tassie again. I am holding our passports in my hand as we speak, and without this *favor*, I will be forced to leave the country and go into hiding to assure my own safety, and naturally, if I go, Itasca goes." He paused to let his words sink in, a trick that he'd mastered in front of the jury years ago, and was sure to have the same effect now on Wynter. "Think about it before you refuse me. You will never know where your daughter is, you will never see her again. You will be dead to her, I will make certain of that."

The sharp intake of breath on the line told Gregory what he needed to know. *She'll do anything to make sure I don't leave the country with her baby.*

Wynter's words spilled out in a rush, "Give her to me. Please don't let your...your business put her at risk."

"Don't be absurd. I would never leave without her; she is my flesh and blood. I have always protected what is mine and that certainly includes my daughter." His voice dropped to a deadly tone. "Get me what I need, just this once, and there will be no need to worry about Itasca. I will even let you see her... if you help me."

Knowing that his threats weren't idle ones, Wynter sighed into the phone. "Tell me what it is that you want and then I will decide. You promise to let me see her if I help you?"

"You have my word that I will let you see her." *I've won. She will help me because she can't do anything else.*

"Give me some time to think it over and I'll

call you back."

Leaning back in his chair, Gregory relaxed, "You have twenty four hours to decide, and I must have the *product* in my possession in forty-eight hours or less. I expect to hear from you tomorrow. Now let me tell you exactly what I need."

Two minutes later, Wynter hung up the phone on Sister Camille's desk and pulled her jacket from the back of her chair. She walked out of the cubby-holed office to the rear door of the building, and made her way to a stone bench in the rear garden of St. Anthony's Children's Home.

Wynter plopped down on the bench and pushed the hood back from her head, letting her long blonde hair spill over her shoulders. She let her head drop forward, and closed her eyes. Wynter prayed harder than she'd ever prayed before.

God help me. I don't want to offend you but I cannot let him take Tassie out of the country. Help me find a way to stop him please. Show me the way.

CHAPTER 22

Tate and Miss Porter rounded the rear corner of St. Anthony's. They walked through a tall, black painted, iron fence gate. The matching fence surrounded the interior garden behind the chapel and Tate followed the fence line with his eyes. He doubted that anyone could go up and over. *Probably eight feet.* He decided.

Rock pathways marked the garden and meandered past flower beds filled with colorful blooms. Tate and Miss Porter took the closest walkway and following it for several yards. Tate fidgeted and picked his step. *I have no need to see a garden, but I do need to ask a few questions about the girls.* He thought, trying to appear interested while Miss Porter talked.

"The garden was designed after a very famous Italian church garden. All the pathways eventually lead to the center of the garden. The design is really very clever." She leaned close to him, pointed and said, "You can see the top half of the angle statue from here, it's a replica of the Hammarby Angel. Both the garden and the statue were donated by a board member when the school was first built. He thought it would give staff and students a good place to reflect."

"I'm sure it does." Tate muttered. He spied a bench, one of many that they'd passed along the path. *Time to talk Miss Porter.* "Mind if we sit here a minute?" He asked.

Miss Porter blushed and cooed, "Oh, not

at all. I love sitting in the garden when the sun is out like today."

Tate dropped down on the bench and smiled at the women. *Time to talk about the missing girls.* "The sun does feel really good today and it picks up just a hint of red in your hair too." Reaching out Tate let one fingers trail lightly across a shoulder length stand of her dull brown hair before he continued. "Tell me something Miss Porter. From everything you've shown me, St. A's seems like a pretty nice place, as far as orphanages go. I mean the teachers seem nice, the house parents seemed to really care about the kids, so why do you think those little girls would run away?"

The woman looked up at him and blushed, "It's hard to say, but if I had to guess I'd say that the younger girls, Allie and Ivy that is, were persuaded to go by Victoria."

Still smiling at her, Tate kept his voice casual and asked, "Why would you think that? Victoria wasn't happy here?"

"I wouldn't say that she was unhappy, she behaved and did what was expected from her most of the time, but she did talk a lot about leaving to find her mother. She and the younger girls were really close, and maybe they wouldn't let her leave alone or maybe they thought they could all live happily ever after if they just got out and found Victoria's mom."

"So she was like a big sister to them?"

"Allie and Ivy had been here for several years and I don't think they remember any other life, but Victoria did, and all the younger kids wanted to hear what it was like to have a real mom."

"So how long has Victoria been here?"

"She was assigned to St. A's about four months ago when her mother was arrested for drugs. An agent from the county brought her in kicking and screaming."

"There wasn't any family to take her in? No dad?" Tate questioned.

Miss Porter sighed, "None that anyone could find. Seems that the father died five years ago and Victoria's mother spiraled into drug use after his death, lost her job and home, and then her daughter, and finally, her freedom. It's not all that uncommon, but sad none the less."

"So where's her mother now?" Tate asked.

"Last I heard she was remanded to a rehab facility for six months, and that was after two months in jail before her trial. She wrote to Victoria every week and Benni, that's the house mother in the C Unit, said that she'd seen the letters and that the woman promised Victoria that she was getting better, and would come and get her as soon as she got out."

Tate looked thoughtful, calculating the time in his head. "So why would she run away if her mother was coming here to get her in what?

Two months?"

Nodding, Miss Porter continued, "That part bothered me too. But then kids often do things that adults just don't understand, these girls aren't the first to run away and I'm sure they won't be the last."

Tate stood and offered her a hand, "So there have been others?" he casually asked.

"Well, we don't like to dwell on it, after all there's not much we can do other than turn it over to the police, but yes, there have been others."

They walked along the pathway and Tate continued to casually ask questions. *Don't want it to sound like an inquisition.* He reminded himself. "So how many others have there been?"

"Oh, I don't know the exact number but I do remember a brother and sister a couple of months ago, and then last year there were a few." Ms. Porter turned to face Tate, "It's not that unusual you know. Many of the children here came from the streets, and some of them would rather go back to the streets than try to conform to the rules here at St. A's. That's especially true of the older ones."

Tate nodded and then asked, "So none of them were found? They just disappeared and no one's seen them since? That seems odd. I mean with the Amber Alert system, and all the other resources available now, you'd think that someone, somewhere, would have reported at least seeing one of these missing children, especially if they were on the streets."

"Occasionally a runaway is found but many times they are not returned to us, they go to Child Services over at the county. It just depends on the child and the situation."

Tate changed the subject, "Thank you for showing me around today. I need to get back and see if my friend has finished her meeting with Dr. Garrett."

Sharon Porter glanced at her watch, "Yes, I too need to get back. Let's walk around the path so that you can see the angel statue before going inside, it's really quite beautiful."

"Certainly." Tate agreed.

They strolled in the afternoon sun and finally rounded a curve in the walkway near the angel. Tate stopped. A tall blonde woman had just stood up from an aged stone bench in front of the angel statue and was pulling the hood of her jacket up. *It's her! The blonde haired gazelle! So do I approach her or follow her?* He thought, before he quickly dropped down on one knee, pretending to tie his shoe. *Don't want her to see me just yet.* He thought.

Covertly, Tate watched the woman until she walked away and entered one of three doors leading from the main building to the garden. He stood up and gazed after her. Not wanting to seem eager, he walked around the statue and admired it while his eyes followed the woman to the buildings entrance. Casually he asked, "Are the garden's open to the public?"

A bit surprised by the question, Miss Porter replied, "Oh no. Only staff and students are allowed on the property."

"So the woman who just walked away works here?"

"Yes she does. That's Sister Camille's assistant."

Tate continued to look up at the angel's sad form and asked, "So Miss...what's her name?"

"Wynter. Wynter Burgland, why do you ask?"

I have a name Em! And she's neck deep in this mess. Knows the traffickers, works at an orphanage where kids go missing and are never seen again, oh yeah, she's in deep. Tate smiled at the woman and replied, "No particular reason, just comparing her job with the Sister to yours with the director. Shall we head back now?"

Her being here might explain why the missing kids aren't spotted on the streets. They're not on the streets. Tate thought. *They're locked up, somewhere totally off the grid and in the hands of evil; otherwise some of them would have been found, or at the least their bodies would have been found. Damn. Someone in this place, probably Wynter Burgland, is working both sides of the fence! But if she is, why did she kill*

Navarone? Why didn't she kill Em? Or me? Maybe she just knows too much and is looking for a way out. The questions swirled as he fought his instinct to chase the woman down.

Miss Porter walked at Tate's side, and paused for him to open the door when they'd reached it. "Our jobs are really quite different." She boasted. "She's a general assistant who does filing, errands and such while my job with the director is more detailed. I do all of his correspondence, assist with record keeping for the facility, set his appointments and greet his visitors among other things."

Tate and Miss Porter reached her office and he'd just taken a seat in the small square room when the director's door opened and Emma stepped out. He watched her turn to smile and shake hands with the man. "Thank you so much for seeing me on such short notice Dr. Garrett. You have my contact information and please do give me a call if you think of anything further regarding the disappearance of the children."

When Angels Cry

CHAPTER 23

Victoria pushed the door to her room closed and crossed to the windows overlooking the garden. Even from the second story window she could still see the blood red stain on the walkway below, in her mind she could still see Bethany laying there, her body twisted and the blood pooling beneath her. Shuddering she moved to the bed and lay down on top of the covers to think, in case Ms. Anderson came in to check on her.

"What are you going to do?" She quietly asked herself. *Bethany said to go to the gazebo; there must be something there that will help you. You can't get into the study because you don't know the door code. Miss Anderson keeps her cell phone in her pocket all the time, and you haven't found a phone anywhere else in this whole house.*

Suddenly an idea popped into her mind and Victoria jumped up to sit on the bed's edge. *There must be a phone in the bedrooms where they sleep!* But she couldn't go in there. *Bethany said I was never to go in there. I have seen movies and grownups in bed together kissing and doing other stuff. I think that is what happens to girls in his room and I am not ever going in there. Never. Even if Chloe says it was fun spending the night with Daddy, she lies. Mama said that kids are not supposed to be doing that stuff and she doesn't lie to me.* Flopping back on the bed Victoria squeezed her eye's tight forcing the threatening tears back. "Crying is not going to get you out of here." She muttered.

Muted voices outside the door alerted Victoria that she someone was coming. She curled her body against a pillow and pretended to be asleep; her eyes relaxed and her mouth slightly ajar. The door creaked lightly, and she could feel someone staring her. She turned to her back and let her eyes flutter open slowly; then she raised one arm in a mock stretch.

Ms. Anderson stood next to the bed looking down at her. "Feeling better?" She asked.

Victoria sat up and curled her legs underneath, Indian style. "You were right. A nap did help, I don't feel sick anymore."

Jerri dropped down on the bed and sat next to the girl. "Would you like to come down and have something to eat? You missed lunch. The other girls are getting ready to have some outside time this afternoon and if you want you can join them after you eat."

Victoria nodded, "I am a little hungry. Can I have a peanut butter sandwich?"

Jeri smiled and stood, "You can. Slip on your shoes and bring a sweater down with you. It's still a little chilly outside. I'll go make your sandwich and see you downstairs in a minute."

Victoria watched the woman leave her room, and then scrambled for her shoes and sweater. "I've got to get to that gazebo." *This could be the chance you've been waiting for.*

Victoria forced herself to slow down and not seem too excited when she went into the kitchen. Chloe and Nora were seated at the table and Chloe looked up when she entered. She didn't say anything but Victoria could see the hate in her eyes. She looked around and asked, "Where's Allie and Ivy? Don't they want to go outside too?"

Nora shrugged, glanced at Chloe, lifted her chin a notch and said, "Not that it matters where those *little* girls are, but they're watching TV in the family room. Ms. Anderson will call them when we get ready to go out. We finished our lunch a long time ago but Ms. Anderson said we *had* to wait for you, so hurry up; you're ruining everything."

Victoria sat down at the table and picked up her sandwich. *So now both of them hate me.* She thought. *Well I don't care, I just want out of here.*

Chloe chimed, "We want to pick flowers today so that we can make ring thingy's for our hair. Daddy is coming home tomorrow and we want to surprise him. I'm sure he'll like mine the best."

Victoria took a bite of her sandwich and watched Ms. Anderson come into the room. Looking at the woman she asked, "Can I feed the ducks instead? I want to see them swimming and if they've got any babies."

Jeri dropped a paper napkin next to Victoria's plate and asked, "Don't you want to make a flower ring for your hair too? It would look so pretty with your auburn hair. Surely you don't want the other girls to be all dressed up and not join them."

"I think I'm allergic to flowers. When I helped in the garden at St. A's I would always sneeze and get a runny nose and I don't want to be sick."

Breaking into the conversation, Nora rolled her eyes and said, "That's just silly. You can't be allergic to flowers, they're too pretty."

Allie and Ivy pushed into the room and Allie immediately came to Victoria's defense. "She is too 'lergic, but me and Ivy aren't, are we Ivy?" Allie turned and looked at her friend waiting for confirmation.

Ivy's head bobbed, her blonde curls bouncing as she slid into the chair next to Nora, she confirmed, "Nope, we're not 'lergic to flowers but I remember one time that Victoria sneezed until her nose turned red and her eye's dripped. She used a whole box of tissue and Sister Camille said she was going to blow her head off!" The two younger girls giggled at the memory.

Jeri frowned at Chloe and Nora. She interrupted the pre-teens before they could chime in. Jeri firmly said, "Some people are allergic to flowers Nora. We'll just have to get Tori tested, and if she's allergic then we can get her some medicine. That way she can enjoy the garden like the rest of you do. For now, you girls can pick the flowers you need for your project and Tori can feed the ducks."

Afraid her excitement would show, Victoria took a bite of her sandwich, and then covered her mouth with the paper napkin effectively hiding her smile.

Allie stared across the table at Victoria, her blue eyes soft with sympathy, "I'll feed the ducks with Victoria, that way she doesn't have to be all alone." A thought struck and she brightened, "Ivy will pick enough flowers for me too, won't you Ivy?"

Victoria swallowed hard, and before Ivy could answer, said, "It's okay Allie, you don't have to come with me. You like flowers. The pond isn't far and I can feed the duck and watch you pick flowers too." She turned to Ms. Anderson and continued, "Can I have some bread for the ducks, please?"

Jeri held up a bag of bread and smiled at Victoria, "I've got it all ready for you." She turned to the other girls and said, "Now put your sweaters on and let's get going. I'm going to sit in the garden and read my book while you gather your flowers. And girls, I will be asking you to tell me about the flowers that you pick, that's going to be our lesson for today. Tori, since you're not picking flowers, your lesson will be about the ducks and the pond."

The girls scrambled to put their sweaters on and see who could get out the door first.

Victoria snatched the bag of bread from where
Ms. Anderson had placed it on the counter
rushed to join them.

CHAPTER 24

Standing at a lone window in Sister Camille's office, Wynter peeked through the blinds and watched the grey Toyota back from its parking spot in front of the center. "It's time Emma Gage-Echo. I need that favor now." She muttered before turning back to her desk and the stack of files waiting to be sorted. Before taking a seat at her desk, another thought invaded. What if they think I took those girls? *Oh God, please don't let that be why they were here.* Wynter's stomach roiled and she prayed harder.

Side by side, Tate and Emma walked down the wide hallway and back to the heavy wooden doors marking the entrance of St. Anthony's without speaking. Once they were settled in the car, Tate turned to Emma and asked, "Well?"

"That man is a master in the 'cover your ass' department and as tight lipped as they come. Says that the girls are runaways, and that as far as the center is concerned, the police can handle it like any other missing minor case. I got the official 'for the press' speech." Emma scrunched up her face up and speaking in a deadpan tone, she continued, "It's regrettable that the children are missing, but the center holds no responsibility in the matter. St. Anthony's has a state of the art security system in place, and it appears that these girls bypassed the system by sneaking out a basement window." Emma pulled her seatbelt around and clicked it into place, then continued, "He said that the basement doesn't have security cameras since the only thing housed there are a few 'dead' files and the laundry facilities. The basement door lock had been jammed open with a piece of wadded paper which kept the lock from engaging. As far as he's concerned this was a well-planned exit on the part of these girls."

Tate started the car and asked, "You think that's the truth? I mean about them jamming the door?"

Emma shook her head and replied, "Nope, I think it's a very convenient story to cover his ass. I mean really, a nine year old and two seven year olds thought about the alarm system and planned to bypass it? That's a little too much for me to buy. I asked to see their files and he gave me some bullshit line about the files being misfiled, and with a *limited* staff they have been unable to locate them. Sounds to me like the files went wherever the girls went."

Tate slid the car into reverse, and stared in the rear-view mirror as he backed the car out. He said, "I think I had better luck than you. I know who the mystery woman is *and* I know where to find her."

Emma's jaw dropped, "What! How?"

"She was in the garden behind the school today when Miss Porter took me on my tour. She didn't see me but I am positive that it's the same woman. Same jacket, same long blonde hair. She works here."

"Turn around!" Emma shouted. "I want to talk to her."

Tate shook his head and said, "Not here Em. We need to take her by surprise, and I don't think it should be here. I'm still having issues with what her involvement is exactly. It's hard for me to believe that she's working for the traffickers since she's saved you from Navarone, gave you that warning note and then did the same for me when that guy was breaking into your house. But then Sharon Porter said that there were other kids that disappeared from St. A's too, and when I questioned her, she confirmed that very few of them were ever located or returned to the orphanage."

Tate stopped the car at the end of the street, looked left waiting for a break in traffic and then moved the car into the flow. "I can't believe that with all the people in this city, and law enforcement practically on every street corner, that most of the missing kids were never seen again, or even found dead at some point. Kids do not just disappear. They've got someone on the inside Em. Someone who's taking the kids and making sure that they're not found. I don't think that it's our mystery woman, but somehow she must be involved, she knows too many of the players in this game. We need to call in a favor and find out who she is before we talk to her."

Emma slumped back in her seat and grudgingly agreed, "Okay, so we do a background on her, then we talk face to face.

What's her name?"

"Wynter Burgland."

"That's an unusual name, shouldn't be too hard to track her history down, assuming that's her *real* name. Hurry up and get us home so I can find out everything there is to know about Wynter Burgland."

Tate grinned at her excitement, "I'll get us home quick enough, but I'm stopping for something to eat. It's well past lunch and I'm starving." Tate wondered if Emma realized that she'd said 'get them home' rather than 'get back to her house'. *Well it could've been my house too, if I'd just stayed in Virginia instead of bailing on her, and going back to Pine Ridge. Push it down Echo you know it wouldn't have worked.* Tate knew in his head that he'd done the right thing for both of them, but today, working together again, Tate's heart wanted this. He wanted Em and it made him question that decision. .

Emma sensed Tate's mood change and refused to ask, or acknowledge that something was bothering him; instead she stared out the car window in silence. *Let him have his thoughts. You can't change the past and you don't have a future, just be happy that he's here to help you now.*

Tate maneuvered Emma's small car through the take out lane of the Burger Barn. He fished a twenty from his pocket and eased up to the window to pay. Without a word, he handed the bag containing their dinner off to Emma and waited while a young girl made change and handed it back to him.

By the time Tate swung the car into the driveway at Emma's house; the sun had shifted and hung impatiently in the afternoon sky waiting for its day to be over. He reached across Emma's legs and grabbed the bag of food from the floorboard. They left the car and walked to the back door of the house neither breaking the uncomfortable silence.

Tate dropped the bag of burgers on the counter and Emma went to disable the alarm. Over her shoulder, she said, "I'm going to grab my laptop and I'll meet you back at the table."

Tate gave her a brisk nod and went to the refrigerator. He pulled two cans of cola out and on his way back to the table he snatched several paper towels from a spindle perched on the counter, and the take out bag. He plopped everything onto the dining room tabled and sat down to wait for Emma.

Emma returned carrying her laptop and sat it down between them before she sat down. Tate pulled the burgers out and handed one to her. Between mouthfuls, she said, "Let's see if we can stir up anything in through the Information Services office. CJIS will pull the records from all the databases and at least one subsystem. If the mystery woman has ever been in trouble, we should be able to find it here, and if she hasn't then we still get a background check."

Tate watched while Emma pulled up the Criminal Justice Information Services Division's web site and typed in her credentials.

"Any idea how she spells her name?" Emma asked.

"None" Tate said, and suggested, "Try Win and the wildcard for the first name. The last name shouldn't have more than a couple variations. Burgland with a 'u' or Bergland with an 'e'?"

Emma's fingers flew over the keyboard and seconds later the screen populated with names of Richmond residents ending in Burgland and beginning with any variation of Win and Wyn. She scrolled down the list of names and then forwarded to the next page. Emma stopped and pointed, "Got her. There's only one Wynter Burgland who currently resides in Virginia." Emma double clicked on the name and her computer screen cycled through before a picture of their mystery woman's State of Virginia driver's license populated the screen.

Tate leaned in close to Emma and scrutinized the photo on her computer screen. "That's her. Now that you've got the correct spelling and her license number, let's run her through the system again and see if anything comes up in her history."

Emma pulled up a second window and retyped the woman's name. Seconds later the screen loaded with everything that the Justice Department had on Wynter Burland.

Emma read through the information, "U.S. citizen, Swedish parents, private school at St. Catherine's here in Richmond and community college. No record of any marriage or divorces. Seems she's been a pretty good girl. No warrants, no arrests, not even a traffic violation." Emma turned to Tate, "So how do you think she's involved with scum like Quinto Navarone? I mean she had to hate the guy to empty my gun on him and then spit on him like she did. It was definitely personal for her. So what's their connection?"

Tate swallowed a gulp of soda and said, "I don't know but I think it's time we found out. Map the address on her license and let's see where she lives."

Emma pulled the address on Wynter's driver's license and entered it on MapQuest. "She's only a few blocks from St. A's. What say we go back to the orphanage and then follow her home when she leaves?"

Tate stood and reached for the empty paper bag and their soda cans. He walked into the kitchen to dispose of them, but answered through the open doorway, "I've already had one foot race with the woman and she moves like a gold medalist. We don't want her to spot us, because you can't run, and I can't catch her. If she lives that close to St. A's then she knows the neighborhood better than either of us. It would probably be better if we just show up at her house after she's gone home. More opportunity for a private conversation that way too."

Emma turned when Tate reentered the dining room. "Yeah you're right. I'm just running out of patience, I need to hear what she's got to say and soon."

The earlier tension seemingly forgotten, Tate smiled and said, "In the mean time we need to change your bandages and figure out what we're going to do if she's not as cooperative as we'd like. Specifically, are you going to arrest her for killing that guy or pat her on the back for saving your life? Have you thought about that? I'm betting she has, and given the chance she'll run."

Emma didn't hesitate with her answer, "I need her testimony to clear me, and put me back on the active duty list. Navarone was a damn child trafficker and God only knows what else; he deserved to die. I've got about a million questions for her. What's her relationship with Navarone, why'd she 'off him, what's her part in the disappearance of the kids, specifically the ones that were in St. A's?...and that' just for starters."

Tate grinned, "I've got a couple questions for her too. Like what was she doing outside the night I shot that guy, and why'd she run? What's up with the cloak and dagger shit, and all the notes and secrecy? Maybe we can work it so that she doesn't face any charges for killing Navarone and get her to talk."

Emma nodded agreement and continued, "On the other hand, if she doesn't come up with the answers that I need pretty quick, I might let her think that she's going down for murder, but in reality that's not my goal. I just want to get back to work and ultimately nail these bastards to the wall."

Tate pushed his chair in and leaned on the back of it, "I want to know if she can help us find those three little girls that disappeared from St. A's, she's got to have some idea about what's going on there, otherwise she wouldn't have been at the warehouse. Miss Porter told me that the little red-haired one has a mother, a mother who was supposed to get out of rehab in a couple months, and who took the time to write letters to her daughter promising to come for her. I keep going back to that. Why'd the kid run if she knew that her mother would be coming there to get her? It doesn't fit. Have you considered the traffickers have someone on the inside at St. A's?"

Emma replied, "I hadn't considered it before, but it certainly makes sense. Could be Ms. Burgland is their inside help."

Tate nodded indicating he'd thought the same thing.

"Don't know why she's helping us but it might be a 'good person, bad situation' kind of thing, and she wants out. I've been on the task force for four months and Clay gave me access to all the files and reports for the last six months, there wasn't any mention or link to St. A's in the history of our case, in fact, it all seems fairly random. Most of the kids are truly runaways, teens and preteens that have been on the streets, that kind of thing. If is it some kind of organized group, then there should be a pattern. The target age for traffickers is twelve and up, so it always seemed strange to me that these younger girls were taken. The case files appear to be random, with no precise association to any particular person or place. Did Ms. Porter say how many kids have disappeared from there?"

"Not exactly, but she did say that there was a brother and sister earlier this year, and a few late last year. I think we definitely need to dig in and find out just how many a few is. First we need to change your bandage, you go get ready and I'll grab my gloves and the bandages."

Emma lay face down on her bed and waited for Tate. Her mind spun with all that she knew about this case. *What am I missing?* She wondered.

Tate stood at the door to Emma's bedroom and thought that he had never seen a more beautiful site. He let his gaze drift up her bare legs to her ass, barely covered by pink bikini underwear. *Damn. Shake it off Echo, just shake it off.*

"You ready?" Emma lifted her head and glanced back at him.

Oh yeah, I'm ready alright. Tate thought before he moved to the edge of the bed with the supplies.

Tate carefully removed the bandage from Emma's leg and from where it disappeared under those silky panties. "It looks better Em. A few more days and I think you'll be able to go without the bandage."

Tate gently rubbed the area with antibiotic cream and covered it with a new bandage and then he slid up next to Emma on the bed. Emma turned on her good side to face him. She locked eyes with him and whispered, "Thanks for taking care of me Tate."

Tate reached out and pushed an errant strand of hair behind one ear. "I'll always take care of you Em. You're important to me." No more than a foot separated them on the bed, and Tate could feel the heat of her body, smell the fresh scent of soap and shampoo, and something else, something that was all Emma, and familiar, comforting...arousing. The tiny space between them crackled with unleashed energy and he was pulled into the magnetic field, he didn't care if consumed him.

Without moving her eyes from his, Emma said, "You're important to me too." Then she did the one thing that she'd wanted to do since she woke up in the hospital and realized he was there. . Emma leaned over and kissed him, a gentle meeting of lips at best. "I don't know how I would have handled this if you hadn't..."

Tate wanted so much from her, but a thank you speech wasn't on the list and he refused to let this moment be driven by gratitude. His hand crossed the unseen force field between them and slid behind her neck, drawing her closer and putting them both dead center of the hot electric space. She didn't resist and he saw her mouth open, maybe it was surprise, but he hoped it was anticipation. He took the safe route, and dropped his lips to her cheek where he pressed tiny kisses down the side of her face, then her neck where he felt her heart pulsing against his lips. *Was that a moan?* Bringing his mouth upward along the same trail, Tate stopped when he reached her mouth, pausing only long enough to pull her lower lip into his teeth.

Emma braced one hand on Tate's hip and opened her mouth to the kiss. *Don't think Emma, just don't think. You want this...no...you need this.* She felt his tongue slide into her mouth and at the same time her hand went AWOL. The traitorous hand and slid upward, under Tate's shirt to caress his hard muscled chest, a place she knew well. Tate rolled back and Emma went with him, her body covering his.

Tate broke the kiss, "You're on really shaky ground here Em." He whispered.

She shrugged her shoulders and grinned at him. "Feels like the beginning of an earthquake if you asked me." She sat up, one leg on either side of him, pinning him to the bed and started to unbutton her shirt.

His hands stopped her, "Let me." Tate fumbled with the top button, the one that opened her shirt to a vee at the apex of her breasts. A lacy white bra did nothing to hide the beautiful mounds. The next button opened easier and gave Tate a peek of her taut nipples stretched tightly against the lace. He groaned.

Making fast work of the remaining buttons, Tate pushed the shirt off her shoulders and paused to admire his beautiful Em. "Gorgeous." He whispered and let his gaze roam lingeringly over her lace covered breasts, down to her taught belly and lower....down to the deliciously pink panties that barely covered her.

Drawing his gaze back to Emma's face, he watched as she undid the front clasping bra and let it fall with the already discarded shirt. His hands were instantly on her breasts, caressing and massaging. He felt the tight peaked nipples against the roughness of his palms and paused to gently flick them, watching her strain forward as he did. He pulled her down for a kiss and lost his breath when she sucked his lower lip in between her teeth and tugged.

"Last chance to save yourself, Em." He said, his voice deep and hoarse against her lips.

Emma pulled back and made quick work of his shirt, tugging it up and over his head. She let her hands glide across his chest before sliding them lower, "Too late Echo. I passed the last stop on the 'save yourself' train at the first button." She popped the button on his jeans and leaned forward on one hand, pushing the rough fabric that separated them down and away with

Tate's help; he did the same with the tiny pink panties.

Moving over and up him, Emma straddled his thighs again, and the coarse hairs on his legs teased and tickled her inner thighs. His hands were everywhere and ignited tiny flames each place they paused. Emma was certain she would find fire licking at the ceiling if she looked upward. Slowly she rocked, teasing him with what could be....would be...

"Woman, I don't want to hurt you but you're torturing me, and I think that you're enjoying it." Tate rasped.

Emma sat back and stared down at him, their bodies were touching but not joined, close but not close enough. "Last chance to save yourself, Echo." She tossed his own offer back to him. Before he could speak, Emma rose slightly, separating their bodies only long enough to slide down on his erect and rock hard manhood. "Mmm...too late." She whispered and rocked gently. Together they found their rhythm. Together they felt the earth quake.

CHAPTER 25

Gregory snatched the phone up on the first ring. "Aiden here." The silence on the other end told him what he wanted to know. "Talk to me Wynter. Tell me that you've decided you want to see your daughter."

"You know I want to see Tassie." She whispered.

"Well then, what's the problem? You only need to do one little thing for me and then I'll bring her to see you. You could be holding her in your arms in just a few hours."

Stumbling over her words Wynter spoke, "I can't get you what you want today. I have to wait until it's safe. Maybe tomorrow or early the next day, and even then it will be risky. There are the security cameras and the other staff members to worry about."

Gregorio's voice threatened, "Make it happen Wynter. You really don't have a choice if you ever want to see Itasca again." Picking up the black passport folders from his desk Gregory fanned them in the air. "I'm holding a passport and airline tickets in my hand right now, and unless the delivery is made on time, I will be forced to use them."

Wynter's reply was choked, "No. Please don't. I will do it. I just need a little time to make sure that it's done correctly." Her voice hardened, "I cannot afford to be caught and you wouldn't want that either. If I am arrested then I will be forced to tell the police everything that I know *and* show them what proof I have."

The passports landed on Gregory's desk with a thud, "Don't threaten me Wynter. You don't *know* anything and the proof that you have could easily be passed off as something you created to force me into giving you Itasca. It would be best if you remember who I am and what I can, and will, make happen if you push me too far. You are only alive now because I allow it."

Wynter swallowed her anger and spoke softly, "I'm not threatening you Gregorio. I am taking a very real risk, and I must wait until I am certain that I can do what you ask without putting myself in danger. Surely you understand that I must take the time to do this with great care?"

His harsh laugh crossed the phone line and Wynter felt a bone cold chill climb up her body and settle in her heart. His words were clipped, "Time is something that I don't have much of. The delivery must be made the day after tomorrow and I need to know that the *product* is in place before then. Take it home with you and call me. I will set up the time to pick it up and then you can see Tassie."

The line clicked and Wynter swore under her breath. "You must do it. For Tassie, you must." She knocked on the interior office door across from her desk and waited for the aged voice of Sister Camille to invite her in.

"Wynter, you don't look well, are you okay?" The elderly Sister asked.

Shaking her head Wynter replied, "I don't feel well Sister. I would like to go home now if you are alright with that."

Sister Camille stood and walked to where Wynter had stopped, just inside the door. She placed one wrinkled hand on Wynter's forehead and commented, "You don't seem to have a fever but you are certainly pale. Please do go home and get some rest. I pray that you are not coming down with a case of the flu. It's been going around you know."

"Thank you Sister. I am just a little sick to my stomach; it's probably just something that I ate. I will see you tomorrow for sure." Wynter turned from the room and hurried to her chair, grabbed her jacket and pulled it on, picked up her purse and left the building.

The tiny apartment she lived in was only three blocks from St. Anthony's, but she wasn't going home. She needed to collect on a favor.

I must be patient and watchful in case Gregorio has me followed. He cannot know that I have asked for help or he will take Tassie and run for sure. She raised her hand for a taxi.

Twenty minutes later the cab jerked to the curb in front of a restaurant just three blocks from Wynter's final destination for the night. She paid the driver and then walked into the restaurant and took the same seat she'd sat in just a day before. She ordered a cup of tea and worried about how this would work out. *What if she won't help me? She is the police and they have rules. What if she arrests me for shooting Quinto?* The sun hung low in the sky and seemed to wait for its replacement before giving up the day and Wynter waited with it. *I must save Tassie. I will save Tassie. Nothing can stand in my way, nothing. If Agent Echo won't help me then I will do what Gregorio asks. Then I will kill him with Quinto's gun and run.*

Fifteen minutes passed, Wynter paid the check and stepped out of the building. The night air swirled around her, stealing the warmth from her skin. She shivered and stepped around the corner and into the shadows of the alley. Wynter followed the same path she'd used the night that the man had shot Gregorio's henchman, and when she reached the woman's house, she stopped behind a huge oak tree and sucked in a steadying breath. She stared at the house and whispered, "Emma Gage-Echo, please help me." She whispered. Without giving herself a chance to change her mind, Wynter stepped from behind the tree and quickly made her way to the porch. Wynter pushed the button and stepped back when she heard the old fashioned chime ring inside the house.

Tate snuggled against Emma's back, their bodies spooned together, warm and satisfied in the afterglow of the most amazing sex he could recall. The doorbell chimed and Tate frowned, now on full alert. "You expecting more company?" He whispered in her ear.

Emma turned over and stared at him, her eyes wide. "No. No company expected." She ran a hand over his jaw, "Or wanted." She added. "Last night's visitor was more than enough and I hope this isn't round two of the same game."

Tate rolled over and swung his legs off the bed. He pulled on his jeans and slipped into his shirt. "Probably not. Don't think a would-be killer would just march up and ring the bell. Just in case, you wait here and I'll go see who it is." On his way out of the room, he snagged his service revolver from atop the dresser and tucked it in his jeans at the small of his back. He saw that Emma was already rolling out of bed and fishing for her clothes.

When Angels Cry

CHAPTER 26

Halfway to the pond, a partial loaf of bread bouncing against her leg, Victoria turned to the small blonde girl at her side, "Allie, you really don't have to come with me. I know that you'd rather be picking flowers with Ivy and the other girls."

Allie glanced back at the other girls gathering flowers in the garden, then turned to Victoria, "You sure it's okay Victoria? I'll go with you if you want me to."

Victoria grabbed the younger girls hand and gave it a squeeze, "You'll still be my best friend. Now go get those flowers before the other girls find all the best ones."

The little girl laughed and hugged Victoria, before she turned and raced back to the garden.

Jeri pulled her shades down to block the afternoon sun and sat on a bench in the garden, a closed book sat next to her. She watched the girl's race around the yard searching for the perfect flowers. In the distance she could still see Victoria's glossy red hair shining in the sunlight as she turned to say something to Allie and the younger girl turned away and ran back to the garden. An easy breeze dropped leaves down from a large oak tree overhead, and Jeri watched Tori toss bread in little pieces to the ducks in the small pond.

"Did you change your mind about feeding

the ducks Allie?" She asked as Allie returned.

Allie nodded and smiled, "Victoria said it was okay, she'll still be my best friend!"

Jeri smiled at the child then opened her book and leaned back on the bench.

Victoria tossed the last handful of bread in the bag out to the ducks and glanced over her shoulder to see if the others were watching her. She saw the other girls looking for flowers and racing around the yard, and then she glanced at Ms. Anderson. She was still sitting on the bench with an open book in her lap. The gazebo was only a little ways away and quietly she slipped toward the white frame structure. She kept to the edge of the pond and occasionally raised her hand as if she were tossing more bread in for the ducks. "Don't be a chicken. It's going to be okay. Just tell her you were out of bread if she asks." Victoria reassured herself.

Victoria slipped inside the gazebo and looked around. The stop-sign shaped gazebo sported padded benches on the side facing the pond, while in the middle of the open space a small table rose from a pole attached to the floor. Two white metal chairs were pushed up to the table.

"The only thing here is benches, Bethany. What did you want me to see?" She softly asked. She thought for a moment. There had to be something. *Whatever it is, I'm going to find it.* Victoria turned at the gate and bent to pick up each cushion from the wooden benches. She looked underneath them one by one. "Nothing." She squatted and looked up at the bottom of the table and both chairs in case something was there. "Nope." She plopped down in one of the chairs and stared up at the rafters overhead.

Victoria imagined Bethany climbing up to hide something there, and then decided she probably hadn't. The roof was steep and made a sharp point in the middle, and without a ladder Bethany couldn't have gotten up there. *Maybe there's something on the ground outside or around the gazebo.* She thought. A fluttering from the pond caught her attention and she stood up, and looked across the water to see what had startled the birds. Victoria froze. Ms. Anderson was looking too. She climbed onto a bench and stood on her knees, her elbows rested on the white wood railing and Victoria stared out at the water, hoping that Ms. Anderson didn't come down to the pond before she had time to search outside the gazebo. That's when she felt it. There was something inside the cushion under her right knee!

Please let it be something that will help me get out of here! Raising her arm Victoria waved at Ms. Anderson. She smiled and held up the bag she'd carried the bread in. *Please don't come down here, please.*

When Ms. Anderson waved and turned back to her book, Victoria sighed in relief. She picked up the cushion and ran her hands over the flowered print fabric feeling for the hard object. "How am I going to get it out?" She worried. She turned the cushion up on its side and saw it, a zipper. She pulled the zipper back just enough to slip her small hand into the opening. At the bottom of the cushion she felt her fingers brush the hard object and she stretched until her hand made contact. She pulled a small square blue book less than an inch thick out of the hiding spot. Victoria turned the book over in her hand and flipped the cover open, glancing at the first few pages. *A journal? That's what you wanted me to see Bethany?* Disappointment raced through her mind then she thought, *Maybe there's a secret in here that can help me get away.*

"Tori!" Ms. Anderson's voice rang across the yard. "Time to go inside now!"

Victoria stuffed the journal into the front of her jeans and pulled her shirt down to cover it. She zipped the cushion and returned it to its spot. As she stepped back she noticed something else. A crack at the edge of the bench. Victoria pulled the top of the bench seat and it opened, a square, hollow box. She glanced inside before closing the bench and straightening the cushion. "Empty." She stepped out of the gazebo and waved to Ms. Anderson, letting her know that she had heard her calling. Victoria walked back to the garden and wondered what could be so important in the journal that Bethany would hide it at the gazebo. "It's got to be something important." She whispered.

The other girls had already gone inside and the table was covered with the flowers that they'd collected by the time that Victoria and Ms. Anderson entered the kitchen. "Did you have fun feeding the ducks?" Ms. Anderson asked.

Victoria nodded and sneezed, "Can I have my bath now? I think I smell like the pond."

Laughing, Ms. Anderson replied, "Sure go on up and get cleaned up while the other girls work on their project. We wouldn't want your allergies to kick in. Once you're cleaned up we can make you a project using ribbons instead of flowers if you want. That way when Daddy gets here, you'll have a project to show him too."

Victoria walked from the kitchen, but she ran up the stairs. She closed the bathroom door behind her and dropped to the closed toilet seat. *No locks..not even on the bathroom. Even St. A's let you go to the bathroom with the door locked.* She thought. She pulled the diary out from its hiding spot and flipped to the first page. *I'd better really take a bath.* She decided and reached over and turned the faucet on.

The words on the first page of the journal were big, and looked to Victoria like something a first grader would do, there were only six words on the first page. 'My name is Beth Ann Cooper.'

The second page was written in the same childish scrawl. 'I am 6 yers old and I want to go home.'

Victoria's heart sank. "Bethany was fourteen when she jumped from that window." Counting on her fingers she added, "Eight years.

Oh God, she was here eight years." Tears filled her eyes and she stuffed the diary under a stack of fresh towels in the cabinet, stripped and sank into the tub.

CHAPTER 27

Tate pulled a slat down on the blinds and peeked out the window, his gun drawn. *It's her! What the hell?*

He tucked the gun back in its resting spot at the small of his back, and reached for the door. *One, two, three.* He mentally counted then snatched the door open and pushed the screen out all at the same time. Tate snagged the woman's arm, jerked her into the entryway and spun her around. He pushed her roughly against the wall and held both her arms behind her.

"Talk to me. Why are you here?" He demanded. Without waiting for an answer he patted her down, searching for the gun she'd stolen from Navarone or any other weapon.

"I don't have any weapon. I need to see Emma Gage-Echo." She said.

Satisfied that she wasn't armed, Tate let go of her arm just as Emma entered the hallway. "Who was...?" She began, and then stopped when she saw who the visitor was.

Turning to face Emma, Wynter pushed the hood back from her head and quietly said, "You owe me a favor and I need it now."

Emma glanced at Tate, and stepped forward, "Let me take your coat and then we can talk. I have some questions for you, and I didn't get the chance to thank you for saving me either."

Wynter nodded and shrugged out of her jacket. She handed it to Tate before following Emma into the dining room and taking a seat at the table.

"Can I offer you something to drink?" Emma asked.

Tate dropped the jacket on the back of the sofa and followed Emma and Wynter into the dining room. He scowled and whispered into Emma's ear, "Dammit Em, she's not a neighbor coming to visit for tea and cookies. She's a killer and she's neck deep in this child trafficking mess. You'd damn well better remember that."

Well, if Emma was going to play the good cop, then that only left one role for him. Bad cop. He plopped into the chair across from the mystery woman and faced her, "I say we call the police and let them have her. After all, she *is* the one who murdered that man and turning her in would clear your name and get you back on the active duty list."

Wynter's face drained of all color and she spoke fast, "You can't. He has my daughter and without your help I will never see her again." Letting her head drop she continued, "Without my help you will never get those girls back." She raised her eyes and continued, "There were others too."

Tate glared through the woman. His voice was even but firm. "Lady, you'd better start explaining this mess. If you know where those kids are and you haven't called the police then you're worse than a murderer. We need to know *who* took those kids, why they took them and most importantly where they are right now. Holding back what you know makes you an accessory to the crime and kidnapping, and God knows what else. You could land in prison for the rest of your life. You might even get the death penalty; you know that's possible in Virginia right?"

Emma stepped in and placed a hand on Tate's forearm. "Give her a minute Tate. I'm sure we'll get to all your questions but let's start at the beginning." She turned to Wynter, "What's your name?"

Wynter snorted and said, "What? You don't know my name?" Glancing at Emma she continued, "I cannot believe that an agent for the FBI could not figure even that out. Maybe you are not the person to help me after all."

Tate opened his mouth to speak, but stopped when Emma shot him a warning look. He pushed a hand through his dark hair and said, "I know who you are, *Wynter*." He tossed the name at her.

Emma pulled a chair out and turned to Tate, "Would you make us some coffee please? Tate clenched his jaw to keep from cursing, nodded and went into the kitchen. *Now it was good cop's turn.* He left the door ajar so that he could hear the conversation. *Guess I really am the bad cop tonight.* He thought.

Once Tate left the room, Emma saw Wynter relax, her shoulders dropped and her hands stilled. Quietly Emma asked, "What were you doing at the warehouse the night that you shot Mr. Navarone?"

Wynter allowed a deep sigh to escape and said, "I don't care about Quinto, I am glad that he's dead. I came here to ask for my favor. He has my daughter and if I don't help him then I will never see her again. Please, you've got to help me."

Emma realized that she wasn't going to get the answers she needed without talking about the favor that she owed. Emma agreed, "Okay, so first we talk about your daughter, then you tell me what I need to know. Alright?"

Wynter nodded and leaned forward. She rested her head on her hands and said, "Itasca, Tassie, she is four years old and I was forced to leave her with her father two months ago. I didn't want to leave her, but it was the only way that I could leave and remain alive."

She looked up nervously when Tate entered the room and handed her a cup of coffee. She nodded her thanks and continued, "Tassie's father is Quinto Navarone's half-brother." She glanced at Tate, "The man that you killed was sent here by Gregorio to avenge Quinto's death," She glanced at Emma, "and in time there will be others. Gregorio will not let you live, and if he finds out that I am the one who killed Quinto then he will kill me as well."

Tate took a seat and asked, "So who is this Gregorio and how does he fit into the story?"

"Gregorio Aiden is..."

Emma swore and then blurted, "*Attorney* Gregory Aiden? That's the man who's threatening you?"

Wynter nodded.

"Yes, he is Tassie's father and he threatens us all."

Tate pushed into the conversation and asked, "You know him, Em?"

Emma shook her head and answered, "Not personally but I know of him. He's a partner in one of the largest law firms in Richmond; he caters to the elite and particularly to several members of Congress. His client list reads like the who's who of politics." She turned to Wynter and asked, "So you're saying that Gregory Aiden ordered the hit on me, he wanted me dead?"

Wynter lifted her cup and took a sip. She nodded, "Wants...he *wants* you dead. I am sorry that you were blamed for Quinto's death, but I cannot let Gregorio know that I did it, not until I get my daughter back."

Tate snapped, "Does he know that you're here? Did he send you to finish his business with Emma?"

The shocked look on Wynter's face told

Tate that her answer was true, "No. I did not come here to hurt anyone. I need your help to get my daughter and I don't have anyone else to turn to. Gregorio has powerful friends. I can't stand against him and win...not alone."

Tate relaxed some and leaned back in his chair. "So how are we supposed to help you? The man's had her for two months; he's an influential attorney with some big friends in high places, what makes you think he's going to hand his child over to us or anyone else? What's to keep him from saying that you voluntarily walked away?"

Tears filled her eyes and Wynter sobbed, "I did voluntarily walk away, it was the only way to save myself. Gregorio would have killed me if I'd tried to take Tassie with me and he would have killed me if I tried to stay. I am only alive now because he is afraid to kill me."

Emma pulled a napkin from a holder on the table and handed it to Wynter. She questioned, "So he forced you to leave without your child, and now you want us to help you get her back. I'm sorry but I have to agree with Tate on this one. There's not a judge in the system that's going to look favorably on a woman who abandoned her child and waited two months, then expects to just walk in and get her back." She paused then asked, "What do you mean he's afraid to kill you?"

"Before I left, I took something that could ruin him. I told him that if anything happened to me or to Tassie, that everyone would know. I have tried to trade what I have for my daughter, but he refuses, and now Gregorio has asked me for a favor. If I don't help him then he will take Tassie and leave the country and it will not matter if I expose him. I have only a few days to get him what he wants or I will never see my daughter again."

Tate pushed back from the table, and asked, "And what does he want from you?"

Wynter lowered her head and whispered, "A baby."

CHAPTER 28

Victoria pushed the silver metal button and watched the water swirled away from her and down the drain before she stood up and grabbed a towel. "Great, now I've got to go make a thingy with stupid ribbons, but I need to finish reading Bethany's diary." Water gurgled down the drain, drowning her words. She tossed the towel down with her dirty clothes and listened at the door before pulling the journal from its hiding spot. Hastily she wrapped the book inside her dirty clothes and stepped out of the bathroom wrapped in a clean towel. Her steps were muffled on the plush carpet and she jogged down the hallway to her room.

Once inside Victoria leaned her back against the closed door and breathed a sigh of relief. *Now where to hide it?* She quickly scanned the room and decided that the book would be safest in the small round trash basket near the built in desk. She pulled the plastic bag from the basket and carefully set the book in the bottom of the trash can and then she replaced the bag. As an after-thought she pulled some tissue from the box atop the desk, wadded it and tossed it into the trash basket. *Looks pretty good.* She thought. Victoria got dressed and snatched her dirty clothes off the floor, and headed back down stairs.

"There you are!" Jeri said when Victoria entered the kitchen. "Just put your dirty clothes in the laundry room, and then we can get started on your project.

Nodding Victoria replied, "Yes Ma'am."

Jeri watched Victoria walk to the laundry room. *That kid's up to something. She's too compliant.* When Victoria returned to the kitchen, Jeri patted the seat next to her at the table. "Let's get your project started. I saved lots of ribbon for you and we have some glitter if you want to glue some of it on the ribbon before you tie it onto your ring."

Victoria dropped into the chair next to Ms. Anderson and picked up the plastic ring that she was supposed to decorate. "So we just tie ribbon all the way around it? Won't that get in my face?"

Jeri smiled and picked up the ring and a long piece of purple ribbon. She pushed a piece of tape on the end of the ribbon and stuck it to the ring. Let me show you how to get started and then you can work on it while I start dinner. Methodically she pulled the ribbon through the ring, and wrapped it all the way around. She held the now purple ring out to Victoria and said, "You just turn the piece that I taped to the back and then start tying your ribbons on." She placed the ring on Victoria's head then pulled it off showing the child where to tie her first ribbon. "If you start here then the ribbons will fall down behind and none will be in front."

Victoria nodded, "Ok, I think I can do it now."

Jeri stood up and smiled down at Victoria, "I'm sure you can, and I'll be close by if you need help. Did you like feeding the ducks today Tori?"

Jeri didn't miss the frown that creased Victoria's brow when she said Tori instead of Victoria, "I did like feeding the ducks. Can I do it again tomorrow?"

"We'll see. We have a busy day tomorrow. Daddy is coming home and we want everything to be perfect for him. Call me if you need help." Jeri walked away.

Victoria's small fingers quickly tied ribbon after ribbon to the hair ring. *I've got to get upstairs and read that book.*

Fifteen minutes later, Jeri returned to the dining room and saw that Victoria had finished tying the ribbons and now stood at the French doors staring out to the back yard.

"You're all finished?" She asked.

Victoria turned and said, "Yes. I think it looks pretty good."

Jeri picked up the hair decoration and replied, "You did a good job. Now that you're finished with your project, I need you to put the extra ribbon and supplies back in the craft box so that we can set the table for dinner, okay?"

"Sure." Victoria replied. *Guess I'm not going to get to read that diary until after dinner.* She thought. *It's probably better that way. I don't*

220

want to get caught.

Just as Victoria closed the lid on the box holding craft supplies and moved it to the countertop, Allie and Ivy entered the kitchen holding hands. "We're going to watch a movie after dinner. You want to watch with us Victoria?"

"Sure I'll watch with you, but I'm going to read my Harry Potter book too."

Chloe walked into the kitchen just in time to hear the other girls making plans for after dinner and added, "Those wizard books are for babies."

Victoria frowned and Jeri stepped in before the girls could further their argument. "Now girls, you are all different and like different things, and that's okay. Chloe, I'd like for you to wipe the table down and put the plates down for dinner." Turning to the smaller girls she continued, "Allie and Ivy, it would be a big help if you would get the silverware and napkins. Tori, you can get the glasses down and pour our drinks. I'm almost finished with everything and I'm going upstairs to check on Nora. When you finish with your assignments, we'll have dinner."

Jeri left the dining room, but she didn't miss hearing Chloe say "Victoria is a baby."

Chloe stepped close to Victoria and whispered, "I bet you're too much of a baby to play the lollipop game with Daddy when he comes home. That's his favorite game but you'll never know because I'm going to make sure that I'm the one he chooses for his snuggle date when he gets home."

Victoria frowned at Chloe, "I've got to get the glasses."

When Victoria reached the kitchen, Ivy and Allie were there getting the silverware and napkins and she pulled them both by the arm into the pantry. "Listen to me. No matter what that man..."

Allie interrupted her, "What man Victoria?"

"Daddy." Victoria hissed, "Now listen! No matter what he says, you are not to go into his room. Do you understand? Pretend you're sick, say you're scared; just don't go in there. I want you to promise me."

"But Chloe says it's fun to be the chosen one." Ivy said. "I want Daddy to like me too."

Victoria sighed, "Later, when everyone goes to bed, I'll come in and talk to you about it, but right now, I want you to promise me. We're best friends, right? Best friends make secret promises to each other and that's what we're doing, okay?"

"We can't tell?" Ivy asked.

"That's right. You can't tell anyone, especially Chloe or Nora."

Both girls nodded their heads and

promised. "We won't tell, not ever."

CHAPTER 29

Tate jumped to his feet, "Look Ms. Burgland, I understand that you've got personal issues with Aiden and he is the father of your child, but that son of a bitch is clearly a major player in this whole child trafficking operation as was his brother." He pointed a finger at Wynter, and continued, "And you, well you're just as guilty as he is if you knew and did nothing."

Startled, Wynter looked up at him, clearly afraid of the rage that she could see in his icy grey eyes. Quietly she said, "I am only guilty of loving my daughter and Quinto was only his employee. Gregorio has many employees around the world. I could do nothing to stop him."

In a rush she continued, "I planned to kill him." She looked at Emma and admitted, "That is why I took Quinto's gun that night at the warehouse. I wanted to kill Gregorio with his brother's gun. But now I am out of time. If I don't bring him a baby, then he will take Tassie and leave rather than face the threat of those who he promised the baby to."

Tate swore, "Dammit. Why didn't you just go to the police?"

Wynter turned her gaze to Emma, "I can't trust the police; they would have called Gregorio. He is a powerful man." Letting her voice drop, Wynter continued, "He threatened to kill my family...my parents. They are old, I couldn't let him hurt them and then there is Tassie. He would take her away, and then I would never be able to get her. Is it wrong to protect your family? Wouldn't you do the same?" She locked eyes with Tate and he glanced at Emma. He would do anything for his family and Em was his family.

"Wynter." Emma began, "I understand your need to save your child, any mother would do the same, but what makes you think that you can't trust the police?"

"Many of the police help Gregorio, he pays them. He knows things before they happen, that is how they have avoided being caught. They cannot touch him without getting caught themselves, and that means that I cannot trust them."

"I see. You say *they*, so Mr. Aiden is working with someone?" Emma asked.

"I don't know for sure but he has said things that lead me to believe that he has a partner. Someone named Captain." Wynter answered.

"How does he expect you to get a baby for him?" Tate asked. "Let me guess, he wants you to steal one from St. Anthony's."

Wynter's head bobbed confirming Tate's assumption. "He expects me to take a boy child from St. Anthony's and bring the child to my home. He has promised to let me see Itasca when he comes to pick up the baby."

"Have you done these types of favors for him before Wynter?" Tate asked.

"Never. I have never taken a child from work or anywhere else for him. When I suspected him of selling children is when I left him. I cannot prove that he has taken any of the missing children from St. A's, but I know that he is on the board of directors for the orphanage and because of that, he handles their legal affairs and has information about the children at the center." Wynter brushed her hair back. "I didn't tell him that there was a male baby at the center, I didn't even know." She whispered. "He told me."

"You understand that I'm a member of the FBI, right?" Emma continued, "I can protect you from whatever cop Mr. Aiden has on his payroll, but I cannot promise to protect you from my own agency. If the FBI finds that you've been withholding information that could have saved helpless children from the hands of a trafficking ring, or that you were actively involved, then they are going to prosecute you and you will go to prison."

Emma frowned and then continued, "The only way to prevent that is if you tell me everything that you know *and* hand over the evidence that you have on Aiden. I promise you that I won't take anything that you share with me outside my own agency. That way the local police won't be tipped off that we're investigating Mr. Aiden."

Wynter raised her watery blue eyes to Emma's. "What guarantee do I have that you will help me after I give you what you need? The flash drive is the only thing that has protected me and giving it to you will mean that I have nothing. Gregorio has many powerful people on his side, people who can make sure that I don't walk away with my daughter...or maybe that I don't walk away at all."

Tate's head snapped up, "It's a flash drive?" he asked, looking at Wynter.

Wynter nodded, "Yes and while I don't understand it myself, Gregorio was livid when he found out that I had it; it is important to him so it must contain information that can ruin him."

Tate braced his hands on the back of a chair and leaned toward Wynter. "So it's in code?"

"I have only looked at it once and there are some names, but most of it made no sense to me."

Emma spoke quietly, "Do you have it with you Wynter? I need to look at it."

Wynter paused a moment and looked them both over as if weighing her options. Finally she pushed back from the table and stood, "I will trust you Emma Gage-Echo." She glanced at Tate and continued, "I will trust you to help me get Itasca back and pray that you can keep me from going to jail." She turned to face Tate, "Or worse as you say. Do you have scissors? I will need scissors."

Emma nodded and then turned to Tate and smiled. "Bottom drawer, under the silverware. Can you grab them for us please?"

Wynter turned and walked away from the dining room, her voice carried back. "I need my jacket. The information you want is hidden, there. I didn't know how else to keep it safe."

"It's on the sofa." Tate yelled from across the room.

Emma stood and followed Wynter down the hallway to where her coat hung over the sofa back. *I'm sure it's not a trick to get away, but it won't hurt to make sure.* Emma thought.

Wynter snatched the jacket from the sofa and turned to find Emma right on her heels, "You don't trust me?" She gave a small smile. "That's okay. I don't totally trust you either, but for now we must help each other. Agreed?"

Emma smiled and nodded, moving aside so Wynter could make her way back to the dining room. Tate stood at the table with the scissors in hand. "Here you go. Now let's see what you've got."

Emma pulled her laptop across the table from where she'd left it earlier, opened it and entered the password.

Tate took a seat and watched Wynter cut a small hole in the seam of her jacket. She slid two fingers in the hole, bunched the fabric for several inches from the hem, and then slid a small blue square of plastic from the hole.

"Got it." She said, and held the flash drive up for Tate and Emma to see. She stared at the device, hesitated for just a second and then handed it over to Emma.

CHAPTER 30

"Tassie, how would you like to take a trip on an airplane?" Gregory asked the little girl bouncing on his lap.

"Would Mrs. Calder come too? Or maybe Nana? Could I take Abigail?"

"Slow down, Love, you ask questions faster than I can give you answers!" Gregorio smiled at his daughter, and tickled her ribs causing her to collapse in a fit of laughter. "Yes, you could take your doll, but Nana Navarone and Mrs. Calder would have to stay home. This would be a trip for Daddy and Tassie only. What do you think?"

A worried frown crossed Itasca's face, and she solemnly asked, "If Mrs. Calder stays home who would make us lunch or take care of me?"

"We would eat lunch on the plane, and when we get off the plane I will take care of you. We will have the whole day to explore and have fun, just the two of us. We might like it so much that we never come back."

"The three of us daddy, don't forget Abigail."

Their talk was cut short when Gregorio's desk phone rang. He sat Itasca down, kissed her on the head, and instructed, "Daddy needs to get this call so you go and play for a while and when I finish with the call I'll come and tuck you in. Okay?"

The little girl nodded and skipped from the room. Gregorio snatched the phone from his desk and answered, "Aiden here."

A male voice streamed through the phone, "I've been expecting your call all day Gregory, but my phone hasn't rang. I trust that you have gotten our little problem resolved and my delivery will be on time."

Gregorio ground his teeth, but assured the man, "Yes, Captain, your delivery will be on time. Two days from now, I'll have the *product* ready for pick up, but we will have to arrange a place for the exchange. I won't bring it into my home and I don't want *anyone* to see you at my home."

"I see." The man said thoughtfully, "You don't consider me suitable company for your family, even though we're business partners? What a shame, and after all that I've done for you. Be careful Gregory, it's not wise to insult the hand that feeds you, so to speak."

Surprised at his own words, Gregorio said, "When this transaction is completed, we're finished. After this, all my business will be conducted in the courtroom or the boardroom." *Dammit, you weren't supposed to tell him that you're finished.*

Laughter filled Gregorio's ears, "I don't think so, *partner.* You'll be through when I tell you that you're through. No one quits and walks away, Gregory, no one."

The phone line went dead, but Gregorio could still hear the laughing in his head. *He's wrong. The Captain is wrong. I will walk away...actually I'll fly away.* He thought. He'd already made the preparations, and everything was ready. He'd chartered a small plane to take him and Tassie to Florida, and once there, they would board a cruise ship to the Caribbean, and from there they would take a commercial flight to Mexico, where another small plane waited to fly them to South America. "Everything is ready." He mused before clicking his desk light off and going upstairs to tuck Tassie in for the night.

Fifteen miles away, the man hung up the phone and looked at his associate. "Have someone tail him. Mr. Aiden has become unstable and I can't trust him to do what he's supposed to do." The paid assistant turned and walked to the door, then stopped when the man spoke again, "If he tries to run, stop him. If that becomes necessary, bring him and his precious daughter to me. If we have to, we'll use her to make sure that Gregory stays in line, at least until he's no longer of any use."

When the assistant had left the room, the man leaned back in his chair and propped one foot atop the desk. "Fool." He said, "You should have ordered him dead. It's only going to complicate matters if the good councilman won't play nice, and you can't afford to let anyone complicate things. There's far too much at stake."

When Angels Cry

233

CHAPTER 31

Allie bounced around the table, and then followed Victoria into the kitchen. "Hurry up Victoria! We're ready to watch the movie."

Victoria rinsed her plate at the sink and placed it in the open dishwasher, "I'm coming Allie, but I've got to run upstairs and get my book first. Why don't you go start the movie and I'll be right there, okay?"

Upstairs, Victoria grabbed her book and looked at the trash basket. She pulled the plastic bag up just enough to see that Bethany's diary was still hidden, then pushed the plastic back down to cover the book. She glanced at the Harry Potter book in her hand and wondered if she could get away with putting the book jacket on the diary and taking it down instead. *You'd better not risk it.* She decided.

When Victoria entered the family room, both Ivy and Allie were sitting on the floor in front of the television, Chloe and Nora played a board game at a table in the corner of the great room and Ms. Anderson sat on one end of a camel colored leather couch reading a book. Victoria took a seat at the opposite end of the sofa from Ms. Anderson and opened her book, but she couldn't concentrate. The minutes passed and all she could think about was the diary hidden in her room. *I've got to read that diary!* She forced herself to focus on the book in her lap, but had to remind herself every few minutes to turn the page. She yawned.

Jeri looked up from her book and asked, "Are you tired Tori?"

Victoria nodded and yawned again, "I think I'll go to my room and read there. Goodnight."

"Sweet dreams." Jeri said, and picked her book back up.

Victoria squatted next to Allie and Ivy, "Don't forget our secret." She whispered. Two blonde heads bobbed up and down without moving their eye's from the television.

Victoria turned to the door and made her way up the stairs and into her room. She pulled the diary from its hiding spot, turned the bed covers back, and slid into the bed.

She flipped past the two pages she'd already read and turned to the next page. The handwriting was large and only a few words were written on each page. "Bethany! How is this going to help me?" Victoria softly whispered and continued to flip the pages and quickly read the childish scrawl. Before she'd reached the halfway point in the journal, things had changed. The print was still that of a small child, but the words were not.

By the time she reached the middle of the diary, Victoria had a first-hand account of some of the vile things that happened to little girls here at Walker Farm. *How could he do that to a little girl? He had sex with her. Like the way married people have sex....over and over again...eight years....eight long years.* She thought. *It sounded scary and painful.* The next page had the word "games" underlined at the top of the page, and listed four things. Victoria imagined that he'd forced Bethany to play these games and she had heard Chloe and the other girls mention them. Bethany had somehow rated them. She'd drawn smiley faces or frowning faces next to each entry.

Lollipop....one frown

Cuddle night...one smiley and a check mark

Touch and hide...three frowns

Ride Horsey...one frown...with tears

Victoria reached up and wiped a tear from her own face. "I don't understand everything you had to do Bethany, but I know it was bad. Didn't your mama tell you not to let people touch you where it was private?"

The next page in the book was blank and Victoria flipped it and was surprised to see much neater, compact, almost adult hand writing. *She must have stopped writing in the diary and then went back to it.* She mused.

Voices in the hallway startled her, and Victoria slipped the book under the covers and replaced it with her own book. The door opened a crack, and Ms. Anderson stuck her head in.

"You're still awake?" She asked, sounding

surprised.

Victoria nodded and replied, "I couldn't fall asleep so I decided to finish the chapter that I was on."

"Okay, but don't stay up too late. Daddy is coming early tomorrow and we want everything to be ready for him. I just tucked the younger girls in and Chloe and Nora have gone to their rooms for the night. See you tomorrow." She slid the door closed.

Once the door closed, Victoria pulled the diary out from under the covers and continued to read. When she read the last page, she was surprised to see tear stains on the page and reached up to wipe her face with one hand. The girl who wrote this book was scared and frightened – and her name wasn't Bethany! Just like my name isn't Tori. Victoria flipped back to the front of the journal. Beth Ann Cooper, Age 6. *Beth Ann, I'm so afraid.* She thought. *Your diary didn't tell me how to get out of here, but I sure know what's going to happen to us if we don't.*

Victoria forced herself to count to one hundred and then got out of bed and opened her door a crack. The hallway was almost completely dark; a sliver of soft light from the bathroom formed a line across the carpet. *Night light.* She thought.

She tiptoed across the hall, and opened the door to the room that Ivy and Allie shared, they'd been offered their own rooms but they chose to share, it's what they were used to, having shared a dorm for years at St. A's.

Both girls sat up when she came into the room and Victoria took a seat on the edge of Allie's bed, and motioned for Ivy to join them.

"Look, I have to tell you some things and it may be hard for you to understand." *I shouldn't understand either.* She thought. "When I was a little girl like you, my mama told me all about this and it's really important that you pay attention and not tell anyone what I'm about to share. Okay?"

Both girls nodded, and Allie solemnly said, "We won't ever tell, Tori. You're our big sister and we love you."

Victoria bristled at the misuse of her name, but that was minor compared to the things that went on here at Walker Farm. "First of all, you should never let anyone touch you where it's private. Do you know what I mean about private?"

Two blonde heads bobbed, "I know because Sister Camille told us that one time." Ivy said.

"Good, I'm glad that you remember what the Sister said, and I don't want you to forget it. There will come a time when someone tries to tell you that it's okay, and that you should let them touch you, but it's not okay, not until you're all grown up and married."

The two girls giggled, "We're not old

enough to get married!" Allie said.

Victoria blew a breath, "That's right, you're not. But sometimes people who are not married do married things, and I don't want you to do that either." She took a hand from each girl and held them in her own. "I know that Daddy seems like a nice man, but he isn't. He touches little girls where it's private and he makes them do things that they shouldn't do. I talked to Bethany and she explained it to me." She lied. "It's really bad things, and the three of us are not going to do them, no matter what he says, or no matter what Chloe and Nora or anybody else says."

"What kind of bad things, Victoria?" Ivy asked.

"I can't explain it exactly, but he wants to touch you where he shouldn't and he might even try to make you touch him like that too. He might even call it a game."

"What kind of game, Tori?" Allie asked. "I like games."

Victoria's voice rose a fraction, "You do not like these games. They are not games for kids. If he tells you that you're going to play lollipop, touch and hide or ride the horsey. Run! Don't believe him."

Both girls stared at Victoria, their eyes wide. She continued, "There's more, but it's too bad to talk about and it hurts really bad. It hurts here." She pointed between her legs. "Just remember that it all starts with touching and don't let him touch you. Run, scream, do anything that you can to stop it. The most important thing is to *never* go into his bedroom or anywhere else alone with him. Promise?"

Both girls nodded and one by one, gave Victoria a hug. "Don't tell anyone what I told you, no one. If you want to talk about it then you talk to me and that's all. We have to stick together, and we can't trust anyone else here, no matter what they say." She pulled the covers up and tucked them around one girl, then the other, "Now, back to bed you two. Remember, I'm your big sister and you can tell me anything. I'll always take care of you both."

At the door, Victoria stopped when Allie called out, "I love you, Victoria." She turned and heard Ivy say, "Me, too."

With one finger to her lips, Victoria nodded and whispered, "Love you too." Then she slipped across the hallway and into her own room. In her own bed, she stared at the darkened ceiling and prayed, *Please don't let them give this away. We've got to get out of here. All of us.*

When Angels Cry

241

CHAPTER 32

Emma pushed the small portable drive into the slot on the side of her laptop and waited for the screen to populate. "It's a spreadsheet." She said, when the computer prompted her to select a program to open the file with.

The file wasn't password protected and the spreadsheet loaded quickly. Emma moved her chair closer to Wynter and turned the screen so that the other woman could see it. Tate stood behind Emma and stared at the screen over her shoulder.

"Okay, so we've got several pages of information, now we just need to make some sense of it." He reached over Emma and touched one finger to the screen and let it slide, first across and then down the page. "I don't think that it's actually a code or anything that's encrypted, looks like Aiden's own brand of shorthand to me."

Emma tilted her head and glanced up at Tate, "I would agree. Now we just need to figure out what he doesn't want us to know. The second row has names, but not every entry has one listed, I'm guessing these are the Vics since there is no consistency or repeat names."

Tate pointed at the first column and said, "This column is obviously dates, he uses the two digit year first followed by a two digit month and day, that's pretty simple." He ran his finger to the right for a few columns and continued, "This one is probably money, what he got for the sale. He didn't use any dollar signs or decimals but the figures are repeated often. He must have a standard price list, or there's some other common factor that we haven't figured out."

Wynter stared at them both, "I'm impressed. I looked at it briefly and only saw a few names and some numbers, it meant nothing to me."

Emma smiled at her and said, "We've seen a lot of things in our careers. Tate," She lifted a thumb back at him, "used to be with the FBI as well, now he's the Chief of Police..."

Wynter slammed her chair back and jumped up, "You could be one of them!" She pointed at Emma, "I thought he was just your man...I've got to..."

Tate grabbed her by the arm, "Just calm down. I am not *one* of anybody. I am the chief of police but not in Virginia. I live in a small town, Pine Ridge, South Dakota. I came here to help Emma after she was shot. That's all."

Wynter froze, and looked at Emma for confirmation. "I'm sorry, it's just that I know there are police helping Gregorio. I can't trust them, surely you understand that."

Tate let go of her arm and Wynter dropped back into her chair. "I am sorry." She said again. "I tried to get the police to help me just after I left Gregorio, and while I was waiting to speak with a detective, he...Gregorio, that is, already knew that I was there. They actually put him on the phone and he laughed, and said that I was a fool if I thought that anyone with the Richmond police would help me." She looked up at Tate and Emma with tearful eyes and continued, "I ran."

Emma reached out and patted the woman's hand, "You don't have to run anymore. I can't promise that we'll get your daughter back, but I do promise that we'll do everything we can to help you."

Tate spoke up, "Yeah, well, it won't be too hard for you to get custody of your daughter if we can prove that Aiden is part of the child trafficking ring. No court in the world would leave a child with a monster like that."

"What can I do?" Wynter asked. "How can I help you to prove that he is a monster?"

"First we need to figure out everything that we can about this spreadsheet, then, we call my SAC." Emma turned back to her laptop.

Tate dropped to a squat between the two woman, "Em, are you sure about that? I mean, do you trust Pruitt?"

Emma stared at Tate as if he'd grown horns. "He's my boss, but more than that, he's my friend. I do trust him. If we go to him with even a shred of evidence against Aiden, or anyone else involved in this mess, then he's going to have our backs."

Tate nodded, "Fair enough." Turning back to the computer screen, he said, "Go to the date that you were shot on the spreadsheet, let's see what's entered for that day."

Emma fingered the mouse and the spreadsheet rolled down, "The dates end a couple months before that."

"That would be because I took the flash drive when I left Gregorio's home, and that was well before you were shot at the warehouse." Wynter interjected.

"Okay, so we have dates, we have possible dollar amounts, we have some names in two separate columns, and what I suspect are ages in one, but we don't know who these people are." Emma summarized. "What else is there?" Emma asked.

The chair scraped against the floor when Tate pulled it out and took a seat again, "We have what appears to be money in and money out, see how the numbers in this column are negatives?" Tate pointed to the screen and then continued, "We have letters and names that repeat, in fact, there only appear to be three or four sets of repeating letters or names in that third column."

Emma nodded her agreement. "Seems that the client list is very small and that they are all repeat customers. Maybe Aiden operates like wholesale, he sells to the same limited customer base and they take it from there. Everyone on this list is dirty as hell either way."

Tate pulled his chair closer to the table. "If you're correct, that the names in the second column are the Vics then you should be able to pull them from the missing person's database, right? I mean, I know you only have first names, but you also have the date they were taken to cross match with."

Emma nodded, "I can do that, and maybe we can fill in the some of the blanks." Her cell phone rang and Emma reached one-handed and picked the device up. She glanced at the caller ID. "It's Clay and since he already said Pruitt would be the one to call me about the IA investigation, I'm going to let it go to voicemail." She put the phone down, then asked Tate, "Maybe I should have told him what we've got here, I mean he is in charge of the team investigating the traffickers." She picked the phone up. "I'll just call him back, because he's going to want to see this."

Tate shook his head, "You can't do that Em."

"What do you mean, I can't do that?" She stared at Tate.

"Well you promised Wynter that you wouldn't share any of this with anyone but FBI and he's not FBI, right?"

Emma scoffed, "You think Clay could be involved? I seriously doubt that Tate. I've been working with the guy for four months and I haven't seen or heard anything that would put out a red flag."

"I don't know the guy and I'm not accusing anyone. But the fewer people who know about this right now, the better. If there's anyone on the task force team who's involved then he might let it slip and the wrong person would find out. Wynter's already certain that Aiden has a long reach and we don't want to give whoever it is, a chance to run."

Wynter cut in, "You promised that you would not involve the police, only the FBI. If Gregorio finds out that I have talked to you then he will kill me, and he will take Tassie and leave the country. Please..." her words trailed off.

Holding her hands up in defeat, Emma said, "Okay. I made a promise and I'll keep it. But I don't think that anyone on the task force is part of this ring. Richmond PD may be feeding Aiden information but he can't be buying off the Department of Justice too."

The cell phone buzzed to signal that a voice mail was left and Emma ignored it. She logged into the DCJS database and clicked on the link for missing persons files. "Let's look at the newest date on the spreadsheet first and see what we get."

Forty five minutes later, Emma declared, "We've matched ten of the entries on the spreadsheet with missing persons files, and that is more than enough evidence to support Aiden's involvement. Seems the good councilman has a thriving business in addition to his law practice. He must have a huge web of contacts throughout the city, there are kids here that are in their teens and last seen on the streets, there are young children, like the three I saw that night, and a few babies. Now we just need to figure out where these kids are now?"

Wynter spoke up, "I don't know what he did with them. I never actually saw any children when I lived with Gregorio."

"That's really no surprise, Wynter. Most traffickers are not willing to bring this kind of business into their home, that's too risky. Do you know if he owns any other property around the city? Some place that he could stash the kids until the delivery is complete?" Tate questioned.

She shook her head and at the same time Emma said, "That's what the warehouse was, a layover point. I'm pretty sure he's not still using that location since it's been a hotbed of police activity since Quinto was killed and I was shot, but I'm betting that he has others."

Emma's fingers stomped over the keyboard, "I'm going to search real estate records and see if anything comes up."

Wynter stood and paced the room, "All of this is searching may help you find the missing children or help you arrest Gregorio, but you need to hurry! I have less than two days left to get him a baby or he will leave with Tassie. How are you going to stop him?"

CHAPTER 33

The real estate search proved a waste of time, and Emma didn't find any property belonging to Gregorio Aiden, Gregory Aiden or Greg Aiden; not even the abandoned warehouse where she'd been shot. Emma changed the search criterion and looked under Quinto Navarone's name and came up equally empty handed.

"We know that both Simon and Navarone were at the warehouse the night that you were shot and we have every reason to believe that they both were working for Aiden. So if the warehouse isn't owned by Aiden, then whose name is on the title?" Tate asked.

Her fingers flew over the keys, "Says here that it's owned by a corporation called Benito Properties." Emma remarked.

Wynter looked up, her face animated with excitement. "Gregorio's father was named Benito! He has pictures of him in his office at home, and I remember his mother telling him that Benito would be proud of the man he is."

Tate pulled his chair close to Emma and demanded, "Can you do a trace to see who the actual owner of Benito Properties is? Or who the board members are if it's a real corporation?"

Nodding, Emma pulled up two screens side by side on her computer. On the first screen she searched for the corporation, and on the other she requested real estate records for any holdings owned or leased by Benito Corporation. Both windows populated with information. She scanned the page on Benito Corp and frowned, "There's very little information on the corporation; it's probably a shell."

The other window finished loading, and Emma moved her mouse over and clicked on one of the files, then leaned in when it opened. "Four properties belonging to Benito." She said. "One in the warehouse district, one downtown and two more near the riverfront. None of these appear to be in residential areas and chances are they are all abandoned property." She pointed at the screen. "These addresses are in some pretty run-down areas."

"Print the listings Em. We're going to need that information when we talk to Pruitt." He leaned back in his chair, "I'm going to do a little recon on these places tonight," He held a hand up to stop Emma before she could speak. "just to see what we're dealing with. I mean...are the buildings occupied or abandoned, rented to legitimate tenants, are there kids there now? I really want to know if they have guards or alarm systems in place, and I think it's time we bring Pruitt into the fold."

The look that Emma pegged Tate with should have scared him, but he only grinned at her. "You know as well as I do Emma that it's easier for one person to recon and gather intell. If we all went, then the only thing that we've accomplished is to raise a big red flag. You and

Wynter will be safe here, and when I get back we'll put everything we know on the table and give Pruitt a call."

Emma glanced at her watch, surprised to see that it was nearing midnight. "Too late to call him tonight." She turned to Wynter and asked, "You'll stay with me?" At the woman's nod she continued, "Tomorrow we'll call my boss and have him come here. I don't want anyone to see us together in case Aiden has you watched." To Tate, she added, "You know this isn't your fight, and yet you've jumped right in the deep end. Why don't you stay here with Wynter and let me scope out the buildings?"

Tate pulled a lightweight coat on and shook his head, "You know that won't work Em. Hell, after the incident at the warehouse, anyone on Aiden's payroll is sure to know who you are. Me? I'm just another down on his luck guy wondering around on the seedy side of town." He dropped a kiss on her head and continued, "I may not be back before daylight. If I get the chance I'll shoot you a text but don't expect it. The other bums might not like it if they found out I have a phone and a car. You got any booze?"

Wynter stood up and looked at him, "You want a drink now? When you are going out to investigate?"

He grinned at her, "I'm not a drinking man Wynter, that is if you don't count a beer every once and a while. I want the bottle for my new friends."

Emma handed Tate a bottle in a brown paper bag and he immediately removed it and wadded the bag. "We want it to look used." He said, answering Wynter's quizzical look. Tate slipped out the back door and listened for the lock being engaged before he stepped off the porch and walked to the car.

Emma busied herself picking up the empty coffee cups. She placed them in the dishwasher and returned to the table where Wynter still sat.

"Tell me about Aiden." She asked.

"What is there to tell?" She said softly, more a statement than a question. "I met him at St. Anthony's annual benefit, and he was charming. The benefit is a big event for the facility and it's our way of saying thank you to the supporters and to get new contributors as well. Everyone on staff is expected to help prepare for the benefit, and as Sister Camille's assistant, it was my job to supervise the smaller children before and after their program. They sing or do a small play; it's something different each year."

Emma nodded, "So how did you come to live with him?"

Tears blurred Winters' vision and she whispered, "We dated for a while and I lived on Eighth Street, he never liked coming there; it wasn't the best part of town and certainly not the kind of place that a rich attorney would hang out. A few months after we started seeing each other, the building I lived it was sold to a company that wanted to build a gas station. They were going to tear down our apartment houses. I was looking for a new place to live, and Gregorio asked me to move in with him. I loved him, or at least I thought I did, and I was so sure that I could make him love me. The next day, I moved in with him."

"Anyone else live there? At Aiden's house?" Emma clarified.

Wynter nodded, "Yes, his mother, who is also Quinto's mother, had a small suite of rooms there, and he has a live in housekeeper, Mrs. Calder. Mrs. Calder is a very nice person and has watched over Itasca since she was born."

Emma stood up, "I'll think I'll make a fresh pot of coffee. I know I won't be able to sleep until Tate gets back. Tell me about Aiden's mother, what's she like?" Emma called through the open doorway.

Wynter sighed, "She hated me, and then when I became pregnant with Itasca she hated me more. She blamed me that Gregorio and I only lived together, and weren't married. She is very committed to her religious beliefs, and to her children. They could do no wrong and no fault could be placed on them." Wynter smiled, "I bet she is hating you more than me right now, since she believes that you killed Quinto."

Emma returned to the dining room with

two cups of coffee in hand, and sat one down in front of Wynter. "It's better that she keep believing that I killed him for now, but eventually, it will probably come out that you did it. How is it that you were at the warehouse that night?"

Wynter stalled, "I followed the ambulance. I had been doing errands for Sister Camille and I had just returned to St. Anthony's. Many of the Sisters don't drive and while I don't have a car myself, I often use the van that we have at St. A's to do errands or drive children to doctor's appointments. I saw the ambulance leaving the rear entrance that night and at first I was afraid that one of the children was hurt. On their way out of the parking lot, they drove near me and I was sure that I recognized the driver as one of Gregorio's men, so I followed them."

"Why didn't you call 911? That would have been the right thing to do." Emma blurted.

"I don't have a cell phone and at first I was only suspicious, I had no proof that anything against the law had happened, and with my last visit to the police I learned that I cannot depend on them for help. I followed the ambulance to see if they went to the hospital and when I realized that they weren't going to the hospital, I couldn't stop to use a phone; I wouldn't know where they were going. It was late and there were very few businesses open and there are no pay phones on the corner anymore, so I just followed them."

"I see. Go on." Emma encouraged.

"When they stopped at the warehouse, I circled the block and parked the van one street over. I walked back to the warehouse and hid behind the dumpster." With a hint of a smile she looked up at Emma, "You were well hidden. I didn't see you until you stepped out from the corner and tried to stop Quinto. At that point, I did the only thing that I could to help. I couldn't save the children, that woman had already driven away with them, but I could save you. Before that night, I only suspected that Gregorio was doing something illegal, and after that I was positive."

Emma sipped her coffee. "So just because you thought you recognized the man in the ambulance as Aiden's associates, you assumed that he was involved? That's a pretty big assumption."

Wynter nodded, "I recognized Quinto right away when he stepped out of the car, and while he is mean and self-important, he is not able to do something like take the children and sell them on his own. He did not have the contacts and would have been caught if he worked alone. Mostly, I knew, because when Quinto would come to the house, he and Gregorio would go to Gregorio's office and when he left, Quinto would be puffed up like a Banty rooster. Once when the bar in the office had no ice and I took them some, I noticed that they stopped talking when I entered the room and Gregorio closed his computer so that I could not see."

Emma looked thoughtful, and asked, "So if you weren't sure that he was doing anything wrong, why'd you take the flash drive?"

Wynter nodded at the question, "Several times, when I lived with him, I saw him remove it from his computer and lock it in his desk drawer. I only took it because it appeared to be valuable to him, otherwise he would not bother to lock it up each time he removed it from his computer, right?"

Emma nodded, "It's a natural conclusion given what you'd witnessed." She looked at her watch, "I wish Tate would call."

"So what is it with you two? I thought you were married, or lovers but now I'm not sure."

Laughter rang out in the small room, "We used to be married but we divorced a few years ago." She blushed, "I guess you could say that we're occasional lovers, I mean, well...we just sort of explode when we're within a few hundred yards of each other."

"So why aren't you together if you love each other?" Wynter queried.

The coffee cups clanked together when Emma picked them up, "That's a hard question. We just didn't want the same things." She thought a moment. "No, that's not true either...we wanted the same things but just not at the same time." She walked to the kitchen to refill their cups, "I mean, Tate wanted me to take a desk job and start a family, and well, I want a family but I wasn't ready for a desk job. After we were married, the Bureau wouldn't assign us to the same cases, as it's too distracting to have a spouse on the same case, and you can't afford to be distracted. Tate obsessed constantly about the cases that I took and it drove me crazy. He thought it was too dangerous. Finally he threw in the towel and left."

Wynter accepted the fresh cup of coffee, and said, "But he's here now."

Emma nodded, "Yes, he's here now and even though we aren't married, he's the one person that I know I can count on unconditionally."

"So you'll make up with him and then you'll be happy." Wynter said.

To Emma, it was more a statement of fact than it was a question but she responded anyway. "No, even though I think about it, I know that it...we...still won't work. I'm not ready to give up my job with the Bureau, and Tate belongs in the small town that he lives in. He fits in there and he's needed, but me? Well, it just wouldn't work, and I won't whisper promises in the dark when I know that I can't keep them in the daylight."

A confused look crossed Wynter's face, "But you love him, and he loves you. I can tell that he does." She stated flatly.

A heavy sigh escaped into the room and Emma replied, "Yes, I do love him and you're probably right about him loving me, but surely you've figured out that love doesn't make the world go 'round, and it doesn't solve all the problems that we have."

Wynter made a huffing sound, "Love may not solve your problems but it would be easier to bear them together than alone. You will learn that this is true one day and I only hope that it's not too late by then.

"Me too." Emma whispered. "Me too."

CHAPTER 34

Tate stood two hundred feet from the fourth warehouse that he'd visited tonight; this one looked no better kept than the last three. All seemingly empty, and all in need of major repairs. He passed the crumpled brown paper bagged bottle to his new friend. "Why don't we go inside that building and get out of the wind?" He pointed to the brown paint and cinder block structure.

"Naw, we can't go there, safer to stay out here. They catch you in that building and you could end up in the dumpster somewhere." A man in his late fifties answered.

"Who's they?" Tate asked.

"Don't know for sure, but I heard that it belongs to some guy called the Captain and his partner. They've got a guy who comes by a few times a night and runs anybody around the building off. Big guy and he totes a gun just in case you don't want to leave the easy way."

"You mean like a security guard? You know who the one they call Captain is? Or where he stays?" Tate handed him the bottle again.

"Well he ain't in no security truck or nothing, but I guess he's some kind of guard. Don't know who the hell the Captain is or anything about him other than to stay off what's his. Why do you care? There's plenty of other places to lay low and have a drink or a smoke.

You got any smokes?" The man coughed and spat on the ground next to Tate's foot.

Tate felt his pockets as if checking, "No smokes. Guess I'm out." He stared at the building; one spot of dim light brightened a dirty window. "I'm going to check it out. I need a dry place to sleep a while." He started toward the building. Two steps later, his new friend snagged him by the arm.

"Come on man, you don't want to go in there. Follow me and I'll show you a good place to rest a while, I'm telling you, that guy will be around any minute now, and if he catches you in there then you'll be sorry. I seen him beat a friend of mine up pretty bad a few months back and since then all us guys on the street steer clear of this building."

Headlights flashed against the side of the building. In the soft light the building looked even worse, graffiti marked the chipped brown paint in several places and even from a distance, Tate could see trash and refuse that had blown against the buildings edge and stayed there. Tate stepped back but didn't look away.

His new friend said, "There he is now, just like I told you. We better move back before he sees us. I don't want to end up like my friend Joey did."

Tate raised the brown paper bag, faked a swig and then passed it to the other man. He watched a thirtyish man step from a Ford Escape and walk to the door of the building. Saw the man pull a ring of keys from a jacket pocket and insert one into the door. Tate watched him push the door open and step inside. *I need that license plate number.* Tate thought. An idea wormed its way into his head. He looked at the man next to him, his coat was torn on one sleeve, most of the buttons were missing and it was dirty, real dirty. "You need a new coat, man." He said to the guy.

The bottle lowered, and the man said, "Ain't nothing wrong with this coat. It still keeps me warm."

Tate shrugged out of his coat, "Here, take mine. I got a friend down at the shelter who keeps me a good coat whenever one comes in. I'll just wear yours until I see him again."

The man was already pulling the worn coat off, he held it out and the trade was made. Tate slipped into the ragged coat and wrinkled his nose at the stench of it. Then he purposefully walked toward the parked Ford.

A few feet away from the vehicle now, Tate stopped and took a swig from the bottle, letting the hot liquid spill on his *new* coat. While he tipped the bottle, he checked the license plate. *Got it.* The door to the warehouse opened and the man came out, saw Tate and rushed at him.

"Get the fuck out of here you bum." He ordered, and planted one fleshy hand on Tate's chest, pushing him back.

"Okay man, I'm going. Just looking for a

warm place to crash, that's all. No problem man, no problem." Tate slurred, and turned to walk back to where his new friend stood waiting.

The man yelled at his back, "Don't let me catch you hanging around here again. No more warnings, you know what I mean, old man?"

Tate raised one hand in the air as if waving and continued to walk away. He heard the man's shoes crunch on the gravel parking lot, heard the car door slam and then the engine fired to life. The twin beams of the headlight's hit Tate in the back and illuminated the space in front of him, including the weathered face of the old man wearing his coat.

"Get out of there man! He's going to run you over!" The man shouted and turned away, hurrying toward the street.

Tate glanced back and saw the Ford move toward him. His long legs ate at the pavement as he ran toward the man he'd just met. *Shit! The old guy was right, the bastards going to run me down.* Tate caught up with the man just as he placed one foot on the curb across the street. He grabbed the older man by the arm and pulled him into a small crevice between two buildings. "Get down." He ordered. "Stay down until I tell you different."

The Ford screeched to a stop just short of jumping the curb. Tate hunkered down beside the old man and watched to see if the driver would get out. One hand slid to the small of his back and the gun hidden there. The headlights blinded him but he didn't hear the vehicle door open, instead he saw the Escape back up, turn and drive off into the night.

"You okay old man?" He asked.

"Yeah I'm okay but I thought for sure that he was going to run us down. I told you not to mess with that building...I told you."

Tate clasped the man on one arm and helped him to his feet. He reached into his pants pocket and pulled out a small wad of bills and pealed several off, handing them to the man. "Go get yourself a warm room and a hot meal. Stay away from this block for a while in case that asshole comes back."

The man stared up at him in surprise. "Damn, where'd you get all that money?" Them suspiciously he asked, "You pushing drugs?"

Tate clasped the man's shoulder, "Nothing like that. I just got my check, I'm a vet. Take the money and get out of here for a while. That's what I'm going to do too."

CHAPTER 35

Emma watched Wynter doze on the sofa in the living room, she was covered with her jacket and had propped her head on the raised end of the couch. Emma sat in a leather chair across from her and balanced her laptop on her knees. She tried to focus on the information in front of her but couldn't get her mind to cooperate. She glanced at her watch. *Four hours. Tate has been gone for four hours. Where the hell are you, Tate? Why haven't you called?*

The whirling of the computer fan and Wynter's even breathing seemed loud in the small room. Emma forced herself to focus on the spreadsheet in front of her. It seemed like she'd been staring at the data for hours since Tate had left. She tried to think like Aiden might. *Okay, so this is my spreadsheet, I've got the dates and some of the kid's names, maybe I don't know them all or maybe I don't care. I've got the money, that's important, how much I'm getting for these drops. What else do I need to know?* Lightening flashed in her sleepy brain. "I need to know who's going to pay me, and who I have to pay for getting me the kids!" *That's it! These are the names or initials of the person who delivered the kids to Aiden and the person he sold them too. That's why some of them repeat.*

Emma struggled to focus on the computer screen. She scanned the third column on the spreadsheet and found the partial name and initials, Quinto N. and Simon A., several times,

"Quinto Navarone and Simon Alvarez." She said, confident that she'd figured this part of the spreadsheet out. "Both dead. If I didn't know that Wynter killed one and Tate the other, I'd think that Aiden was cleaning house." With just a few clicks, Emma sorted the spreadsheet alphabetically by the names and initials in the third column. Other than Quinto and Simon, the bulk of the other entries were one name and one set of initials, initials that she could not identify. *Not yet.* She highlighted the unknown names, Captain S. and NW. "Who are you?" She quietly asked.

Headlights cut across the living room windows, and Emma rushed to the door. She peeked out and saw her Camry pull into the drive. She moved to the alarm panel and disabled the device, then pulled the door open just as Tate jogged up the front steps. *He looks tired.* She thought.

Tate stopped in the entryway and shrugged out of his coat. He started to hang it on a wooden wall peg, but stopped. "I think this one needs to go into the trash." He said to Emma, handing her the coat and dropping a quick kiss on her cheek.

Emma wrinkled her nose and took the offensive jacket with two fingers, "It's filthy and it smells. What happened to the coat you left with?"

He grinned, "I made a trade." Tate followed her down the dimly lit hallway and into the dining room. He dropped into a chair and watched Emma stuff the coat into a black plastic trash bag before opening the kitchen door and depositing it on the back porch.

"So tell me what you found out?" Emma slid into the chair across from Tate.

"Not much. I was able to look inside a window at the first two warehouses, the two at the riverfront, both appear abandoned and there was no sign of kids or anything else going on. Then I went to the building in the warehouse district, it looked a little better, as far as upkeep, but I couldn't get inside or see inside. There was a light on in there but no cars in sight. Had a big padlock on the outside, so I'm guessing that it was empty. Met the guy I gave my coat to near the downtown building, and he says that word on the street is that the building belongs to someone called the 'Captain', and his partner.

Emma's eyes snapped up, "The Captain again. He's on the spreadsheet as one of the suppliers for Aiden. Now we just need to know who he is."

Tate nodded, I asked the old guy but he didn't have a name for me. "There's a security guard who drives through there several times a night. I've got a plate number and if you can pull it, we might find out who's guarding the building. One more piece of the puzzle. If the vehicle is registered to a security firm, then maybe we can find out who's paying for the security. If not, then we'll have to assume that it's internal, and private. There wasn't any logo on the Ford to identify a security group, but the guy warned me off and then tried to run me down when I didn't move fast enough."

"Did you get a look at him?" Emma asked.

Tate laughed, "Oh yeah, I got a look at him when he pushed me. That was right before he tried to run me and my drinking buddy over with his car." Tate and Emma looked up when Wynter entered the dining room and tiredly took a seat.

"Did you find anything?" She asked, looking at Tate.

"Nothing for sure, but I met a guy who made sure that I didn't get too close to one of the warehouses, that's pretty suspicious." He glanced at his watch. "Let's get a couple hours of sleep, and in the morning we review everything that we've got so far, call Pruitt, and bring him up to speed, and then figure out how we're going to catch Aiden without letting him know that we're on to him."

Emma stood and reached for the light switch, "Sounds good. Wynter, you can take the guest room, first door on your right." She turned to Tate, "You're bunking with me, Echo."

CHAPTER 36

The clock on the bedside table glowed red; four in the morning. Victoria tossed the covers back and put her hands over her eyes. "What am I going to do?" She asked the darkness. *He's coming here tomorrow and we've got to act like we love him, and try to stay away from him at the same time.* She walked to the window and pulled the curtain back to stare into the early morning darkness.

She sensed that the door was being opened and turned to see Allie and Ivy peek in. "What's wrong?" She whispered.

The girls ran to Victoria and wrapped their arms tightly around her. "I had a bad dream." Ivy cried. "I don't want to do bad things, and I don't want to go back to St. A's. What if he sends me back?"

Victoria grasped the hands of both girls and led them back to her bed. "It's okay Ivy. You don't have to be afraid of going back to St. A's. He's not going to send you back, because if he did then you might tell on him, and he wouldn't want that." She motioned to the bed. "Get in." She said to the girls, and climbed in beside them and pulled the covers up. "If he tells you that he's going to take you back if you don't do what he wants, then you come and tell me, just don't let him touch you."

Allie yawned. The girls scooted closer to Victoria. "Go to sleep now. I'm going to take care of you and that's a promise. Nothing bad will happen as long as you do what I told you to do."

Victoria stared into the darkness and wondered how she was going to keep her promise to her friends. Once she was certain that the girls were sleeping she slipped from the bed and went to the door. "I've got to find a phone."

She tiptoed out of the room and went to *his* door. Quietly she turned the handle but the door didn't budge. *Locked. There must be a phone in there or why else would he lock the door.* She thought about going to Ms. Anderson's room and saying that she couldn't sleep, hoping that she could get the cell phone that the woman always carried, but changed her mind in case Ms. Anderson liked touching too.

Victoria crept down the stairs and into the kitchen. She stared out the glass double doors into the garden, and knew that if she tried to open the door that the alarm would sound. *How long would it take Ms. Anderson or the gardener man to get down here if the alarm went off?* She wondered. *I need a plan. If I could open the door I could run, but where would I go? I don't even know where I am. I don't think the girls would be able to run very far and I can't leave without Allie and Ivy...I won't leave them.*

The top of the gazebo was just visible in the distance and Victoria stared at it, thought about Bethany and how she had died. *Even being alone in the woods would be better than staying here. There has to be another house or a road somewhere near here.* She thought and her mind was made up. *Tomorrow night, we're leaving here. I don't know where we'll go but anywhere is better than what he has planned for us.*

Victoria walked back to the stairs and felt better than she had in a while. *Tomorrow we leave, no more waiting for someone to save us, we have to save ourselves.*

When Angels Cry

CHAPTER 37

Daylight pushed through the morning darkness and threatened the sky with pinks and blues just as Gregorio Aiden stepped out of the shower. He stared at his image in the mirror and liked the man that he saw. He turned and admired his muscled abdomen and flat stomach before leaning in close and intently scrutinizing his face. *Damn good looking for thirty five.* He thought. He quickly shaved and slipped on his robe. Mrs. Calder would have breakfast waiting for him in the dining room and he had lots to do today.

"Good morning Mr. Aiden. Coffee this morning?" Mrs. Calder asked when her boss entered the dining room.

"Good morning to you as well, and yes, I will definitely have coffee today." He took a seat and waited while she poured the steaming liquid into his cup. "Mrs. Calder, tomorrow I will be taking Tassie on a short trip and I'd like it if you would see that her bag is ready. I plan to get an early start so it might be best if you prepare her things tonight."

"How many days will you be gone sir?" She asked and set a plate of fruit near him at the table.

Gregory sipped his coffee, "No more than three or four days. Just the essentials will be fine, oh and she mentioned taking her doll, so we wouldn't want to forget that. And Mrs.

Calder, please don't mention this to my mother.
I have planned a special trip for just the two of
us and I don't want anything to spoil it."

"You can count on me sir. Shall I pack you
a bag as well?" She asked.

"I'll take care of it. After all, we'll only be
gone a few days. I will be home early today, but
have plans for the evening, so I won't be here for
dinner." Gregorio replied. *The final plans.* He
thought. *Once I deliver the baby, my business
with the Captain will be finished, and Tassie and
I will start a new life in a new place, and with
new names.* Gregory smiled at this.

He'd had a home in South America for
several years now, nothing as grand as this
house, but certainly rich by the local standards.
There was enough money in an account there to
last him for many years. Tassie would be home
schooled by an American tutor that he'd found
on a previous visit, and he knew a certain young
woman who would do anything to make him
happy. *Life will be good.* He thought. *Too bad I
can't take Mama, but she is just too old for this
trip. She will be very disappointed when she
figures out that I won't be returning.* He thought,
and then reasoned. *But she will still have the
house here, and enough money to live well until
she passes.*

Upstairs he dressed for work with the
usual care, he couldn't afford to alter his routine
or raise any suspicion. He glanced at his watch.
Wynter hadn't called, but he was confident that

she would do anything to keep him from taking Tassie and leaving, and if she didn't keep her end of the agreement, then he'd only lost a few hundred thousand. He wanted the money, but nothing was more important than his freedom, he would have that, with or without the baby and the money.

Tassie was at the table having her breakfast when Gregory reentered the room. He stooped to kiss her head. "I'll see you tonight Itasca. You be a good little girl for Mrs. Calder today."

She laughed, "I'm always good Daddy! Mrs. Calder says so."

At the back door, Gregory waved to his daughter and left the house for his office in town.

Across the street from the Aiden estate, a lone man sat in a Ford SUV. When he saw Aiden's car take the turn out of his driveway, he waited. He watched until he saw the big black car turn right at the next intersection, and then pulled his own vehicle into gear and followed a few car lengths behind.

Gregorio saw the blue Ford two cars behind him but he wasn't worried, "Let them follow me. I am only doing what I do every day." He adjusted the radio and listened to the morning traffic report as he maneuvered his car onto the freeway. He actually didn't care if there were traffic problems this morning, today's drive into the office was more about keeping up appearances than it was about work. For weeks he'd been offloading cases, and avoiding court appearances, always with the same excuse; Noah Walker needed something that couldn't wait. Noah's name carried a lot of weight at the firm and his partners were willing to give him free reign, as long as he keep the good congressman happy, and they collected the huge retainer fee that Walker paid.

Gregorio slowed and then stopped at a red light. He glanced in the rear view mirror and saw that the SUV was still following him. So his partner didn't trust him. *No problem.* He thought. *Since I don't trust you either, Captain. We'll play this game for now.*

Three blocks later he maneuvered his car into the parking garage, and eased into his reserved parking space.

CHAPTER 38

Wynter came awake slowly. She looked around the room and it took a few minutes for her to remember where she was. She listened, the house was still and quiet. She slipped from the bed and quickly made it up. Without turning a light on, she opened the door and tiptoed across the hall to the bathroom. On the counter there was an unopened toothbrush and a yellow sticky note with her name on it. She smiled. *Emma is a thoughtful host.* Since she hadn't known that she would be spending the night, she didn't have any clean clothes, but at least she could wash up and brush her teeth.

Finished with her morning ablutions, Wynter walked to the kitchen where she located the coffee and filled the coffeemaker. Minutes later, she heard the water running in the bathroom and knew that someone else was up. She pulled two cups from the cabinet and filled them with coffee.

Tate entered the kitchen and accepted the steaming cup of coffee that Wynter handed him. "Morning." He said. "You ready to put the cards on the table and hope for the best?"

Wynter nodded, "I always knew that the time would come that I had to confess to killing Quinto, but I don't know what I could have done differently. I mean I couldn't let him shoot Emma again, and I would be a liar if I said that I am sorry he is dead. He was evil."

Tate pulled a chair out for her and said, "I'm glad that you were there that night. Even though you didn't do the right thing with what you knew or suspected about Aiden, you did the right thing when you saved Emma." He allowed a little half smile, "Maybe a little overkill...but..." He shrugged.

Wynter looked thoughtful, "What do you think will happen to me? Really?"

Tate took a sip, "I don't know, but it's possible that you could come out of this with nothing more than a slap on the hand. You did save a federal agent, and you're cooperating now. We just have to convince Pruitt that you were afraid for your life, and the life of your child, when he starts asking questions about why you didn't come forward sooner."

Wynter picked up her empty cup and placed it in the dishwasher, through the open doorway, she said, "I need to call St. Anthony's and let Sister Camille know that I won't be at work today. She will not be surprised because she thought I was ill yesterday when I asked to leave early."

Both Tate and Wynter turned when Emma entered the room, "Coffee. I need coffee. When this is over, I'm going to sleep for a week."

Tate grinned at her, and she wondered how he could look so good with so little sleep. "Still not a morning person, huh Em." He said. "Wynter made the coffee and I'm going to make breakfast, then we lay out our plan and call

Pruitt in."

Emma nodded and took a seat, cradling the coffee mug in her hands. "I'm pretty sure I figured out one more column of the spreadsheet, maybe two." She said. "I think the columns that we couldn't figure out are for who supplied the children to him, and the other for who he sold the children to. I mean, he needs to know who he has to pay, and he certainly wants to know who owes him. There are multiple sets of initials and partial names on the spreadsheet and several of them repeat on different dates, specifically there are entries for Quinto N. and Simon A."

"Quinto and Simon." Wynter said.

Emma nodded and continued, "Since we know that Quinto was delivering children to someone that night at the warehouse, and we know that Simon was sent here to kill me, we can work under the assumption that this column is the suppliers, the people on Aiden's payroll. There are also multiple entries in the same column for Captain S. and NW, any idea who that might be?" She asked the other woman.

"No. I don't really know Gregorio's business associates, he didn't often bring people into the house, other than when he was entertaining, and those were mostly other attorneys and clients of the firm. Important people, not child molesters. Quinto was his brother, but even he didn't come to the house other than for Sunday dinners with his mother. Gregorio and Quinto would go into his office after dinner and I just assumed that they were having drinks, until I saw them with the computer open that day that I took the ice in."

The smell of bacon floated in the air, and Tate stuck his head into the dining room, "Let's not discount anyone just because you think they were important. Affluent people commit crimes too. I mean how many people would think that a respectable and powerful attorney like Aiden would be messed up in a child trafficking ring? In fact, I think that we should consider that maybe he had the some of the same people on his client list for both his legitimate and his illegal business." He disappeared back in the kitchen and returned a few minutes later, he carried two plates filled with bacon and eggs, he sat one down in front of each of the woman and returned to the kitchen for his own plate.

"You should have kept him Emma. A man who will cook for you is rare." Wynter said before picking up her fork.

Emma rolled her eyes, and forked a bite of eggs. She didn't reply to Wynter's remark.

Seconds later, Tate joined the women with his own plate and anxious to start the day's work, the three made short work of their food. Wynter cleared the table while Emma retrieved her laptop from the living room where she'd left it the night before. Tate pulled the printed documents showing the location and owner of the four warehouses from the printer in Emma's office, and brought them to the table.

"I called Sister Camille and she was very understanding." Wynter said to no one in particular as she watched Tate and Emma turn the dining room into command central with their papers and computers.

"I've got to get Pruitt before he heads off to some meeting or field OP. It's still a little early, so I'm going to try to catch him before he leaves for the office." Emma said and picked up her cell. "Excuse me." She stepped out of the room.

Tate and Wynter took seats at the table and waited for Emma to return. Tate watched Wynter. He saw her bow her head in what appeared to be a silent prayer and hoped that it helped.   A full ten minutes later, Emma returned, laid her phone on the table, and took a seat. "He'll be here in less than fifteen minutes. He was already on his way into the office, but agreed to detour when I told him that we had the shooter and that she was ready to talk."

"You didn't go into the details over the phone did you?" Tate asked.

Emma shook her head, "I didn't, but if I had wanted to then I would have been comfortable with it. I don't think that anyone has bugged my phone or Pruitt's."

Wynter stood, her face ashy and panic filled, "What will I say to him? What if he doesn't believe me?"

Emma glanced up from her laptop, "He's a fair man, Wynter. You answer his questions as honestly as you can and don't hold anything back. Tate and I will be right here with you. You don't have anything to be afraid of at this point, it's all downhill from here."

"What do you mean 'downhill'? Downhill is bad, right?" Wynter squeaked.

Tate replied, "She doesn't mean it's downhill for you, she means that we've got a good lead on the case and the investigation is going to move now, get easier, like riding a bike downhill. We're going to catch the bastard, and hopefully he'll be willing to squeal on a few of his associates."

Wynter dropped into a chair and buried her face in shaky hands, "I'm sorry. I'm scared, that is all. I don't want to lose my freedom and never see Tassie again while Gregorio goes free."

Emma stood and gave Wynter a quick hug, "I'll do everything I can to make sure that doesn't happen. You have my word."

"Em, pull up the website to Aiden's law firm, maybe they have one of those client feedback pages, you know where clients recommend them. That might give us a clue some of the clients that the firm represents, then we can cross reference any names we find with the initials on the spreadsheet. I'd like to have everything in place before we have to give it over to Pruitt." He turned to Wynter, "You say he only entertained others from the firm or clients, do you have the names of anyone who might have been included on the guest lists?"

"There were several parties when I lived there but I don't recall anyone specifically. I tried to stay out of the way most of the time." She snapped her fingers, "But I know someone who does know the names. I don't know if she would help us, but I can ask."

Emma looked up from the keyboard, "So who is it?" She asked.

"Mrs. Calder. She is the housekeeper, and even though the parties were catered, she was still in charge of making sure everyone was taken care of and that the catering staff handled the job as they should. I'm certain that she would have been the one to order invitations on Gregorio's behalf."

Tate chimed, "Hold up. How are you going to get her to give you the names without throwing a big red flag up? I mean she works for him, why would she help you?"

"She doesn't have to know that she is helping me. I will simply tell her that I want the guest list so that those people can be invited to the annual benefit at St. A's. It's coming up in a couple of months, and I know that she will help me if she thinks that it will benefit the children." Wynter reached for Emma's cell phone. "Let me ask, it may save us time that we really don't have."

Emma and Tate locked eyes and silently

agreed with Wynter's plan. Emma nodded her consent and Wynter made the call.

Two minutes into the call, Wynter mouthed the word "fax" to Emma and repeated the number that Emma hastily scribbled on the corner of her notepad. When Wynter disconnected the call she looked up at Emma with watery eyes. "It was all I could do not to ask to speak with Itasca. I know that she would not have let me, Gregorio has forbidden it, but still...I..." Large tears spilled over and ran silently down her face and she wiped them away one handed.

Before Emma could move to comfort her, the doorbell chimed, and Emma left the room to answer it. "Here we go." She said as she left the room.

CHAPTER 39

Victoria woke up when the door to her room opened. Ms. Anderson poked her head in and seeing the younger girls snuggled and asleep in the big bed with Victoria, she smiled. "I was worried when they weren't in their room." She frowned and whispered.

Victoria glanced at Allie and Ivy and then looked back at Ms. Anderson, "Ivy had a bad dream and couldn't get back to sleep."

"I'm glad that you take such good care of your sisters Tori. Let them sleep and I'll hold off on breakfast for a little while. After all, today is a special day and everyone should be rested and ready for the party." She quietly pulled the door closed.

When she heard the soft click of the door closing, Victoria stood and tucked the covers around Ivy and Allie. She left her room and after a quick trip to the bathroom, she walked downstairs and into the kitchen.

Jeri stood at the sink, absently staring out a small window above it. She turned when Victoria entered the room. "It's a lovely day today. Spring is here and summer's not far behind."

"What kind of party are we going to have? Is it someone's birthday?" Victoria asked, dropping into a chair at the table.

Jeri smiled indulgently, "No birthdays

today, just a welcome home party for Daddy. We celebrate in some way each time that he comes home for the weekend."

"Why doesn't he live here all the time?" Victoria questioned.

"Oh, he'd love that, but he has business to take care of in the city and it would be too hard to travel in each day. He has an apartment in town but this is really his home."

"Can I have milk please?" Victoria asked, and continued, "How far is it to town? It seems dumb to have two houses. Most people just need one."

Jeri sat the milk down in front of her and replied, "It takes about an hour to drive into town from here and then to get downtown would take another hour, what with morning traffic. Your Daddy can easily afford two homes, and there are many people who have two homes or even more than two."

Victoria's mind was spinning. *A whole hour to drive to town. How long would it take to walk there?* She wondered.

Nora entered the kitchen, and Chloe was not far behind her. Both girls were still in their nightgowns and Nora plopped into the chair next to Victoria, while Chloe took a seat across from them. "I've been to the apartment in town. Daddy took me shopping and we spent the night there. It's just lovely and there's a beautiful view of downtown and the river." Nora yawned.

"Me too." Chloe piped. "You have to take the elevator, 'cause it's a penthouse. That means it's at the very top of the building. It takes up the whole floor and everything is all white, the carpet and the furniture, just everything." She screwed her face up and locked eyes with Victoria, "Maybe someday you'll grow up enough to get invited to town, but I wouldn't bet on it."

Victoria opened her mouth to reply, but Ms. Anderson interrupted her.

Jeri scolded, "Girls, it's a day of celebration and we are not going to have any bickering, so just get it out of your systems and start acting like real sisters. Now, I'm going to start breakfast and then we will decorate the family room for our party." She turned to Victoria, "Tori, please go up and see if Ivy and Allie are awake yet." She glanced at the other girls, "By the time everyone is dressed, I should have breakfast ready. Now scoot!"

Victoria followed Chloe and Nora from the room and at the bottom of the stairs she asked, "So what happens when we have the party? Are there games or food? Do the neighbors come too?"

Nora turned, one arm resting on the wood railing, "It's just a family party. Sometimes we grill outside by the pond, and sometimes we have a fancy dinner inside. Tonight we'll all dress up and wear our flower projects so we're probably eating inside. When we eat outside we usually just wear shorts or jeans."

"Don't we ever have company? Or friends over to play?" Victoria asked.

Nora snorted, "Why would we need friends to come over and play? We have each other, silly! And Daddy says he doesn't want company at this house, he sees too many people at work and in the city. He always says 'this place is just for relaxing with his girls'."

Nora and Chloe resumed climbing the stairs with Victoria following behind, "So we never see anyone else? What about church? Don't we ever go to church?"

It was Chloe that turned this time, "Stop asking all these stupid questions. We don't need anybody else and we don't need church. We have everything we need right here. We're *Walker* girls and that's what's really important."

The other girls ran ahead in front of her and Victoria thought about their total belief in living here, and their ignorance about the outside world. *Robots, they're just like robots. They do exactly what they're told and believe that it's right.* She thought.

The door squeaked when she pushed it and entered her room. She closed the door behind her as quietly as possible. Allie and Ivy sat cross legged on the bed, facing each other. They both turned and smiled at Victoria, "We said our morning prayers Victoria, just like Sister Camille taught us to." Allie said, her blonde curls bouncing.

"That's good Allie, we could use some serious prayers today. It's time to get dressed for breakfast, but I want your promise that you won't forget what we talked about last night."

"We *already* promised." Ivy said.

"We promise double." Allie said.

"And cross our hearts." Ivy chimed, her short chubby fingers drawing an X over her chest.

Victoria smiled at them and instructed, "Okay, so go get dressed and hurry downstairs for breakfast. I've got a big surprise for you later. A secret surprise."

CHAPTER 40

Wynter couldn't sit still, her hands worried with the each other in her lap. *Please don't let me go to jail.* Her mind chanted. She looked up when Emma returned to the room, a tall well-dressed man in a dark suit behind her.

"Wynter, this is my supervisor, Jackson Pruitt." Emma said, she made eye contact with Pruitt, and slanted her head in Tate's direction. "This is Tate Echo. Tate, Jackson Pruitt."

The two men shook hands and seemed to size each other up. Tate motioned the older man to a chair. "Before we begin, I do want to thank you for calling me in when Em was hurt."

Jackson Pruitt smiled, showing off perfectly straight teeth and making him look younger than his graying hair suggested. "Just following procedure. As I indicated, you are listed as the emergency contact on Emma's file."

Pruitt took a seat next to Wynter and gave her a hard look. "I understand that you are the person responsible for the death of Quinto Navarone, is that correct?"

Wynter tried to speak, stammered and gave up. She simply nodded. Pruitt continued, "If Emma is correct in her assumptions, and she generally is, then you also know quite a bit about the child trafficking operation that the Department of Justice has been investigating here in Richmond." He paused, "But then I'm getting ahead of myself." He softened his tone, "Let's start at the beginning okay? I'd like you to tell me everything that you recall about the night that you shot Navarone."

Wynter's head bobbed and she began her story. Some ten minutes later, Pruitt leaned back in his chair and crossed his arms. He looked intently at Wynter, then at Emma. "Emma, based on what I've just heard, and effective immediately, I'm closing the IA investigation regarding your conduct that night, and you are cleared for active duty as soon as your doctor says it's okay. Ms. Burgland, as for any charges being brought against you in the death of Mr. Navarone, I will have to hear the rest of the story and give that careful consideration. I can tell you that saving the life of an agent in the field, and your continued cooperation does reflect positively for you." He looked at Tate and Emma, "Now tell me, have you brought Shuler into the fold with the information that you mentioned?"

Emma shook her head, "No sir, not yet anyway. I promised Wynter, ah, Ms. Burgland, that we would only involve the FBI at this point. Ms. Burgland is certain that Aiden has contacts inside the Richmond PD, and she has reported an incident to us that supports her story. Since we didn't know how far Aiden's influence has stretched, I didn't want any of this to go outside this room until I had an opportunity to speak directly with you."

"Fair enough, for now at least. I know that

I don't have to remind you, but I will anyway. This is the type of information sharing that should be handled in a Bureau conference room with a full team to offer perspectives, but given the situation, we'll waive that formality. Now, let's take a look at the spreadsheet and any other information that you have."

Tate excused himself and went to Emma's office to see if the faxed list of names had been received from Aiden's housekeeper. It was on the machine, three neatly typed pages of names, addresses and phone numbers. He pulled the papers from the tray and returned to the dining room with them. Emma had scooted her chair closer to Pruitt and turned her monitor so that he could see the spreadsheet while she explained their interpretation of the data on it. Tate fanned the papers in his hand and pushed them toward Emma.

Pruitt pushed back in his chair, "I don't know Emma. This is very circumspective. We only have Ms. Burgland's word that the flash drive came from Aiden, and in court, I'm sure it would be twisted to insinuate that she fabricated the information in order to obtain access to her daughter."

Tate spoke up, "I *know* that there's something going on at those warehouses; why else would he have security threatening people, and trying to run them over if they get too close? I didn't get a look inside, but I'd bet that there were people being held in that last warehouse." He paused then continued, "We both know that I don't have any authority in this investigation, but I believe that Wynter is being honest. There is a confirmed connection, Aiden's own brother was up to his eyeballs in this trafficking operation, and the only way to know for sure that Aiden himself is guilty is to let her set up the drop, monitor the call and be there when he shows up for the baby."

Until now, Wynter had remained in her chair, silently watching and listening while Tate and Emma explained their findings to Pruitt, but at this, she jumped up. "I cannot do that. Even if I had a baby I could not give it to him. Not even to save Tassie, that is why I came to you in the first place."

Emma spoke up, "You don't have to *actually* deliver a baby to Aiden for us to be able to arrest him. We only need to witness the call when you tell him that you have the child, and intercept him when he comes to what he thinks is the pick-up. There will be no baby waiting for him, just the FBI."

Jackson Pruitt stood up, "I agree with Tate. The only way to clearly implicate Aiden is to have Ms. Burgland go along with him. I'm going to need a team available for the arrest and we'll need to brief them. At this point, I'm keeping it strictly with our agents and on a need to know basis only, so there's no need for you to contact Shuler. The task force can take credit for the arrest, since you worked with them for the last four months, but if there is indeed a leak, I don't want to give anyone the chance to warn

Aiden." He turned to Tate, cleared his throat and said, "Echo, given your current level of involvement with this case, I'll expect you to serve the Bureau as an active member of the team." Tate looked surprised, then nodded as Pruitt went on, "With your past experience with the Bureau, and the fact that you are already involved deeply in this case, it would be foolish on my part to exclude you now."

Tate grinned, "In that case, my first suggestion would be that we work it out so that the drop coincides with active raids on all four of the warehouses belonging to Benito Corporation. If you send teams in to all four places at the same time, then no one will get any advance warning."

"I agree and will set the arrangements in motion when I get to the office. I'll return at two this afternoon with the necessary equipment for the phone call. We will of course block the caller ID so that Aiden can't identify the phone that Ms. Burgland uses to call him." He turned to Wynter, "Did Aiden give you any specific time that you had to deliver the baby? Or a place?"

"No, he just said that I had to get him the child in forty eight hours or less, that would mean no later than tomorrow. And that I was to take the child to my apartment."

Looking thoughtful, Pruitt said, "I think we can work with that. When you call him back, you'll tell him that he has to come and get the child right away, that your neighbors are suspicious, and that you are worried that they'll report the noise, something like that. When he arrives, we'll be waiting."

Emma smiled, "We also think that we may be able to figure out who he sold some of the children to. If this works out, we may just get some of them back."

"How so?" Pruitt asked.

"It was Wynter's idea really. We're working under the premise that some of his associates and clients at the law firm may also be his clients in his trafficking business. Wynter reached out to Aiden's housekeeper and asked for his private guest list for parties at his home so that the same people could be invited to a benefit at St. A's. We just received a fax from Aiden's housekeeper showing the names and addresses of many of his business associates and friends, and before you return, we'll have compared the names on the list to the partial names and initials on the spreadsheet that we believe to be the buyers of these kids."

"We will be extremely lucky if that pans out." He said and turned to Wynter, "Ms. Burgland, please accept my gratitude for your part in saving Agent Echo, and for coming forward with information that may assist us on our investigation. Your cooperation is indeed appreciated."

When the door closed behind Pruitt, Wynter buried her face in her hands, "I was so afraid that he was going to arrest me. I didn't know what to say to him."

Tate spoke up, "You did fine, and in a few hours we'll have Aiden in custody. That Pruitt walked out of here without taking you with him bodes well for your continued freedom."

Emma turned, "Tate, if you'll start the comparison on the spreadsheet, I want to brief Wynter on the process that will occur when she makes the call to Aiden. We need her to come across naturally."

Emma and Wynter spent the next hour perfecting a relaxed script that Wynter would use when she called Aiden. "You don't want the conversation to sound forced. We don't want him to have any idea that the call is being monitored."

Wynter bunched her hair on one shoulder and absently twisted it. "He expects me to be hesitant because he knows that I am afraid of him. If I sound confident or like I am reading," She shook the papers with Emma's notes on them in front of her, "then he will be more suspicious, I need to do this in my own way."

Emma leaned back on the sofa, "Okay, so convince me. Show me how you'll handle the call, act it out."

After several tries, Wynter had memorized what she would say, and Emma was satisfied as well. "Gregorio is arrogant. He will believe me because he thinks that I am too afraid to disobey him. He knows that I will do anything to see

Tassie. He knows that I am afraid to go to the police, and since he doesn't know that I was at the warehouse when Quinto was killed, or that I was here when Simon was shot, he has no reason to think that I have come to you for help."

CHAPTER 41

In downtown Richmond there were three men in three different offices, in three different buildings. Each with their own unique set of thoughts for the day.

The first man, Noah Walker, leaned back in his chair, and thought about his girls. "It's time." He whispered. *Tonight, Ivy will be the chosen one. She'll come to my room and even though it's too soon to play all the games, we can have some quality snuggle time, and when she falls asleep...."* Just the thought of the bubbly blonde pressed against him brought him to a full erection. *But before that, I'll introduce her to the games that we play in Daddy's room.* He instantly saw the child sitting astride him, bouncing as they played *ride the horsey...ride daddy.* He thrilled at the thought of running his hands up her small legs and onto her naked thighs, of grasping her buttocks and bouncing her harder, up and down, up and down... of course it wouldn't be nearly as gratifying as the full version of his game, but it would get her used to his touch, she'd laugh, that shy little giggle and he'd grind her hard against him.

Memories of a younger Bethany seeped in and filled his mind. She had been a beautiful child, and such fun to teach the ways of life to. He remembered the first time that they'd played the games to a finish, the shocked and hurt look that she'd given him, and how she struggled at first. . How she cried on his shoulder when it was done. She was, and would always be his, as were all his girls. He loved the power, the feeling of complete and utter control. He could name them each, more than thirty now – with more to come, starting tonight with Ivy.

I hope Ivy struggles...and screams. Oh yes, the little screams were an exciting part of the process...he needed to hear them, to know that she was his. *All just part of the game.*

"Shit." He exclaimed and glanced at his watch. *Two hours and one meeting before I can leave, at least an hour to drive home and then the party with all the girls. I hope I can stand the wait.* He stood up and adjusted his manhood, willing it to a flaccid state. A quick thought about any grown woman was enough to accomplish that. He snatched a leather bound portfolio from the desktop and briskly walked from the room.

The second man, Gregorio Aiden, a mere ten blocks away, sat hunched over his personal shredder. He'd gone through all the personal files that were in his desk and fed them one by one into the machine. "Nothing left behind." Gregory murmured as he fed another page of legal sized paper into the shredder. He'd already performed this same task in his office at home. He looked around the room, a bookshelf lined one wall, the dark wood and the equally dark binders on the books were a firm reminder of the struggles that he'd encountered on his way to a partnership at the firm. On one ivory coated wall, a plethora of gold framed degrees and accomplishments stared back at him. He'd have no need of them now; still he was thankful that the years of learning and working to distinguish his self, had brought him to this place in time.

"No regrets." He laughed; a hollow sound in the empty room. He'd never see this place again, and he wouldn't miss it. A small gold framed picture of Itasca sat proudly on his desk and he tossed it in his open briefcase. That was a memory that he would keep.

He leaned back in his chair and ripped individual sheets from his personal journal. There really wasn't anything incriminating in the journal, just his notes and perceptions of the people that he'd dealt with over the years. But still, it was better if someone, someday, couldn't piece together how his mind had worked during his time at the firm. He looked at the growing stack of paper, "You should have moved on to the electronic journal, or even your smartphone, years ago, and then you wouldn't be doing this. You could have taken that with you or erased it with the click of a button."

His phone! The GPS mechanism had been disabled but still he couldn't afford to take it with him. He needed a disposable cell, something that he could use to call out but that no one would be able to trace back to him. He rush-fed the remaining paper into the shredder, its growl echoed in the quiet room. Satisfied that there was nothing else to be shredded, he pulled the mechanical unit off the paper basket and picked it up. He left his office and took the elevator down to the basement where he dumped the baskets contents into the incinerator. Even with the nine cross cut blades, he wouldn't trust this trash to the building custodian.

On his way back to his office, Gregorio thought about what he was doing and smiled. He felt good about his decision to leave. *It's time to move on.* He thought. The elevator stopped and Gregorio prepared to step outside the moving box, his path was blocked by Charles Mayer, the senior partner at the firm, who was waiting to enter the elevator, "You taking the trash out now Aiden? I thought you had an important engagement with Walker."

Gregory looked at the empty shedder basket and said, "Cleaning crew failed to dispose of the paper in my shredder basket and I don't like it left overnight. I have a late lunch scheduled with Walker in," he glanced at his watch, "thirty minutes. I'm on my way there now." The other man nodded and entered the elevator. "Well make sure you pick up the tab Aiden, we want to keep the congressman happy."

There was no meeting with Walker, but he'd use that time to get the cell phone that he needed.

The third man, known on the streets as Captain, tried but failed, to concentrate on the meeting speaker. *I need to touch base with Aiden, make sure he's got my delivery ready.* He thought, then shook his head and forced his eyes back to the speaker. His contact had assured him that Aiden reported to work as usual this morning. *There's nothing to worry about. He's not stupid enough to stiff you on this deal. He knows what the consequences are and he's not willing to risk it.* Still, a niggling of worry bounced in his stomach, churning up an acid burn. There was no room for error with this sale. The buyer had agreed to a fee of more than double the usual price just to have a healthy baby boy delivered for his distraught and very barren wife. The Captain shook his head at the thought of how far some men would go to please a woman, and how money could cut through the red tape and get you what you wanted when you wanted it, no questions, no paperwork, no background checks or home visits. No waiting, even if you wanted a baby. The man and his wife were returning from an international business trip today. They had plans to introduce their "adopted" son to their friends and family tomorrow. This child would indeed have the best of everything that life had to offer.

The speaker droned on and the man pretended to jot down notes on a yellow pad of paper, but there were no words, only doodles that emphasized his distracted state.

His thoughts shifted and he thought about killing Aiden, if the man wanted out, then he could make that happen. In fact, he could make it happen and make sure that no one ever placed his involvement; he had ways, lots of ways. After all, Aiden wasn't the first man to think he could walk away and realistically, he probably wouldn't be the last.

The scrape of chairs being pushed back startled him and he looked up to see that the meeting had been adjourned. He quickly left the room, and the building. Outside he sucked in a breath of exhaust infused city air, and jogged to his vehicle. Inside the car he checked his gun. He smiled, at some point on his walk to the car, the decision had been made. "Aiden will get his wish; he'll be out of my business and out of my way." He shrugged. *I'll have to find a new business associate.* That wouldn't be a problem either, there were people already on his payroll who'd do anything for a share of the big money.

The car fired to life and he pulled it into gear. *Fuck Aiden. And once he's gone, I'm making a few changes, taking the whole thing mainstream. No more babies, and no more phony adoptions, just some streetwise kids twelve and up from here on out.* He settled things in his mind. As soon as Aiden made the delivery, he'd dispose of the man. *Maybe I'll intercept the delivery; then it will be a total surprise, no time for confrontation and no going back.*

CHAPTER 42

Victoria couldn't concentrate on today's literature lesson, her mind raced with what she planned to do. *Please don't let them catch us.* She silently prayed, her eyes drifting to the closed glass door leading to the garden. All through breakfast, she'd watched the younger girls, hoping that they didn't forget her warning.

"Tori, I asked a question about the story. Can you answer it?" Ms. Anderson asked. She'd seen the child looking outside, and knew that she wasn't paying attention. In fact, none of them really were. *Pre-party excitement.* She thought.

"I'm sorry. I didn't hear the question." Victoria answered.

Jeri closed the book in front of her and said, "I think we've had enough for today. After all, we have a party to get ready for, and I know it's hard for you to concentrate on school work with all the excitement."

"Can we go outside?" Victoria asked. "I want to see how much the baby ducks have grown."
Jeri glanced outside and back at Victoria, "I've got to make some preparations for dinner and you," She looked around the table at all the girls, "have to be dressed and ready for dinner at six. We still have a few hours, so why not!"

The table erupted with cheers from the girls. "I'm going to pick some flowers for the vase in the family room." Chloe said.

"That would be a nice touch Chloe, now all of you, run upstairs and grab your sweaters, it's still a little chilly outside and we wouldn't want anyone getting sick." Jeri stacked the books on the table, and watched the girls run from the room. Even she hadn't been able to concentrate today, a trip outside would do them all good.

Upstairs, Victoria grabbed her sweater and ran back to the door. She stopped. *I've got to put Bethany's journal back in the gazebo. If they never found it in all the time that she was here then that's the best place to keep it.*

She pushed the door closed and quickly retrieved the diary from her trash basket and stuffed it inside her jeans before pulling her sweater on and buttoning it so that the bulge of the book was hidden.

At the top of the stairs, she waited for Allie and Ivy to catch up. "Come on slow pokes! Don't you want to go outside?"

Downstairs, the five Walker girls waited for Ms. Anderson to grab her book and lead them outside. Victoria held a plastic bag half full of bread that she planned to feed the ducks, and Bethany's journal was safely tucked in her jeans.

Once outside, the girls split into their usual groups, Chloe and Nora picked flowers while Allie and Ivy chased a butterfly in the garden. Victoria took the small path toward the pond but her mind wasn't on feeding the ducks or even returning the diary to its hiding spot. All she could think about was how she was going to get Ivy and Allie out of here, and how far they would have to go before they found someone who could help them.

At the ponds edge, she threw a handful of bread into the water and smiled when the ducks bickered over the pieces. *You don't even know where the road is. And if you just go down the driveway they'll catch you for sure.* She worried. *You need to know where to go so that you won't get caught. Maybe you could hide until they give up...nah...that probably won't work. They'd never give up.*

She glanced back to the garden and saw that Ms. Anderson was on the bench with her book so she slipped around the ponds edge and into the gazebo. Quickly, she unzipped the cushion and returned the diary to its hiding spot. Once she'd replaced the cushion, Victoria climbed up on the bench and stood looking out over the pond. From here, she could see the whole pond, the garden, and the house. She could even see into the woods surrounding the property. She squinted, then pulled one hand up, using it to shade her eyes. "I can't see any neighbors, nothing but woods...." She muttered.

Walking on the benches she used the beams that supported the roof to keep from falling and went to the other side of the structure. The sun was behind her now and she looked out at almost the same view on this side of the gazebo. In the distance she saw a patch of sandy colored dirt. The ground stood out in stark contrast to the grass and pine covered ground around it. She felt sick and dropped to sit on the bench. "That's what they did with Bethany. Oh God, we have got to get out of this place." She whispered. *Tonight. No matter what, we are leaving tonight. Getting lost in the woods or eaten by an animal is better than what will happen if we stay here.*

Victoria left the gazebo and instead of taking the trail from the pond to the garden, she walked along the edge of the woods and looked for anything that might help her get the girls to safety. She stopped behind the gardener's tool shed on the west side of the yard. The door wasn't locked and she stepped inside and waited for her eyes to adjust to the darkness. *Nothing in here but yard tools. Maybe I could take one and use it if we see any wild animals in the woods.* She thought. She pulled a small shovel off a worktable and peeked outside to make sure that no one could see her before stepping out with the tool. She walked to the back side of the shed and leaned the shovel up against the wooden building. A sparkle of light flashed in the trees, Victoria shivered. *Something's out there. Maybe there are wild animals, God I hope not.*

Victoria walked along the edge of the yard until she reached the corner of the house. *Maybe I could slip around to the front yard and see the road from there.* She thought.

"Tori! It's time to go inside now." Ms. Anderson called. She stood up and shielded her eyes but didn't see the child anywhere around the pond. Fear settled in her stomach, *What if she fell in? Could she swim?*

"Here I am." Victoria said.

Jeri turned, "I couldn't see you and I was afraid that something happened to you." She smiled, "Girls!" She called to the others, "Thirty more minutes and that's it. We've got lots to do, and Daddy will be here in just a few hours."

CHAPTER 43

Satisfied that Wynter would be able to handle the call with Aiden, Emma returned to the dining room, Wynter trailed behind her. At the table, Tate continued to compare the guest list to the names on the spreadsheet. He looked up when they entered the room.

"You find anything yet?" Emma asked.

"Nothing yet, but the comparison has been relatively easy. The list that Aiden's housekeeper sent is in alphabetical order and I sorted the spreadsheet that way too. So far I'm down to "S" with no match other than Quinto Navarone. Maybe we're chasing our tails with this one, Em."

"I'm going to pull out some sandwich stuff so that we can eat before Pruitt gets back and you keep looking. I'd rather do the review and find out that it's a waste of time than not do it and have overlooked a connection."

Tate made a face at her, "I'm too far into it to stop now anyway. I can say one thing for the man, he does have some high powered friends, the guest list is chock full of judges, politicians and even some celebrities."

Wynter dropped into the chair across from Tate, "Now you understand more of why I could not fight him alone. Gregorio has power and money on his side, along with all these people that trust him."

Tate stared at Wynter, "What I don't get is why? I mean why is he involved in the buying and selling of children when he obviously has a lucrative career, and with friends like this he could probably move up to a political career too if he wanted."

Tate could see the sadness in her eyes, Wynter shrugged and said, "I don't know why. Gregorio was always trying to prove his worth, not to others, but to himself. He was never satisfied with what he was or what he had, and always talked of more."

Emma came into the room carrying a plate rounded with sandwiches in one hand and a bag of corn chips in the other. She sat the sandwiches in the middle of the table and returned to the kitchen to grab paper plates.

Tate snagged a sandwich from the plate and took a bite, his eyes never leaving the spreadsheet. "I think I found one!" he whooped, then continued, "But if this is right then there are going to be heads rolling at the State Capitol."

Emma returned to the dining room, paper plates forgotten for now, "Who is it?" She asked.

"The only match is for Virginia republican, Congressman Noah Walker." Tate leaned back in his chair and took another bite from his sandwich. "So how do we confirm the link?" Tate questioned. "I mean we can't just walk into his office or home and demand to know if he's a child molester."

"First we find out everything that we can through the system. I doubt that I have the right level of access for anything too personal, but Pruitt does." Emma said excitedly. She nudged Tate from his chair and sat down in front of the computer.

Thirty minutes later, Emma was almost ready to admit defeat, "The man has a squeaky clean record, not even a parking ticket. Never married and no children. Didn't have the greatest childhood either, no father listed on his birth certificate, one sister, Sara, died in a hit and run accident when she was eleven and he was five. Walker was a witness and the driver was never caught. His only remaining relative, his mother, died in a house fire believed, but never proved, to be arson, when he was eighteen. Went to state college and thanks to a hardship scholarship finished his education."

Tate leaned forward, "Guess you could say that he made it the hard way. What about property, does he own any warehouses? If he does, it's not likely that they'd be in his name but you might as well look."

Emma pushed the keys on her laptop and waited while the information loaded, "He has an apartment here in Richmond, nice neighborhood too, and is listed as the owner of a place about fifty miles north of here, probably his real home."

"With Gregorio for his attorney, it does not surprise me that you wouldn't find anything on his record. I mean, what value is there in having a very high priced attorney if he can't *fix* things for you." Wynter said.

Tate nodded his agreement with Wynter, "I think she's right Em, anything that might have reached out to bite him in the ass has been cleaned up by Aiden. The only way that we're going to confirm the relationship, assuming that there is one, is to get Aiden to admit to it."

Emma frowned, "I don't know if Pruitt will go for that kind of fishing. He's going to call this whole comparison flimsy as far as evidence goes, and he's not going to let us implicate a U.S. congressman with so little proof."

Tate grinned, that heart stopping grin that Emma dreamed about, "I see the wheels turning Tate. What are you thinking?" Emma asked cautiously.

"Pruitt's due here in what? Two hours?" He said.

Emma glanced at her watch and nodded. "So if you were a known political figure and you had a place in town and one in the country, where would you keep stolen goods...or kids? I think I'm going to take a little drive to the country and have a look around, what do you think?"

"I'll get the keys." Emma was on her feet, and returned a few seconds later, handing her car keys and a small pair of field binoculars to Tate, who waited at the back door.

"Lock up and I'll be back before you miss me. If Pruitt gets here first, tell him I had to run to the store or something." He kissed her hard on the mouth and left.

"You make a good team." Wynter declared, then added, "Do you think Tate will find the evidence that your boss needs to arrest this congressman?"

Emma crossed her arms over her chest and tilted her head, "Oh, he'll find a way to get into the house, or see into the house, that's for sure. Other than his years with the FBI, Tate was a Marine, and he knows how to blend in and check things out without getting caught. He's damn good at it in fact."

"So you believe that there are children being held by the congressman?"

Emma shrugged, "I don't have any way of knowing at this point, but I don't think that we should overlook the possibility; that would be foolish. I do know that if there are kids out there, then Tate will report that back to Pruitt and the congressman will become an official part of the investigation. Tate wouldn't take any action without Pruitt's buy in because one screw up and the whole thing would get thrown out of court on a technicality, and that's something that Tate wouldn't be able to live with...not if it were his fault."

"You know him so well. It's too bad that you cannot work out your differences. I can see that he loves you..."

Emma cut her off, "That's not going to happen, Wynter. Neither of us could take the failure a second time, and we would fail. He hasn't changed...I haven't changed." She stammered. "Excuse me, I'm going to go freshen up before Pruitt gets here, jeans are not my usual agents uniform."

Wynter shook her head, "This one," She pointed at Emma. "is ruled by the mind, if only you would let your heart be in charge, then you would find a way to work things out with Tate."

Emma felt tears spring to her eye's as Winter's words hit her in the face like a cold freezing rain. She shook her head and turned away, leaving Wynter alone at the table.

CHAPTER 44

Tate stared at the GPS system in Emma's car. He'd punched the address for Noah Walker's country home into the system and the machine mapped out the shortest route for him. The early afternoon traffic was light, and before long the freeway disappeared and gave way to two lane traffic; skyscrapers were replaced by forests of trees just filling out with spring growth. Tate thought that in any another situation the drive would have been relaxing, but today he continued to watch the time, marking the miles off in his mind. Gut instinct, he reasoned, "It's always right. Go with it." He pushed the gas pedal a little deeper.

Less than ten miles later, the GPS directed him to turn on a smaller two lane road, this one was topped with white caliche rock and reminded him of some of the county roads around Pine Ridge. Thick stands of trees lined both sides of the small road, their branches reaching out and shading the road, creating a canopy of shadows across the space. He glanced in the rearview mirror and saw a thick layer of white dust billowing behind the Toyota, and slowed the car. "No advance warning." He muttered. He didn't see any houses, or pass any driveways, nothing but woods.

The GPS chimed to signal that he had reached his destination and Tate slowed, but drove past the lone driveway that marked the entrance to the Walker residence. He could see the house about a quarter mile up a hill from the road.

"You'd think he'd have it gated if he were holding kids there against their will. Maybe he thinks he's far enough out that they won't run." Then another thought found its way in. *Maybe they don't want to run.*

He drove another half mile and didn't see any other houses, "No neighbors. Not sure if that's a lucky break or not." He parked the Toyota on the side of the road and got out. He tucked the binoculars into his jacket pocket, calculated the distance and cut a path through the dense woods.

Tate walked in a straight line parallel to what he'd calculated would be the edge of Walkers property. Ten minutes into his walk, he stopped. *Damn.* He heard voices and laughing, *Sounds like the gut instinct wins again.* He trudged on, keeping to the tree line. Fifty feet later he stopped and hunkered down in a patch of dense underbrush, pulled the binoculars out and focused on the back yard of Noah Walkers house.

He watched four girls playing in the yard, two older children picked flowers and two younger blondes chased something that he couldn't see. A woman of about fifty sat on a stone bench with a book. Movement at the northwest corner of the property caught his attention and he turned.

Tate watched a red-haired child of nine or

ten slink along the edge of the yard. *That's got to be the girl from the warehouse, but what's she up to?* He watched her stop at the shed and go inside only to step out seconds later with a small garden spade. The child walked to the back of the shed and propped the tool against the building, she looked around and then the woman called out and she took off.

Tate had seen enough, Noah Walker was just as guilty as Aiden. He jogged down the hill and back to the Toyota. Inside he cursed, "Dammit, I should have snatched that girl. I could have taken her out of there in thirty seconds flat."

He jammed the car in gear and made a three point turn on the small road. He punched the gas, not caring if anyone saw the white fog billowing behind him this time.

When Angels Cry

CHAPTER 45

Gregorio Aiden closed his briefcase, took one last look around his office and saw nothing that mattered any more. He walked out and closed the door behind him. "Jena, I'm catching a late lunch with Congressman Walker and won't be back today. Please forward my calls only if you deem it urgent."

The girl at the desk nodded and watched Aiden enter the elevator.

In the dim parking garage, Gregorio slid into his car and drove ten blocks north. He didn't see the car that had followed him to work this morning. *He must think he's got me where he wants me if he called off the watchdog.* He mused.

After a quick stop at a strip mall where he bought three disposable cell phones, he drove home to wait for Wynter's call. *If she doesn't call by five then Tassie and I are out of here. I won't chase it down, I'll let it go and get the hell out.* He promised.

He jogged up the stairs and peeked around the door jamb at Tassie's door. He smiled when he saw her sitting in front of a three story dollhouse happily placing tiny furniture inside the rooms. Gregorio cleared his throat and she turned around, jumped to her feet and ran. He caught her to him and dropped kisses across her face. She laughed. "You're home!"

He settled the girl on the floor and dropped to one knee. "I am home and tonight I'm taking my favorite girl into the city for dinner." He brushed a stray lock of dark hair from her face.

The child bounced with energy, "That's me! I'm your favorite girl, you always say so." At his nod, she continued, "Can we have pizza? At the place where the man throws the dough? I haven't had pizza in a long time. Mrs. Calder says she doesn't know how to cook it."

Gregorio laughed, "We can have pizza Miss Tassie. I have to grab a quick shower and then I have just a little bit of work to do." He glanced at his watch, "Ask Mrs. Calder to give you a snack, and then you can take a bath and put on your prettiest dress."

"I know just what I'll wear." The little girl beamed. "Love you Daddy." She yelled back, already headed for the stairs.

Gregorio watched her go, and wondered at her joy in such small things as going out to dinner. Was he ever that happy as a child? He turned when he heard a door open. His mother stepped into the hallway.

"Why do you let that child run in the house? You should discipline her more Gregorio, or send her to school where they can teach her to act as a lady should."

He wouldn't let his mother's sour disposition or controlling advice ruin today,

"Perhaps I will send her to school, Mother. We can look into some of the better parochial schools in town next week." He turned and walked to his own room, firmly closing the door behind him. *After today, you won't be disturbed by Tassie, and I doubt that either of us will miss you.*

The small piece of luggage that he'd filled with a minimum of clothing snapped shut with a metallic click and Gregorio placed it near the door. He'd showered and dressed in a pair of worn jeans and a western cut shirt. Staring at the clothes hanging neatly in his closet he frowned. *It's okay, you don't need a closet full of designer business suits where you're going.* He glanced at his watch and jogged downstairs to his office. He poured a drink into a short crystal glass and sat down to wait for Wynter's call.

Across the street in a white van with a cable company logo on the side, the Captain waited. *It's the beginning of the end Mr. Aiden. All I need is the baby that you promised me and then I'll set you free.* He whispered.

CHAPTER 46

"Daddy's home!" Chloe yelled down the stairs. "I just saw his car come up the driveway." She ran down the stairs and stood impatiently at the double doors waiting for him to enter. Nora stood a few feet behind her, equally excited.

Victoria ran from her room and ducked into the room belonging to Allie and Ivy. "He's here." She said. "Remember what I told you. Don't go into his room, no matter what."

Both girls nodded and ran to Victoria when she held her hands out to them. "Now we have to go downstairs and we're going to pretend that we're glad to see him, but it's only *pretend*. You can do that right?"

"Sure we can." Allie said, "It'll be just like when we was in the play at St. A's. We'll pretend real good, won't we Ivy?"

Victoria glanced from one to the other and sucked in a deep breath. *Please God, help us. Sister Camille says you watch over the little children and we really need someone to watch over us now.*

The three girls walked slowly down the stairs and had just reached the landing when the front door opened and Noah Walker entered.

Chloe and Nora immediately wrapped him with hugs and demanded his attention. He knelt and pulled both girls to him. From where his head rested between the two girls he could see the three new comers standing at the bottom of the stairs. He watched the two little blondes and felt his manhood spring to life, he pushed closer to Chloe, and smiled when he felt her hand slide down and cup him. *Tonight little Ivy, tonight we begin a new journey. You will love it.* He silently promised.

Victoria gave a little push to the two girls standing in front of her, "Let's go say hello to Daddy." She said.

Noah stood when the girls approached him and smiled down at the trio. "Hello girls, I'm really glad that you came to welcome me home." He stared at Ivy, "Do you think I could have a hug Ivy?" He asked and held his arms out to the child. Ivy glanced at Victoria and then moved toward the man, he scooped her off her feet and wrapped her in a tight hug. One finger found its way to Ivy's mouth and she drew it in, sensing her hesitance Noah pulled the finger free from her mouth and pulled it to his own. "Let me taste that finger, it looks yummy." He teased. The child laughed and he spun her around, letting his hand cup her bottom as he turned. *Oh yes, Ivy will be so much fun once she gets the hang of the game. And tonight we begin.* He thought. Gently he let one long finger slide between the girl's legs. Caressing her through her clothes while he spun.

"Stop it!" Victoria demanded. She stopped herself and changed tactics. "I mean, you're going to make her sick, Ivy has a very sensitive stomach and she's never allowed to spin at the playground because she throws up."

Noah stopped and looked at Victoria, "That's very good to know Tori. I wouldn't want her to be sick." His glanced flittered across the girls, "We have a party tonight and everyone should be feeling their best." He plucked Ivy down and continued, "Now how about you Allie, do you have a hug for Daddy?"

The blonde stepped behind Victoria and peeked around her at the man, and shook her head. Seeing Noah's surprise and worried that Allie was going to mess things up, Victoria stepped forward, "It's okay Allie. I'm going to give Daddy a hug now, and then it will be your turn."

Noah smiled, "Thank you Tori, it's so important to help your sisters and it really shows me just how grown up you are." Victoria fought the urge to run when he wrapped her in his arms. She forced herself to hug him back and to stand still when he covered her lips with his and shoved his tongue in her mouth. She moved to step away but Noah had other ideas, he pulled Victoria to his side and casually draped and arm around her shoulders, one finger grazed a not quite there yet breast, and he grinned.

"It's fun Allie." Ivy chimed in. "I liked it when he spinned me around and hugged me."

Chloe snatched Allie by the hand and pulled her toward Noah, "We all *like* it when Daddy comes home. Now give him a hug so we can get the party started."

Allie moved into the space in front of Noah and wrapped one arm around Victoria's leg. "Welcome home Daddy." She whispered.

Noah bent and kissed the hesitant little girl on the forehead, "Thank you Allie. Now let's go see what Ms. Anderson has planned for us."

CHAPTER 47

Emma heard the doorbell chime and rushed to pull her shoes on. "I'm coming!" She yelled out. At the doorway to the dining room, she glanced in and saw Wynter still sitting at the table. "Step into the kitchen, just in case it's not Pruitt, we don't want to advertise that you're here." She ordered. Wynter looked surprised but rushed to do as she was told.

At the door, Emma peeked out the window and saw that the caller was indeed Pruitt and that he had two agents with him. She pulled the door wide and said, "Come in. We'll set up in the dining room if that's okay with you. There's room for everyone around the table."

At Pruitt's nod, she led the way. "You've worked with Tolbert and Grimes before Emma?" Pruitt asked.

"It's been a while, but yes." She glanced at the two men and said, "Thanks for coming to help guys. Now what do you need for the set up?" She asked.

Tolbert, appropriately labeled a techno-geek at the office, grinned at her, "Phone line and an electrical outlet should do it Emma." He pushed his large wire glasses up on his nose and shifted his blue canvas bag to the other shoulder before extended a hand to Emma.

"We've got both near the table. Make yourself at home." She pointed through the open doorway. The men opened the blue canvas bags that they carried and began setting up their equipment for the call.

Wynter stared through the open doorway and watched the men in Emma's kitchen. *Please don't let me mess this up.* She thought. *This could be my only chance to get Itasca back.*

Emma saw Wynter watching the men and knew that she was nervous. She smiled at her and waved her into the room. "Gentleman," she started, "this is Wynter Burgland. She's our witness and will be making the call." Both men looked up from their work and smiled at Wynter. Emma felt no need to further explain that Wynter had been the actual shooter that night at the warehouse. *Need to know only.* She reminded herself.

"Nice to meet you ma'am." Slade Tolbert said. "If you have any questions about all of this, then be sure to ask before we start the call process."

Wynter stepped hesitantly into the room, "Emma has already explained what will be done and I think I am ready. I just want this to be over." She slipped into a chair and watched the men work.

Emma folded her arms across her chest and glanced nervously out the window. *Where are you Tate?*

"So did you reach any conclusions with the review of the guest list?" Pruitt asked, noticing that Emma looked worried.

"Yes and maybe." Emma unfolded her arms and let them drop to her sides. "Tate should be back any minute now, and I'd rather wait..."

A car door slammed outside and Emma returned to the window, "He's here now." She watched Tate walk across the yard and up the rear steps of the house. He entered the crowded dining room, locked eyes with Emma and gave her a barely perceptible nod.

Her confidence renewed, Emma confirmed, "We do have another suspect that should be part of the sting, and you're not going to like this one."

Pruitt raised an eyebrow at her, "Go on." He ordered.

"The only match we found on the comparison of the spreadsheet and guest list was Virginia Congressman, Noah Walker."

The room went still, all eye's turned to Pruitt. He cleared his throat and measured his words, "You are certain that Walker is part of this trafficking ring? I don't have to tell you that there is absolutely no room for error with this accusation."

Tate stepped forward, "I'm one hundred percent positive sir. I just came back from Walkers house in the country, and while I was there I personally observed five underage girls on the premises."

"Go on." Pruitt urged.

"One of them is Victoria McEvers. I was close enough to confirm her identity based on the pictures that were shown on the news. I also saw two young blondes that I believe to be Allie Barrow and Ivy Tambrey, I wasn't close enough to positively identify them."

"And the other two girls? Do you have a make on them as well?"

"No sir. They appear to be somewhere between the ages of ten and thirteen, but I don't know who they are. There was a woman there as well, late forties, early fifties, she appeared to be the nanny."

Wynter spoke up, "She was tall and big boned with streaks of gray in her hair and she wore glasses?"

Tate looked at Wynter with amazement, "Exactly. You described her to a T."

All eyes turned to Wynter, "She is the woman who drove the car away from the warehouse the night that Emma was shot."

Emma moved to Wynter's side and rested one hand on the other woman's shoulder, "That's true. I saw her but couldn't have described her as well as Wynter did. I was pretty busy trying not to get shot."

Pruitt rubbed a hand over his face, "This

is going to get really messy and soon." He turned
to Tate, "At your suggestion, I have four teams
set to enter the warehouses owned by Benito
Corporation at seven tonight, we need the
meeting with Aiden to happen between six thirty
and seven thirty, and now we need a team to hit
the congressman's house as close to the same
time as possible."

"Gregorio...ah, Mr. Aiden," Wynter spoke
up, "He knows that I don't have a car and he
told me to take the baby home with me. I think
he will expect to pick the child up at my
apartment." She pulled a worried lip between
her teeth, "He is supposed to bring my daughter,
Itasca. That was our trade, he would get the
baby and I would be allowed to see Tassie."
Wynter pushed back from the table and stood, "I
can't do this! What if Tassie is hurt?"

"Sit down, Ms. Burgland." Pruitt ordered.
"Not only can you do this, but you will follow
through as we've already discussed." He
softened his voice, "I give you my word that we
will take every precaution to protect your child
during the arrest."

Tolbert and Grimes had finished with the
phone line and call capturing equipment and
joined the others at the table. Pruitt turned to
the two men, "All set up?" At their nod, he
continued speaking to the group, "My original
plan was for myself, Tate and Emma to be at the
drop and pull Aiden in, however, with the raid
expanding to include Walkers home, and we'll
need additional man power. Tolbert, Grimes, I'll

need the two of you stationed at the drop with Ms. Burgland."

Wynter jumped to her feet and interrupted Pruitt, "You can't be serious? You're sending the telephone repairman to protect me and my daughter? That is not..." She stopped when the room erupted with laughter.

Emma was the first to speak, "Wynter, these men," she pointed to the two men across from her, "are not telephone repairmen, they are trained and *armed* FBI field agents. Any one of them is more than capable of protecting you and Itasca and the two of them together will provide more than enough fire power to take Aiden down *and* protect your daughter."

A slow red flush crept up Wynter's face and she looked at the two men with renewed interest, "I'm sorry." She apologized. "I didn't know. I just thought..." Her words trailed off.

Grimes grinned at Wynter and teased, "It's okay ma'am. We get mistaken for phone repairmen all the time, but like Emma said, we are trained and armed. We won't let anything happen to you or your daughter tonight."

Pruitt forced his way back into the conversation, "As I was saying, Grimes and Tolbert will shadow Ms. Burgland, and take Aiden down when he arrives. There is no need to wait for him to admit to anything. We have the flash drive and we'll have the phone conversation as evidence. Tate, I want you on the perimeter as backup. If Aiden does show up with her daughter," He nodded at Wynter, "then your primary function is to secure the child, get her out of there and to a safe place. Emma will go with me to Walker's house. I'll have a team of three additional agents meet us there as well. Now, let's get this party started." He looked at Wynter, "You ready to make the call?"

CHAPTER 48

Gregorio smiled when the phone on his desk rang. "Right on time." He picked the handset up and answered, "Aiden here."

Wynter stalled, her panic stricken face flew around the table in Emma's dining room. She cleared her throat, "It's me." She squeaked.

"Of course it's you Wynter, and just in time too. If I'd had to wait much longer I might have been tempted to change our agreement. You do have what I asked you for, right?"

She faltered, "Yes, I have the baby you asked me to get, but Gregorio, I beg you, please don't do this....it's wro..."

He cut her off, the harshness of his voice bellowed into the room, "I don't need a lecture from you. If you want to see your daughter, then shut up and listen."

Pruitt nodded at her and Wynter whispered, "Okay, I'm listening."

"I trust that you took it home with you as I instructed?" He questioned.

"Yes. I did exactly what you told me to do, but please..."

"Enough!" His voice thundered. "I will be by to pick it up at six forty five, so make sure that it is well cared for until then. My client expects a healthy and well cared for child." The phone clicked and the call disconnected.

Gregorio stood and refilled his glass. He flinched when the phone rang again. "Aiden here." He answered.

"Do you have my delivery Aiden?" The deep male voice questioned but didn't wait for an answer. "It's not a good thing to make me wait, you know."

Gregorio sat his glass on the desk and pinched the bridge of his nose, "I will have it for you tonight. I've already confirmed the pick-up and everything is in place." His voice dropped, "Now let me give you some advice. Don't threaten me. One phone call and you're ruined, so back off."

The man's laughter sounded hollow even through the phone lines and Gregory shuddered. Tossing threats with this man was not a game that he wanted to play. "Meet me at the warehouse on the riverfront at nine and don't shoot your mouth off Aiden, we both know that you can't touch me, not without implicating yourself." Captain disconnected the call and smiled. *You'll never make it to the warehouse Aiden. All I have to do is follow you to the drop, take what's mine, and leave you drowning in your own blood.*

Gregorio downed his drink, opened his desk drawer and stuffed his and Itasca's passports into his briefcase, he pushed them under the nine millimeter Ruger that he hoped he wouldn't need. He left his office and jogged up the stairs to his room where he retrieved the bag that he'd packed earlier and went back downstairs. Mrs. Calder had left Tassie's packed bag in the laundry room just off the massive kitchen. Her favorite doll sat next to the small pink suitcase, and he picked them both up and exited to the garage, where he dumped everything into the trunk of the car.

He returned to the house and climbed the stairs. At least he could say goodbye to his mother. He knocked lightly on her door and entered without waiting for permission. "I'm taking Tassie into town for pizza tonight and I wanted to say goodbye since we might not return before you go to bed."

He bent and kissed her on the cheek, and almost changed his mind about leaving. She was old and she had no one else. *You can't stay...you don't even want to stay.* He thought, scolding himself for feeling sentimental towards the woman who criticized him at every turn.

"You should be spending the evening with a beautiful woman, not that child Gregorio. How will you find a suitable wife if you don't even try?" Theresa Navarone scolded.

"I don't have time to argue the fine points of marriage with you tonight Mother. I hope that you have a pleasant evening. Goodnight." *And goodbye.* Gregorio turned and left the room. He crossed the hall and popped his head inside the door of Itasca's room. "You ready Sweetheart?"

Itasca ran to the door and grabbed him by

the hand, "Come on! I'm ready for my pizza."

Gregorio laughed and allowed the child to pull him down the hall and the stairs.

CHAPTER 49

Tate drove Emma's car and Wynter rode with him to her apartment, Grimes and Tolbert followed in a federally issued sedan. At the complex, Tate waited for the two men to park down the block and return to escort Wynter to her apartment. Once they were safely inside the building, Tate parked the Toyota across the street so that he had a good view of the complex. He saw a light come on in a second story window and assumed that to be Wynter's apartment. When she crossed to the window and opened the blinds, he relaxed. *Now we wait.* He glanced at his watch and slid down in the seat.

Thirty minutes passed before a blue BMW pulled into the parking area. Tate watched as Gregory Aiden stepped out of the car. He saw the man open the rear door and bent down to talk to someone. Tate frowned, he couldn't see anyone in the back seat but if it were a small child that Aiden were talking to, he shouldn't expect to see a head through the rear window. *The bastard actually brought his kid with him while he's committing a felony.* Tate was livid. *Is he that confident or just that stupid?* He wondered.

Tate figured that he had at least forty five seconds once Aiden entered the building before the man climbed the stairs, and reached Wynter's apartment. He wanted the kid out of that car and safely in his own in case Aiden somehow managed to get away and make it back to the car. He silently counted the seconds in his

head and when he reached thirty his hand
moved to the door handle of the Toyota.

Tate had just opened the car door when a
white van with a cable company logo made the
turn into the parking lot and slid into the spot
next to Aiden's BMW. Tate pulled the door closed
just enough that the interior lights went off. He
watched a tall blonde man jump down from the
driver's seat. *He looks familiar. I know I've seen
that guy before? The warehouse? No, that's not
right.* Then it clicked. "Shit. Clay Shuler should
not be here." Tate raised the console between the
bucket seats and slid across to the passenger
side of the car; he quietly opened the door and
got out. *I should have known that he was the
leak. Should have trusted my instinct when we
first met. He doesn't show up when Em is shot,
he's too friendly and the only witness in the case
conveniently had a heart attack after meeting
with him.* Tate hunkered behind the door and
watched Shuler exit the van, and enter the
building. As soon as the door closed behind him,
Tate ran. He didn't stop at the BMW, the child
was safer in the car than Wynter was in her own
apartment with two FBI agents to protect her.

Tate opened the exterior door and entered
a dimly lit hallway. He pressed his back against
the wall and listened. He heard the man's
footsteps ascending the stairs. *He's not in any
hurry.* Tate thought. He pressed his back to the
wall and side stepped his way up the stairs
behind the man.

Sixty miles away, Emma and Pruitt cut a

trail through the wood on the north side of Walkers house, while three additional agents entered the property from the south side. They were almost an hour late arriving at the site because an accident on the freeway had blocked traffic for miles. With no way around, they'd been forced to wait along with all the other impatient motorists. Darkness covered them and without the night vision goggles they each sported, they would have been walking blind over the rough landscape. Emma and Pruitt hunkered down just outside the perimeter of the yard.

Emma lifted a pair of Steiner tactical binoculars and focused on the house, "He's here. I just saw him pass the kitchen doors." Pruitt spoke quietly into the microphone attached to his collar and conveyed Emma's finding to the rest of the team.

Pruitt ordered everyone to hold their positions and wait for the house to go dark. Now that they knew Walker was in the house, he felt it would be safer for the children if they waited until it was lights out at Walker Farm before they approached. The primary concern was to get the children out safely, and then to arrest Walker and his female accomplice without incident. "We wait." He whispered to Emma. "Everyone is in place, and we're ready to go when the time is right."

CHAPTER 50

"That was an amazing dinner girls and I love the project that you did this week. The flowers and ribbons just made you look even more beautiful than you usually do." Noah Walker leaned back on the sofa in the family room. He couldn't help but notice that the little girls were following whatever lead that Victoria gave them. If she engaged in conversation, then they did as well; if she were silent, so were they. He chalked it up to their newness at the house, but he didn't change his plans for the night. Ivy would sleep with him, of that he was certain.

"Are we going to play a game tonight Daddy?" Nora asked.

Noah yawned, "I don't think so Nora, it's getting late. I had a really busy day at the office and," He yawned again, "I think we'll turn in early and tomorrow we'll have lots of time together."

Chloe slid closer to him on the couch and he wrapped one arm around her shoulders, and pulled her close. She whispered something in his car and Noah shook his head. "Not tonight Chloe, if I recall, you were the chosen one last week." Chloe stuck her lips out in a pout and scooted away from Noah. He noticed her pout and the cold stare that she gave him. *That's the way it goes and Chloe and Nora will both just have to get used to sharing.* Noah thought.

Jeri considered this her queue to get the

girls ready for bed, "Time to get ready for bed girls. Chloe, come into the kitchen for a minute, I want to show you something. The rest of you, go on up and get your pj's on and I'll be up to check on you in just a few minutes."

"I'll stop in after my shower to say goodnight to each of you as well." Noah said. *I'll say goodnight and pick up my little snuggle bear for the night.* He thought.

Jeri waited until the girls turned for the stairs and then she pulled Chloe aside. "Chloe, I don't want you pouting because you're not the chosen one tonight. You know that everyone gets their special night with Daddy, and it's selfish of you not to want to share with your sisters."

Chloe jerked her arm free from Jeri's grasp, "Those brats are not my sisters and I hate them all, especially that red-headed witch! I'm the oldest here now and I they should be asking me for permission, just like we used to have to ask Bethany. I hope they all fall out the window just like she did."

"Chloe, you don't mean that!" Jeri admonished. "You know that as the oldest Walker girl you have a responsibility to take care of the younger girls."

Chloe cut her off, "Me and Nora talked about it, and we don't need all these babies here. Me and her are the only true Walker girls and we're not sharing Daddy with anyone else. Those three are just brats that needed a home. Tori doesn't want to be here, let her go back to her mother or wherever she came from. She can take her sister's with her. We Don't Want Them Here!"

"Stop it." Jeri ordered. "You will go to your room now and get ready for bed. I will not permit you to upset Daddy on his weekend at home. Either you follow the house rules or you will be punished. I doubt that's what you want."

Looking down at her feet, Chloe bit back her reply and let out a long and frustrated breath. "Fine. I will go to my room." She turned away from Jeri and headed to the stairway. *I do hope they fall out the window and I might just help them if I get the chance.* She thought. After all, why should she have to share her Daddy with them, wasn't it enough that she'd always shared with Bethany and Nora? *I am the oldest now and I will make sure that those girls know it and follow my rules, or else.*

CHAPTER 51

Victoria cornered Allie and Ivy at the top of the stairs. "Grab your pajamas and come in my room. If anybody asks you about it, tell them that you're afraid you'll have another bad dream. Bring your shoes with you too."

The girls nodded and rushed to do as Victoria instructed.

In her own room, Victoria waited until the younger girls returned. "We are leaving." She whispered to them. *I should have left when he wasn't here, now I have to worry about two people chasing us instead of one. Maybe three if the man who works in the garden is at home.*

"Do we put our pajamas on now Victoria?" Allie asked.

"No, didn't you hear me? We're leaving. Put your shoes on, and be sure you tie them good, because we are going to have to run." She pulled the girls close and whispered to them. "As soon as Ms. Anderson comes upstairs, we go downstairs. I'm going to get us out of here and we'll find a place to get help."

The girls stared at her with wide eyes, "It's dark outside Victoria. I don't like the dark." Ivy said.

"I'll be with you Ivy, and you don't have anything to be afraid of outside. In this house, you have everything to be afraid of. I need you to be brave because we *are* leaving. All of us. Now hush so that I can hear."

Victoria leaned against the door jamb and pulled the door open a crack. She saw Noah walk down the hallway and into his room, and Ms. Anderson followed a few seconds later, turning into her own room. Victoria flicked the light off in her room and pulled Allie and Ivy by the hand. "Be very quiet. Not one word." She ordered then slipped out the door and ran, pulling the girls with her.

Victoria didn't slow down at the bottom of the stairs, she turned toward the kitchen. She could hear Ivy or Allie or maybe both of them whimpering. She pushed them in front of her to the kitchen sink, "Stay here and don't move." She rummaged inside a cabinet and found it. The porcelain coated, cast iron skillet was heavy and she lifted it with two hands. "Now listen to me. Stop crying and listen. This is important. I'm going to break the door and when I do, the alarm is going to go off. It's going to be very loud but that's okay. As soon as you hear the ringing, you come to the door, but be careful, don't touch anything with your hands because there's going to be glass, okay?"

Both girls bobbed their matching blonde heads and Allie popped a finger in her mouth. "I'm scared Victoria." She whimpered.

Victoria squatted in front of the two girls and gave them a quick hug. "I'm scared too, Allie, but we have to go. If we don't get out of this house, very bad things are going to happen to us all. I've tried to wait to for help, but I don't think anyone is coming to help us. We've got to help ourselves, before it too late. Remember, when the alarm rings, run to the door, I'll be waiting for you and I'll make sure you get out safe."

CHAPTER 52

At the top of the stairs, Tate stopped at the corner, where the stairs and the hallway intersected, and waited. He didn't hear Shuler moving and he hadn't heard him knock on Wynter's door. *He's waiting for Aiden to come out. Dammit, Grimes and Tolbert are going to open the door and walk right into him. I've got to stop him before that happens.*

Tate turned the corner, his gun leading the way and at the same time, the apartment door opened. He saw Aiden being propelled out the door and he saw the man at the end of the hall take a step back and raise his weapon. The two men in the hall fired at the same time. Tate's aim was true and the man at the end of the hallway went down; so did Aiden. Somewhere in the distance he heard Wynter scream.

Tate ran to the mess in front of Wynter's door, he yelled, "Two men down out here. Someone call an ambulance!"

"Is that you Echo?" Grimes yelled from inside the apartment.

"Affirmative and get me some help out here. Now!" Tate ordered.

Tate rolled Aiden over onto his back, the man was still alive but barely, "Tassie?" He gurgled around the blood pooling in his mouth.

Grimes looked at the other shooter; he was in a sitting position, his back against the wall. The man's head hung at an unnatural angle and a small round bullet wound on his forehead seeped blood. "He's dead." Grimes confirmed. "You know him?"

Tate looked up and nodded, "That's your leak. The bastard." He turned back to Aiden. "Shuler was your partner? Right? Answer me, dammit." He demanded.

Aiden's eye's widened, "Clay Shuler, yes...partner...Captain..." he struggled with the words, "but Tassie?" His body jerked and his eyes closed. He was gone.

The apartment door opened a crack and Tolbert stuck his head out. "We all clear?"

Tate nodded, "Escort Wynter down to the parking lot. Her daughter's in the back seat of a blue BMW parked next to a white van. Keep them both there until this mess is cleaned up, especially the kid."

CHAPTER 53

Emma stared at the house through the binoculars, "Three lights remaining sir. All upstairs, probably bedrooms." Emma dropped the binoculars and made eye contact with her SAC. He gave her a rare smile. He was a quiet man, but she'd never worked with anyone more capable of leading a team of agents through a mission. He took his job seriously and made it his personal mission to ensure the safety of everyone on the team. He thought before he acted, considered the options and the repercussions of his actions, and Emma hoped that one day she would be more like him.

Pruitt spoke quietly to the rest of the team, "Two minutes and counting."

Turns out that they didn't need two minutes, because thirty seconds later, all hell broke loose. From where she sat hunkered in the trees, Emma heard the sound of glass breaking and immediately the house alarm sounded, the ear splitting sound pierced into the quiet night. *What was that?* She thought she saw something move in the yard but it disappeared so quickly that she wasn't sure.

"Go now!" Pruitt yelled as he and Emma cleared the woods and entered the yard.

Emma reached the back door just as a shirtless Noah Walker stepped outside. She pushed him against the cool brick façade of the house and pointed her gun at him. "Turn around and don't move." When he'd complied, she continued, "Noah Walker, you are under arrest..." She saw Pruitt move past them and enter the house.

"Do you know who I am? You can't just come into my home this way." Noah thundered.

Emma slapped the cuffs on his wrists and turned him around. "I know who you are, and I know *what* you are too. Sit down and don't move." She shoved him and he slid down, coming to rest with his butt on the sidewalk.

Noah twisted and tried to stand, "Uncuff me now!" He ordered. "I am an honored member of the Virginia Congress and I refuse to be treated in such a manner. What the hell are you doing here anyway?"

One of the three man team that had come into the yard from the side opposite Emma and Pruitt, approached. Emma pointed at Walker and ordered. "Keep an eye on him and if he moves even a little, shoot him."

Emma stepped over the broken glass at the kitchen door and entered the house, she moved through the kitchen and into the foyer just as two agents escorted the woman from the warehouse down the stairs, they were followed closely by Pruitt who led two girls by the hand. The taller of the two struggled against him, trying to break away.

"Where are the others?" Emma asked.

"We're clear up here. No one else in the house." Pruitt said.

Emma stopped in front of the two girls, she spoke to the older of the pair. "What's your name? Do you know where the other girls are? Ivy? Allie? Or Victoria?"

The lady of the house twisted against the agents grip, "Do not say a word Chloe. Not one word. Daddy will take care of this...this... mistake."

Without taking her eyes from the girl, Emma jerked her head toward Jeri and ordered, "Get her out of here. Put her outside with her partner."

Emma struggled to keep her voice soft and tried again, "We know that the other girls were here earlier today. Where are they now Chloe?"

The child turned her head and refused to look at Emma. Refusing to give up, Emma turned to the other child. "Will you tell me your name? Do you understand that we are the FBI? The police? We're here to help you. Please, if you know anything about the missing girls, tell me."

Her lower lip trembled but the girl didn't look away. "My name is Nora and the other girls were here just a little bit ago...we all went to our rooms to get ready for bed, and they were here then."

"Shut up Nora! Just shut up!" Chloe demanded. "I told you that they are not our family! They will never be our sisters. Wherever they went, just let them go. I hope they get lost and never come back!"

"Shit, that must be what I saw run across the yard when the alarm sounded. You'll take care of these two?" Emma questioned Pruitt, asking for his permission to resume the search. At his nod, Emma ran through the kitchen and into the back yard. She followed the stone pathway through the garden and stopped near the pond. "Victoria McEvers!" She called, "Victoria! This is Emma Gage-Echo with the FBI, if you're out here honey, it's okay, you can come out. We're here to help you."

Twenty yards away Emma saw movement, a flash of red. The little girl stepped through the tall reeds surrounding the pond, her pants legs were soaked up to the knees; she'd been standing in the pond. Emma opened her arms and the child launched herself into them.

"I remember you. You were at the warehouse, you tried to save us. That man shot you...he shot you!" Tears ran down the child's face. "I remember you." She cried, "I remember." She wrapped her arms around Emma's neck and held on.

Emma pulled back, "Honey, do you know where the other girls are? Ivy and Allie?" At the girls nod, Emma continued, "Can you show me?"

Victoria led Emma around the pond and into the gazebo. She lifted the bench seat and Emma stared down at two curly haired blonde children huddled in the small compartment. Gently she lifted them out. She pulled her shirt tail free from her slacks and used it to wipe their tear stained faces. "It's okay now, you're going to be okay, I promise."

One of the girls looked up at Emma, she wasn't sure which one, and said, "Victoria saved us. She broke the door and made us hide 'cause Daddy is a bad man."

Emma brushed a hand over the girl's curls, "Victoria is very brave. You all are."

I have something for you. Victoria said. She unzipped the cushion and pulled Beth Ann Cooper's journal from inside and handed it to Emma. Her name was Beth Ann and she jumped from the window," she pointed, "right over there.

They took her away in the garden cart and told us she went to the hospital, but she didn't." Victoria choked back a sob, "She died and no one even called 911, they just rolled her in a blanket and drove her away and into the woods."

"Oh honey, I'm so sorry that you had to see that, but it's going to be okay now. He won't ever hurt another child. I promise you that...I promise you that."

CHAPTER 54

By the time that Emma returned to the house with the three girls, Walker and Anderson were safely tucked away in separate vehicles. Pruitt wanted to question them separately and he wasn't giving them any opportunity to talk with each other. Nora and Chloe were at the kitchen table with an agent, while they waited for Social Services to arrive. Emma insisted that it was better to keep Allie, Ivy and Victoria away from the other girls based on the angry outburst from Chloe. Clearly they did not fit in with the rest of the house, and thankfully they had been found before they could learn to be part of the family. She sat on the stone bench in the garden with Ivy held securely on her lap and Victoria and Allie snuggled on either side of her.

Pruitt had already called in a team of agents to take the house apart, brick by brick, if necessary, to find any relevant evidence that would strengthen their case. They'd arrived a few minutes ago and started the process in Walker's office, beginning with his computer and a collection of photo albums, both digital and printed.

"Em?"

Emma looked up at the sound of Tate's voice. "No, don't get up." He bent to kiss the top of her head, and then squatted in front of her and the girls.

"Tate, I'm so glad to see you. Did everything

work out at Wynter's?" Emma questioned.

"It's all over. We can talk more about it later, but right now, I have Pruitt's authorization to take you and the girls out of here. The team will be here for hours and there's no reason that you beautiful ladies should be stuck here until they finish."

At this, Victoria looked up. "Are we going back to St. A's?"

Tate grinned at the child, "Not tonight. Tonight we're all going to stay together at a hotel in town." He tipped his head at Emma. "SAC Pruitt, that's Emma's boss, is going to have some questions for you three, but not until you've had a good night's rest. Is that okay with you, Victoria?"

"I want to go to St. A's, my mom..." The child's face crumpled and she started to cry. "He told me my mom was dead, he said she was run over by a taxi. Is she? Do you know?"

"Oh sweetie, don't cry." Emma pulled her close. "I happen to know that your mother is fine. SAC Pruitt received a call from the office a bit ago letting him know that they had located your mother and assured her that you were safe."

Large eyes peered up at Emma, "I knew he was lying...I knew it!"

Tate held a hand out to Victoria, "Let's go now. Em and I will take really good care of you girls tonight and everything else will be worked out tomorrow. You'll see."

Once the girls were secured in the backseat of her car, Emma excused herself. "I'm just going to grab a few essentials from the house for the girls. A change of clothes and a toothbrush."

Minutes later they were moving down the long driveway and Tate reached over to clasp Emma's hand in his. "We did good today, Em."

She glanced in the rear seat at the three little girls and nodded, "Yes we did Chief Echo. I'm so glad that you were here through all of this."

He squeezed her hand, "Wouldn't have it any other way."

At the bottom of the driveway, a circus of media cars and van's vied for position. Some half-dozen cameramen raced forward and tried to snap pictures of them as they exited the driveway. Tate slowed and made the turn onto the white rock road and then accelerated beyond their camera's reach.

Less than half way from Walker Farm to Richmond, the girls had fallen asleep in the rear seat of Emma's car. Glancing back at them and certain they were not going to overhear him, Tate had filled Emma in on what had happened at Wynter's apartment.

"I can't believe it!" Emma said. "Shuler? How could scum like that get named to lead a child trafficking taskforce?"

"I understand he was just in it for the money, but who knows." Tate said, "What really bothers me is that he left you hanging out to dry at the warehouse that night on purpose."

Emma pursed her lips but said nothing.

"He wanted Navarro to kill you Em, and he almost did."

"So are you saying I told you so?"

"No," Tate said. "I'm just glad he didn't succeed." He squeezed her hand.

An hour later, the girls were safely tucked in a king-sized bed together, their hair, a mass of blonde and red, hid the pillows beneath them. "What do you think will happen to them now?" Tate asked Emma.

Emma took a seat and began pulling her boots off. "I don't know about Allie and Ivy, I suppose that they will go back to St. A's, or some other place like it. Pruitt says that Victoria will be released to her mother in less than a week. She completed her drug abuse training, went through some serious counseling and has had a job for a month now."

Tate wasn't too happy with the answer, but he nodded. "Go grab a shower Em. We can get a few hours' rest before morning. Tomorrow's going to be a long day sorting this out. I'm going to call home and check on things while you shower."

Tate was stretched out on the bed when

Emma returned from her shower, the television droned quietly in the background. "News spreads fast." He told her as he flipped to CNN just in time to see a picture of the good congressman flash on the screen.

"I know. I'm worried about that too. I mean, how's it going to be for the girls now? I can just picture some reporter sneaking around the orphanage and trying to catch an interview with one of them."

Tate patted the bed next to him and Emma dropped down and rested her head on his shoulder. One hand slid across and she rested her palm against his heart.

The room went dark when Tate flipped the television off. "Don't worry about it tonight Em. I'm sure Pruitt's thought of that too, and together, we'll come up with something to keep them safe."

Tate and Emma slept without moving until morning when whispers and giggles from the next room woke Tate.

"Time to rise and shine." He whispered against Emma's ear and dropped a kiss on her cheek.

Emma rolled to her back and Tate sat up on the side of the bed. He smiled when he saw three heads peaking around the corner at him. The smallest child spoke first.

"You snore, Mister." Giggles erupted into

the room.

Trying to keep a straight face, Tate said, "Of course I snore. After all, at night, I'm a great big grizzly bear. Arhhhh!!" He roared and rose from the bed.

Screams and laughter filled the room as the three girls ran back to their bed and hid under the covers.

He turned on Emma. "And now, Chief Grizzly Bear is going to steal a kiss from the lovely Agent Echo." He jumped at her, but Emma spun away from him and quickly pinned him to the bed.

"Okay, Chief Grizzly, here's your kiss." She moved over him and slowly sucked his lower lip between her teeth, teasing him, before kissing him full on. "Now that the morning kiss is out of the way, I'm going to help the girls get dressed. How about you order up some breakfast for us? We've got a long day of questions and Pruitt is expecting us in his office in less than two hours."

"Yes ma'am, Agent Echo. A kiss like that will get you just about anything you want."

More laughter and giggles from the adjoining room.

CHAPTER 55

An hour and forty five minutes later, Tate and Emma escorted the girls into a conference room where SAC Pruitt waited for them.

"Come in and have a seat please, and we'll get started." Pruitt gestured to the large conference table situated in the center of the room.

There was a man already seated at the table. "Emma, I believe that you know Garrett Preston from the Department of Justice." He nodded toward the man at the table. "Garrett, this is Tate Echo, current police chief of Pine Ridge, South Dakota and previously a Bureau agent. We also have a couple of representatives from the Department of Social Services in an outer room. We'll ask them to join us after the initial interviews have been completed."

Emma nodded at Preston, she had met him when she first joined the task force. He was Clay Shuler's boss. Taking a seat, Emma pulled Ivy into her lap and Allie clung to Tate. Victoria took a seat between them.

Tate turned to the children. "Girls, these are the good guys. They work with Emma and need to ask you some questions. Is that okay?" All three nodded solemnly.

Allie and Ivy had very little information. They were just too young to understand exactly what had happened to them. After just a few questions, Pruitt called a female associate in and had the younger girls removed to a visitor's room, allowing them to watch television while the interrogation continued.

Gently, Pruitt spoke to Victoria. "Victoria, please tell me everything that you can remember about the night that you were taken from St. Anthony's."

She nodded, "The man that drove the ambulance came into our dorm room and told us that Sister Camille had sent him to get us. He said that we were getting new parents and had to go with him. He picked Ivy up and we just followed him."

"Go on." Emma encouraged.

"I didn't want to go, and when he went down the stairs to the basement I knew that we shouldn't go, but he had Ivy and when I tried to tell him to leave us alone, he said that if we made any noise, that he would hurt her...I didn't know what else to do."

Fat tears pooled in the child's eyes. "You did the right thing." Tate said. "Tell us the rest of what you remember." His heart broke for the child, but he knew that getting the whole story was a necessary evil if they wanted to build a strong case.

Victoria took them from the shooting at the warehouse, to the bitter apple juice when she first arrived at Walker Farm, the story about her mother being run over by a taxi, how she hid in the closet and overheard the plan to send Bethany to Texas, her talk with the older girl and her death. She told how she saw them roll the body in a blanket and load her in a garden cart, how she'd planned their escape. In the end her body shook with tears, and she was exhausted and drained.

Emma gave the girl a quick hug. "You did good sweetie. How about you join the other girls for a little bit and then we'll come and get you. Tate will show you where they are."

SAC Pruitt leaned back in his chair, "Just heartbreaking. I am so happy that you and Tate were able to find them before they were brainwashed like the other girls. I'm not sure that those two will ever be children again. I sent a team out first thing this morning with a cadaver dog and before this meeting began, they had recovered the body of Beth Ann Cooper, and one other. We don't have an identity on the second body, but it was clearly a young female. I hope to God that there are no more."

Garrett Preston had been silent during Victoria's statement, but spoke now. "I have a hard time understanding how Clay Shuler became involved in all this. There was no indication that he was anything but a good agent...a good man. I have a team looking through his financial data, as well a team at his house in case there's additional evidence there." He turned to Pruitt, "I believe I have everything that I need to close my case." To Emma, he continued, "We'd be more than happy to have you continue your work with our team, Agent Echo. Sad, but there are still more traffickers out there. We stop one and there are two more waiting to take his place. Give me a call and we can talk about that further."

Pruitt and Emma reviewed all the information they had, beginning with the night she was shot and working through to the prior night, when Walker had been captured. A woman in a blue three piece suit with a badge clipped to her jacket sat in one corner, recording the questions and answers that flew around the room. Thirty minutes later, Wynter joined the group in Pruitt's office and added her side of the story. She'd turned over the gun that she'd taken from Quinto and Pruitt had rushed it off to the lab to confirm that it was indeed the gun that Emma had been shot with.

In the end, Pruitt cautioned Wynter about taking the law into her own hands, gave her a business card, and told her that if she ever found herself in trouble that she could call him directly. Wynter walked out a free woman, with no threat of jail time and she had her daughter.

She stopped to hug both Tate and Emma in the small office. "I can't find the words to tell you how much you mean to me. Both of you." She looked between them, "Because of you, I can live without being afraid and I have my daughter." She glanced down at Tassie, and then gave them both another hug. "If you ever need a favor Emma Gage-Echo, you can count on me."

Tate and Emma watched her walk away, Tassie chattered up at her and Wynter smiled down at her daughter.

Tate, at Pruitt's request, escorted the ladies from Social Services into the conference room, behind them Emma spotted a familiar face.

"Karlee!" Emma exclaimed. Tate's mother rushed forward and folded Emma into an embrace.

Emma stepped back, "What are you doing here? Tate?"

Tate grinned and winked at Emma and his mother before pulling two chairs out for the ladies from Social Services.

An hour and a half later, the officials from Social Services had agreed to leave Victoria with Emma for the next week, until her mother was released from the rehab facility.

Special arrangements were made that allowed Karlee to take Allie and Ivy to South Dakota, where they would be fostered in the elder Echo's home for an undetermined time frame. Jackson Pruitt had made it clear that not only would the children be targeted by the media, but that there were concerns for their physical safety if they were remanded to any facility or foster home in the state of Virginia.

"Consider it a safe house. Witness protection for the children." Tate said, addressing the two women. "Karlee and my father have been fostering children for years and are certified."

The arrangements were finalized and Pruitt agreed to present the paperwork allowing the children to be transported out of state to a judge before the end of the day.

"We should have all the necessary documents ready by tomorrow morning, and your mother," Pruitt looked at Tate, "can leave with the girls as soon as she wants."

Karlee and Emma both stood and one by one, reached to shake hands with the women and with Pruitt.

"Now let me see those baby girls!" Karlee exclaimed.

The car ride to Emma's house was a happy one. The girls giggled and laughed at Tate's impression of various animals, including the bear that they'd met that morning.

Ivy snuggled next to Karlee, "Do you have animals at your house?" She asked shyly.

"I sure do, sweet girl, and you will get to meet them all very soon. You and Allie will love South Dakota."

Allie frowned and questioned, "What about Victoria, isn't she coming with us?"

Situated in the middle, Victoria clasped hands with the two younger girls. "My mom is coming to get me next week. I can't go with you this time, she's going to need me and it's my job to be there, and to help her. You know, like she took care of me when I was little."

Fat tears rolled down Allie's face. She lifted her eyes and looked at Victoria. "I love you Victoria."

The little red-head pulled the girl in a tight hug, "Love you too. Always will."

Tate maneuvered the car into the driveway at Emma's house and the group filed into the house. The girls would have this one last night all together and Emma was determined to make it a good one.

"Girls, I'm just too tired to cook. How about we call for pizza delivery!" Emma exclaimed and was rewarded with gleeful shouts all around.

CHAPTER 56

Karlee and the girls boarded a plane at three in the next afternoon. Victoria, Tate and Emma waved them off. Tate promised to stop by and check on the girls as soon as he returned home, and Emma promised to call regularly. The drive home was quiet but happy. They'd stopped at an outlet mall where Emma bought Victoria enough clothes to fill a closet of her own.

"That was sweet of you." Tate whispered in Emma's ear. "It's going to be hard enough on her mom getting out of rehab and finding a place to live without having to worry about whether her daughter has clothes for school."

"I've got some ideas about that." Emma grinned. "I'm hoping that Victoria's mom and Wynter will hit it off. They could both use someone that they trust to help them out with the girls. Just so happens that the apartment next to Wynter's is vacant, and the manager has agreed to hold it for a week."

Tate grinned at her, "I see you're capable of making secret plans too, Em."

"Well, nothing like you sneaking out and calling Karlee in to rescue the girls, but I've got my ways."

They laughed and made their way to the car. Victoria skipped in front of them, packages dangling from both arms. Emma remarked, "Just look at her. No one would know the horrors that she's lived through in the last week."

"She's got a chance now, Em."

Fifteen minutes later they were back at Emma's house and Victoria was excited to get a call from her mother. Tate made grilled cheese sandwiches and they all piled in front of the television with paper plates.

The second time that Emma noticed Victoria dozing off, she said, "Come on Sweetie. Let's get you to bed."

Tate smiled watching Emma lead Victoria down the hall to the guest room. *Someday you're going to be the best mother.* Tate thought.

Emma returned to the living room a few minutes later and silently held her hand out to Tate. Without speaking he pushed the remote and the room fell in darkness. He took her hand and let her lead him to the bedroom.

As soon as the door closed behind them, Tate pulled her into his arms and kissed her on the neck. "Come to bed Tate." Emma whispered against his cheek and with no modesty or fanfare, began to undress. She dropped her clothes in a chair next to the bed and watched as Tate did the same.

She reached for the light and Tate dropped down on one side of the bed. "Leave it on, Em."

Emma hid her grin, but did as he asked. She

moved toward him and stood between his legs. The hair on his thighs tickled her legs and she bent to kiss him. Her full breasts swung down and Tate dropped his head, letting his tongue slide across one taught nipple before drawing it into his mouth.

A moan escaped and Emma pushed him down onto the soft bed and covered his body with her own. "Tell me what you want." She demanded.

"Nothing. I want for nothing." His breath was sharp. He wrapped his arms around her and pulled her closer. "Everything I've ever wanted is right here, in my arms."

He reached down and cupped her, his fingers found her and he smiled when he heard her suck in a breath. *I remember what you like...I remember everything about us.* He thought.

He pulled her upward, over him and kissed every part of her, lavishing her with his tongue and his hands until he thought he would explode. He rolled her to her back without letting go and buried himself in her fire. They rocked, slowly at first, letting the flames build. Higher and higher, the fire licked at his soul and threatened to suffocate him if he didn't unleash the power of his love.

"Now Tate. Come with me." Emma choked the words out. A fine sheen of sweat covered them both and skin on skin moved without friction.

"Let's do this." Tate ground out. His body moved to the tempo that she'd set. Faster, harder, faster...until they collapsed together, their breath the only sound in the room.

Spent, Tate tucked Ema's head under his chin. One arm held her close as heir reathing returned to normal and sleep overtook them.

CHAPTER 57

The sun had just pushed its way through the darkness and Tate and Emma lay cuddled in each other's arms. Their lovemaking had been slow and sweet, and flaming hot. Emma opened one eye and glanced at the man she loved. *He's going to leave, you know that. Unless you do something. He'd stay if you asked him to,* Emma thought.

Tate felt her stir against him and he knew that she was awake. "It's been a long night Em. Go to sleep for a little bit." Tate whispered.

She snuggled closer and Tate waited until he heard her breath even out, slow and soft, then he slipped from the bed and walked to the living room.

Martin Crawley answered the phone on the second ring. "Crawley here, that you Tate? How's Miss Emma?"

"Emma's doing good Martin. I just wanted to touch base and let you know that I'll be home soon. I've got a meeting with Emma's SAC later today to wrap up a few things and then I'll be on my way. I should be there tonight or at the latest, tomorrow."

"I suppose you want me to pick up that damned dog for you." Martin said.

Tate chuckled, "That would be a big help buddy, I'm sure he's ready to get home too."

"More like Doc Snider can't wait to get rid of him."

"So you'll take care of that for me?" Tate pushed.

"Ahh hell, you know I will. See you tomorrow Tate." Martin said.

Tate disconnected the call and walked to the kitchen to make coffee and breakfast for Emma and Victoria. *She'll be back to power bars and juice in no time at all.* He thought.

Victoria, her hair a mass of red curls, entered the kitchen and gave Tate a smile. "Good morning." She said. "Only four more days and I'll get to see my mom."

Tate grinned at her. "That's right. You keep counting the days down and it'll be time before you know it. Have a seat, I'm going to wake Emma up and then we'll eat. Breakfast is almost ready."

"No need to wake me. I'm up." Emma entered the kitchen wearing a robe and Tate supposed nothing else.

"Okay girls. Get ready for the best breakfast you've ever had." Tate moved to the table with plates piled high with bacon, toast and eggs. "Let me grab the juice and we'll be all set."

Pushing a fork full of eggs into her mouth, Emma said, "We did good Tate. Wrapped it up with a pretty little bow."

"And the bad guys aren't so bad anymore, now that they're locked up or dead." Tate replied.

"There are plenty more out there, bad guys, that is. You ever think of coming back to the Bureau?" Emma asked.

He shook his head, and Emma didn't need any further explanation, he belonged in Pine Ridge, they needed him...but she needed him too. "You're leaving soon?"

"Tonight." He answered. It sounded so final and he guessed that it was; what else could he do? *You could ask her to come with you.* He thought.

Pushing back from the table, Tate picked up the empty plates. "You girls go get all prettied up for the day and I'll take care of the dishes. We've got one last stop at Pruitt's office to pick up the paperwork that I need to take to Karlee and I've got to be at the airport by five.

Emma and Victoria left the dining room and Emma stopped when she felt Victoria pull at her arm. "Why is he leaving? Don't you want him to stay?" The girl asked.

Emma felt tears stinging the backs of her eyes and threaten to spill out. "It's complicated Sweetie." She gave the child a quick hug. "Don't worry about us, okay? It's going to work out for the best. You'll see."

The morning slipped away and the afternoon came too quickly. Tate dropped his blue bag in the backseat of Emma's car and watched to make sure that Victoria buckled up.

"Guess it's time to go, Ladies." He said.

Fifteen minutes later, Tate pushed the door to SAC Pruitt's office open and they filed in. As promised, Pruitt had the appropriate paperwork for the children in Karlee's care. He pointed to a black duffle bag at the end of his desk.

"I had someone run by St. A's and pick up the girls belongings. Thought it might help if they had some of their own stuff."

Tate nodded and shook hands with the man.

"You know Echo, if you ever decide you want back in, we've got a spot in the Bureau for you." Pruitt said.

"I appreciate it, but I've got a town depending on me back in South Dakota. If that ever changes, I'll look you up."

"Fair enough." The older man replied.

Tate turned to Emma and Victoria, "Ladies, I've got a plane to catch. Think you can get me to the airport in time?"

Victoria piped up, "You're driving, silly. Think you can get yourself to the airport in time?"

They laughed as they exited the Richmond offices of the FBI.

Tate placed the Toyota in park outside the passenger drop off area of the Richmond Airport. He already felt hollow. Leaving was tearing him apart and he couldn't help but question his own sanity. *Why are you leaving? You know you love her? Just take the job Pruitt offered and live happily ever after...not. Stop it. You know that it won't work. She's no more ready to back off the heavy caseloads today than she was the day you left her. Two weeks and you'd be crazy with worry and obsessed with what she's doing... what cases she pulled. Just let it go.*

He shook his head, trying to clear his thoughts. "There's no need for you to park and come in Em. My flight leaves in forty five minutes, and by the time I make it through security, it'll be time to load."

Emma got out of the car with him and took the keys when he offered them, "Thank you for coming Tate, I..." *Dammit Emma, just tell him you love him. Beg him to stay...no...he'd smother you, remember? Pack up and go with him? You know you love him. Do something! I...I...I can't.* She let a long held breath escape.

Tate pulled his bag out of the trunk and closed it, he reached for her then. She came willingly and he wrapped her in his arms, their lips met and the kiss was tender, a soft goodbye.

Emma stepped back and watched Tate

walk away. He didn't look back and she didn't run after him. Tears streamed down her cheeks and dropped from her face. "Loving you is like running down a dream, Tate Echo....running down a dream."

Epilogue

Eight months later:

Noah Walker stood silently while a guard at the Red Onion State Prison violated his person, looking and poking in places that no man had a right to touch. Handcuffs bit into his wrists and shackles around his ankles ensured that he could only walk at a brisk shuffle. *I shouldn't be here.* He thought. *This has got to be a mistake, another holding place…something. State prison is not for federal offenders.*

Without a word, the guard pointed to a stack of neatly folded clothes on a white plastic chair against the wall. He shuffled to the chair and waited while the guard unlocked one leg and one hand, allowing him to slip into the orange jumpsuit; state issue, provided for all Virginia's inmates. He slid his sockless feet into a pair of white tennis shoes, sans laces.

He knew all about this place, he'd seen the reports and the complaints, and he knew that the SuperMax facility had been subject to public scrutiny and a Department of Justice investigation for their supposed *overuse* of solitary confinement. Some human rights groups wanted the public to believe that inmates were suffering from mental deterioration because they weren't socialized enough. *Shit.* He thought. *I'll take the private room and like it.*

The guard reattached his cuffs and shackles, and then jabbed him in the back and pointed to the steel door, he heard the lock mechanisms metal clink and knew that this was it. He walked through the doorway into the sally port and heard the lock engage behind him. He shuffled in front of the guard to the next door and waited for the sound indicating that it was open.

They passed into a long, gray painted hallway, the floors were cheap tile and the lighting, a bright white fluorescent, did nothing to make any of it look better. Noah glanced at the guard, *Couldn't the man talk?* "Where are we going? Are you taking me to my cell now?" he asked, hoping to force a conversation.

The man only stepped around him and swiped his identification card on a panel that prompted another door to open. Noah looked up at the camera suspended above the door and smiled, a big, toothy grin, the same one that had drawn voters to him during the election, but this one was special, it was for whoever sat in some little room somewhere, watching that particular camera. *Rot in hell. I'll be out of here in six months flat.*

The walkway was wide and on both sides, barred cubicles lined the hall. *My room awaites.* He thought. *No more community showers and no one looking up my ass. Just some quiet time to figure out how to best word my appeal. Those bastards at Gordon, Mayer and used to be Aiden, can kiss my ass. Sorry Mr. Walker but we don't handle criminal cases...fuck them.*

When they reached the end of the hallway and the guard still hadn't directed him to his cell, Noah began to worry. *Where is he taking me? Maybe I'm in a different wing.* He reasoned and relaxed.

They walked through another set of doors, another sally port, the second one refusing to open until the first had been secured.

This door opened to a large dormitory of sorts, a community room. On one side of the massive room, three tables were set up, each surrounded by four chairs, other prisoners looked up from their card and domino games to stare at Noah and the guard when they entered. A man picked up the remote and muted the television that hung overhead, killing all background noise in the room. Institutional steel framed beds lined one wall, twelve in all.

The guard stopped in front of one of the beds and finally spoke, "Here you go Walker, your home sweet home for the undetermined future." He pointed to a small metal bed made up military style with a faded blue wool blanket. "This is yours."

The guard turned to the other prisoners in the room, "Gentleman, don't forget to welcome the ex-congressmen to the unit. You've got the next fifty years to get to know him, and I really hope that some of you get to know him very, very, well." With that final statement, the guard left the room, following the same path that he'd entered, he didn't look back. Didn't care what happened to Noah Walker in the community room, in fact, he was hoping for the worst.

"Wait! You can't leave me *here!*" Noah yelled at the man. The guard didn't stop or even slow down and Noah sank down on the bed. *This is not happening. What about my private cell?*

Consumed in his own world of despair, Noah looked up in surprise when a burly man jabbed him in the chest. "Look here guys, we've got a *Chester* in the badlands. A real live Diaper Sniper in the B-unit." He wrapped one beefy hand under Noah's chin, forcing him to look up.

Noah's eye's flittered from the man holding his face to the others surrounding him. *Where had they come from?* He slapped at the hand holding him but failed to push the man away. *Shit.*

"Show him how we welcome Diddlers, Mason, show him!" A thin man behind Noah hissed.

Mason shoved Noah, forcing him to fall back on the thin mattress of his bed before flipping him face down. Two meaty hands pulled his arms out, stretching him in his prone position.

"No! Stop! Guard!" Noah's cries were lost in the laughter and grunts of the other prisoners. He felt hands on his legs, his arms, his back....everywhere....felt his prison issue pants being pulled away. "NO!!

In a small monitoring station two floors up, the technician stood, stretched and rubbed his eyes. He left the room for a coffee break, his replacement entering at the same time he exited. They nodded as they passed, but didn't speak. The replacement dropped into a chair just as one of seven monitors on the table flickered, and then caught a view of the B-unit. He glanced at the screen for a few seconds, cranked the volume down, and spun his chair around so that he faced the door.

"Welcome to Red Onion, Beast."

A Note From The Author:

When Angels Cry is a fictional work providing only a brief glimpse at the growing problem of human trafficking, and specifically the exploitation of children. This modern version of slave trade is a growing problem worldwide and in the United States people are being bought, sold and smuggled on a daily basis. The victims are forced to work as prostitutes or to take grueling jobs with little or no pay, while the traffickers have found a profitable method of supporting themselves.

In 2003, the FBI in conjunction with the Department of Justice, launched the Innocence Lost National Initiative and as of June 2012 they have recovered over 2100 children, commonly referred to as "throw away children". Currently there are forty seven task forces or working groups dedicated to recovering America's children across the United States and over 1000 traffickers have been convicted and sentenced for their crimes.

Many of the arrests resulted from tips and reported sightings from the public. If you suspect that underage children are being sexually exploited, report it. Contact the FBI or the National Center's hotline at 1-800-THE-LOST because America's Children Are Not For Sale.

http://www.fbi.gov/aboutus/investigate/vc_majorthefts/cac/innocencelost

About the Author

Tammy Cheatham grew up in rural East Texas and learned to love books and reading at an early age. Her writing career began in the fifth grade when she won second place in a UIL writing contest, but was put on hold while she pursued a career and raised a family. In 2010, Tammy elected to retire from her full time job and return to her first career choice, writing fiction. Today, Tammy lives in South Texas with her husband.

www.ingramcontent.com/pod-product-compliance
Lightning Source LLC
Chambersburg PA
CBHW030359180626
46812CB00005B/1839